Ruth

About the Author

ANDREA BUSFIELD is a British journalist who first
traveled to Afghanistan to cover the fall of the
Taliban in 2001. She is now a full-time writer living
in Bad Ischl, Austria. *Born Under a Million Shadows*
is her first novel.

D0017899

Born Under a Million Shadows

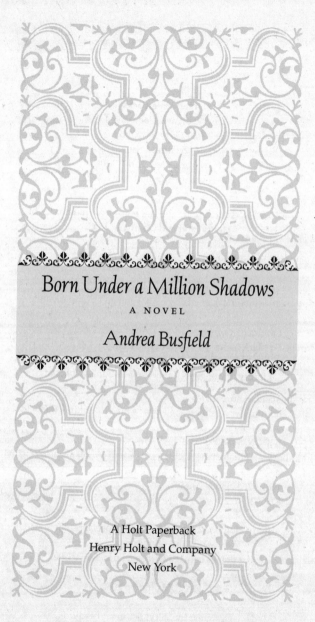

Born Under a Million Shadows

A NOVEL

Andrea Busfield

A Holt Paperback
Henry Holt and Company
New York

Holt Paperbacks
Henry Holt and Company, LLC
Publishers since 1866
175 Fifth Avenue
New York, New York 10010
www.henryholt.com

A Holt Paperback® and 📖 ® are registered trademarks of
Henry Holt and Company, LLC.

Copyright © 2009 by Andrea Busfield
All rights reserved.

Distributed in Canada by H. B. Fenn and Company Ltd.

Originally published in the United Kingdom in 2009 by
Black Swan, an imprint of Transworld Publishers

Library of Congress Cataloging-in-Publication Data

Busfield, Andrea.
    Born under a million shadows : a novel / Andrea Busfield.
        p. cm.
    ISBN: 978-0-8050-9061-1
    1. Boys—Afghanistan—Fiction.   2. Kabul (Afghanistan)—Fiction.
I. Title.
    PR6102.U785B67 2009
    823'.92—dc22   2008055287

Henry Holt books are available for special promotions
and premiums.
For details contact: Director, Special Markets.

First U.S. Edition 2010

Designed by Meryl Sussman Levavi
Printed in the United States of America
1 3 5 7 9 10 8 6 4 2

For my mum, my dad, and my sister

Born Under a Million Shadows

Part One

I

My name is Fawad, and my mother tells me I was born under the shadow of the Taliban.

Because she said no more, I imagined her stepping out of the sunshine and into the dark, crouching in a corner to protect the stomach that was hiding me, while a man with a stick watched over us, ready to beat me into the world.

But then I grew up, and I realized I wasn't the only one born under this shadow. There was my cousin Jahid, for one, and the girl Jamilla—we all worked the foreigners on Chicken Street together—and there was also my best friend, Spandi. Before I knew him, Spandi's face was eaten by sand flies, giving him the one-year sore that left a mark as big as a fist on his cheek. He didn't care, though, and neither did we, and while the rest of us were at school he sold *spand* to fat Westerners, which is why, even though his name was Abdullah, we called him Spandi.

Yes, all of us were born during the time of the Taliban, but I only heard my mother talk of them as men making shadows, so I guess if she'd ever learned to write she might have been a poet. Instead, and as Allah willed it, she swept the floors of the rich for a handful of afs that she hid in her clothes and guarded through the night.

"There are thieves everywhere," she would hiss, an angry whisper that tied the points of her eyebrows together.

And, of course, she was right. I was one of them.

At the time, none of us thought of it as stealing. As Jahid

explained, because he knew about such things, "It's the moral distribution of wealth."

"Sharing money," added Jamilla. "We have nothing, they have everything, but they are too greedy to help poor people like us, as it is written in the Holy Koran, so we must help them be good. In a way, they are paying for our help. They just don't know that they're doing it."

Of course, not all the foreigners paid for our "help" with closed eyes. Some of them actually gave us money—sometimes happily, sometimes out of shame, sometimes just to make us go away, which doesn't really work because one group is quickly replaced by another when dollars are walking the street. But it was fun. Born under a shadow or not, me, Jahid, Jamilla, and Spandi spent our days in the sun, distributing the wealth of those who'd come to help us.

"It's called reconstruction," Jahid informed us one day as we sat on the curb waiting for a 4×4 to jump on. "The foreigners are here because they bombed our country to kill the Taliban, and now they have to build it again. The World Parliament made the order."

"But why did they want to kill the Taliban?"

"Because they were friends with the Arabs and their king Osama bin Laden had a house in Kabul where he made hundreds of children with his forty wives. America hated bin Laden, and they knew he was fucking his wives so hard he would one day have an army of thousands, maybe millions, so they blew up a palace in their own country and blamed it on him. Then they came to Afghanistan to kill him, his wives, his children, and all of his friends. It's called politics, Fawad."

Jahid was probably the most educated boy I'd ever known. He always read the newspapers we found thrown away in the street, and he was older than the rest of us, although how much older nobody knows. We don't celebrate birthdays in Afghanistan; we only remember victories and death. Jahid was also the best thief I'd ever known. Some days he would come away with handfuls of dollars, taken from the pocket of some foreigner as us smaller kids annoyed them to the point of tears. But if I was born under a shadow, Jahid was surely born under the full gaze of the devil himself because the truth was he was incredibly ugly. His teeth were stumpy smudges of brown, and one of his eyes danced to its own tune, rolling in its socket like a marble in a box. He also had a leg so lazy that he had to force it into line with the other.

"He's a dirty little thief," my mother would say. But she rarely had a kind word to say about anyone in her sister's family. "You keep away from him . . . filling your head with such nonsense."

How my mother actually thought I could keep away from Jahid was anyone's guess. But this is a common problem with adults: they ask for the impossible and then make your life a misery when you can't obey them. The fact is I lived under the same roof as Jahid, along with his fat cow of a mother, his donkey of a father, and two more of their dirty-faced children, Wahid and Obaidullah.

"All boys," my uncle would declare proudly.

"And all ugly," my mother would mutter under her chador, giving me a wink as she did so because it was us against them and although we had nothing at least our eyes looked in the same direction.

Together, all seven of us shared four small rooms and a hole in the yard. Not easy, then, to keep away from cousin Jahid as my mother demanded. It was an order President Karzai would have had problems fulfilling. However, my mother was never one for explaining, so she never told me how I should keep my distance. In fact, for a while my mother was never one for talking full stop.

On very rare occasions she would look up from her sewing to talk about the house we had once owned in Paghman.

I was born there, but we fled before the pictures had time to plant themselves in my head. So I found my memories with the words of my mother, watching her eyes grow wide with pride as she described painted rooms lined with thick cushions of the deepest red; curtains covering glass windows; a kitchen so clean you could eat your food from the floor; and a garden full of yellow roses.

"We weren't rich like those in Wazir Akbar Khan, Fawad, but we were happy," she would tell me. "Of course that was long before the Taliban came. Now look at us! We don't even own a tree from which we can hang ourselves."

I was no expert, but it was pretty clear my mother was depressed.

She never talked about the family we had lost, only the building that had once hidden us—and not very effectively as it turned out. However, sometimes at night I would hear her whisper my sister's name. She would then reach for me, pulling me closer to her body. And that's how I knew she loved me.

On those occasions, lying almost as one on the cushions we sat on during the day, I'd be burning to talk. I'd feel the words crowding in my head, waiting to spill from my mouth. I wanted to know everything; about my father, about my brothers, about Mina. I was desperate to know them, to have them come alive in the words of my mother. But she only whispered my sister's name, and like a coward I kept quiet because I was afraid that if I spoke I would break the spell and she would roll away from me.

By daylight, my mother would be gone from my side, already awake and pulling on her burka. As she left the house she would bark a list of orders that always started with "Go to school" and ended with "Keep away from Jahid."

In the main these were orders I tried to follow out of respect for my mother—in Afghanistan our mothers are worth more than all the gold that hides in the basement of the president's palace—but it wasn't easy. And though I knew she wouldn't beat me if I disobeyed her, unlike Jahid's father, who seemed to think he had a God-given right to hit me in the face on any day the sun came up, she would have that look in her eyes, a disappointed stare I suspected had been there from the day I crept out of the shadow.

I am only a boy, but I recognized our life was difficult. Of course, it had always been the same for me; I knew no different. But my mother, with her memories of deep-red cushions and yellow roses, was trapped by a past I had little knowledge of, so I spent most of my days on the outside of her prison, looking in. It had been like this for as long as I could clearly remember, yet I like to think she was happy once: laughing with my father by the clear waters of Qargha Lake, her green eyes—the eyes I inherited—smiling with love, her small hands, soft and clean, playing with the hem of a golden veil.

My mother was once very beautiful—that's what my aunt told me in a surprising burst of talking. But then the shadow fell, and although she never said so, I guessed my mother blamed me. I was a reminder of a past that had dragged her into the flowerless hell that was her sister's house, and from what I could tell, my mother hated her sister even more than she hated the Taliban.

"She's just jealous!" my mother once screamed, loud enough for my aunt to hear in the next room. "She's always been jealous—jealous of my ways, of the fact that I married an educated man, of our once happy life . . . and I long got over apologizing for it. If Allah blessed her with the face of a burst watermelon and a body to match, it is not my fault!"

"They're women, they're born that way," Jahid told me one afternoon as we escaped once again from the screams and insults flying around the house to steal from the foreigners in the center of town. "They are never happier than when they are fighting with each other. When you are older you will understand more. Women are complicated, that's what my father says."

And maybe Jahid was right. But the argument that had just taken place had more to do with money than being women. My aunt wanted us to pay rent, but we could barely afford the clothes on our backs and the food in our bellies. The few afs my mother earned from cleaning houses along with the dollars I picked up in the street were all we had.

"Maybe if you gave a little more of your dollars to your mother she wouldn't be so angry with my mother," I suggested, which was obviously the wrong thing to suggest because Jahid punched me hard in the head.

"Look, you little bastard, my mother gave your mother a roof when you had no place to stay. Coming to our home begging like gypsy filth, forcing us to give up our room and put food in your idle fucking bellies. How do you think we felt? If we weren't good Muslims, your mother would be pimping your ass to every fucking homo who passed by. In fact, you want to help? Go pimp your own fucking ass! Pretty boy like you should make enough afs to keep the women happy."

"Yeah?" I spat back. "And maybe they'd pay just as much money to keep the donkey's ass that's your face away from them!"

And with that I ran off, leaving my cousin shouting curses about camels and cocks in my direction while dragging his dead leg in fury behind him.

That day I ran from Jahid until I thought my legs would die. By the time I reached Cinema Park I could barely breathe, and I realized I was crying—for my mother and for my cousin. I had been cruel. I knew that. I understood why he was saving his money, why he buried it under the wall when he thought no one was looking. He wanted a wife. "One day I will be married to the most beautiful woman in Afghanistan," he always bragged. "You wait. You'll see." And that's why he needed the money, because with a face like his he'd have to come up with a hell of a dowry to make that dream come true. It's not even as if he could rely on the force of his personality to win over a wife. He had the foulest mouth I had ever heard, even more so than the National Police who cluttered the city's round-abouts, barking curses and demanding bribes, even from crippled beggars. In fact, the only other thing that could have saved Jahid was school, where he'd shown an unlikely talent. He threw himself into his learning as only a boy with no friends can do. But then the torment and the beatings he took day after day finally drove him away, and he became increasingly hard.

My country can be a tough place to live in if you're poor, but it's even tougher if you're poor and ugly. And now Jahid was like stone, a stone that knows he will never find a woman who will willingly marry him, but whose father might agree for the right price.

"Come on, Fawad, let's go to Chicken Street."

Through my tears I saw Jamilla standing before me, the sun throwing an angel's light around her body. She was small, like me. And she was pretty.

Jamilla reached for my hand, and I dragged myself up from the ground to stand by her side, wiping my face dry on the sleeves of my clothes.

"Jahid," I said by way of explanation.

Jamilla nodded. She didn't talk much, but I guessed she would grow into that if Jahid was right about the ways of women.

Jamilla was my main rival on Chicken Street. She cleaned up with the foreign men, who melted under the gaze of her big brown eyes, while I cleaned up with the women, who fell in love with my big green eyes. We were a good team whose pickings pretty much depended on who was passing by, so if we found ourselves working on the same day we would split our money.

Fridays were the best, though. It was a holiday, there was no school, no work, and the foreigners would come, stepping out of their Land Cruisers to trawl Kabul's tourist area for souvenirs of "war-torn" Afghanistan: jewelry boxes made of lapis lazuli; silver imported from Pakistan; guns and knives apparently dating back to the Anglo-Afghan wars; *pakols*, *patus*, blankets, carpets, wall hangings, bright-colored scarves, and blue burkas. Of course, if they walked twenty minutes into the heaving mess of Kabul's river bazaar, they would find all these items for half the price, but the foreigners were either too scared or too lazy to make the journey—and too rich to care about the extra dollars that would feed most of our families for a week. Still, as Jahid noted, their laziness was good for business, and Chicken Street was their Mecca.

Along with the aid workers, now and again we would see white-faced soldiers hunched over the counters of stores selling silver, looking at rings and bracelets for the wives they'd left behind in their own countries. They were mainly tall men with big guns, metal jackets, and bowl-shaped helmets strapped to their heads. They came in groups of four or five, and one would always stand guard in the street as the others did their shopping, watching out for suicide bombers. "America good!" we would shout—a trick that always earned us a couple of dollars. Money in hand, we would then move away, farther down the street, just in case there were actually suicide bombers around.

Most of the other foreigners, though, were less interested in America, so we used different tactics to win their dollars, following them as they weaved their way from shop to shop and yelling out all the English we could remember. "Hello, mister! Hello, missus! How are you? I am your bodyguard! No, come this way, I find you good price." And we would take their hands and drag them to a store where we could earn a few afs' commission. Most of us were on the payroll of four or more shopkeepers, but only if we brought in customers. Therefore, if the foreigners didn't bend to our thinking, we would follow them into stores, tutting and shaking our heads in pretend concern, but carefully out of sight of the owners. "No, missus, he is thief, very bad price. Come, I show you good price." We would then lead them to the shops that paid us, telling the owners of the figure given by one of their rivals so that he could begin his bargaining at a lower but still profitable price.

Meanwhile, as the foreigners argued a few extra dollars away, the women who also worked the street but knew no English would descend, hovering in shop doorways to reach out with their dirty hands, grab at elbows, and cry into their burkas. They all come from the same family, but the foreigners don't know this, and as woman after woman would come to break down in tears pleading for money for her sick, dying baby, this would usually be the point when it became too much for the Westerners and they would climb back into their cars, trying to avoid our eyes as their drivers sped them away from our poverty and back to their privileged lives.

However, as the Land Cruisers screeched out of Chicken Street and into the gridlocked traffic of Shahr-e Naw, Spandi would appear to tap his black fingers on their windows and hold out the bitter, smoking can of herbs that we call *spand*, the smell of which is so unbelievably foul it is said to chase away evil spirits. Without doubt this is the worst of all our jobs because the smoke gets in your hair and your eyes and your chest and you end up looking like death. But the money is pretty okay because even if the tourists aren't superstitious it's hard to ignore a boy at a car window whose scarred face is the color of ash.

On a good day on Chicken Street we didn't need to hustle.

The foreign women would happily hand over their bags as they struggled with headscarves they had yet to grow used to, and I would carry their shopping until they called it a day, sometimes earning five dollars for my trouble. Jamilla would smile prettily and get the same for carrying nothing.

"And what is your name?" the women would ask slowly. Pretty white faces with smiling red lips.

"Fawad," I would tell them.

"Your English is very good. Do you go to school?"

"Yes. School. Every day. I like very much."

And it was true, we all went to school—even the girls if their fathers let them—but the days were short and the holidays long with months off in the winter and summer when it became too cold or too hot to study. However, the English we learned came only from the street. It was easy to pick up, and the foreigners liked to teach us.

And even if Jahid was correct and they did come to bomb our country and rebuild it again, I quite liked the foreigners with their sweaty white faces and fat pockets—which was just as well really, because that day I returned to my aunt's house to be told we were going to live with three of them.

2

I T DIDN'T TAKE us long to move out of my aunt's house, possessing as we did only one blanket, a few clothes, and a copy of the Koran. We would have taken more, but my aunt seemed to think that the few pots and pans we'd gathered over the years now belonged to her.

Thankfully, my mother was in no mood to argue that day and simply spit at her sister's feet before lowering her burka and dragging me out of the door.

"Good-bye, Jahid!" I shouted behind me.

"Bye, Fawad jan!"

I looked back, surprised by the affectionate "jan" added to my name, and just in time to see my cousin wipe something from his one good eye.

"Don't forget us, you donkey cunt!"

It was a quick extra that earned him an equally quick blow to the ear from the fat fist of his mother.

It took us two whole hours to walk from Khair Khana on the edge of the city to Wazir Akbar Khan, the location of our new house, in which time I managed to get from my mother that we were to live with two women and one man. She said she only knew the name of one of the women, the one who had invited us; her name was Georgie. And apparently, she had been washing *Georgie*'s clothes for weeks.

I couldn't believe she hadn't mentioned this before.

"But why were you washing her clothes?" I asked.

"For money, what do you think?"

"Why doesn't she wash her own clothes?"

"Foreigners don't know how. They need machines to wash their clothes."

"What kind of machines?"

"Washing machines."

This sounded incredible to me, but my mother wouldn't lie. Okay, she didn't talk much, but when she did it was always the truth. I also knew that foreigners were a Godless people, so I had to assume that as well as going to Hell they hadn't even been blessed with the common skills given to ordinary Afghans like us.

"Does she sew?"

"No."

"Can she cook?"

"No."

"Does she have a husband?"

"No."

"I'm not surprised."

Mother laughed and dragged me into a hug as we walked. I looked up, but I couldn't see her face through the screen of the burka, so I held her hand tighter, my ears burning at the thought of having made her smile.

This was fast turning into the best day of my life.

Although I had no real memories of what it had been like before my aunt's house, I knew my mother was miserable after we moved from Paghman. Locked in one room with a thin carpet that offered no comfort from the cold scratches of the concrete floor, we lived, ate, and slept like tolerated prisoners under my aunt's roof. The toilet was also a constant torment to my mother, smattered as it usually was by the missed aims of four careless boys and a man whose bowels were as loose as a slaughtered goat's; and we were plagued with illness, from malaria in the summer to flu in the winter, as well as the worms and bugs that permanently lived in our stomachs. Yet we had to appear grateful because my aunt had taken us in on the night we lost everything.

Every year, people around us died from disease, rocket attacks, forgotten mines, the bites of animals large and small, and even hunger. And even if you did have food, that was no guarantee of coming out of the day alive. Mother cooked our meals on an old gas burner that sat in the corner of our room threatening to explode and knock the heads from our very necks. That's what happened to Haji Mohammad's wife three doors away. She was cooking chickpeas in the kitchen when the burner exploded into a ball of flames. It then shot from the floor like a rocket, taking her head clean off. It took him weeks to clear the blood and brains from the black remains of the kitchen. Even today, dents from bullet-propelled chickpeas scar the walls of the house, and Haji Mohammad won't eat anything but salad, fruit, and naan. Anything, in fact, that doesn't need cooking. Thanks be to Allah, though, because he'd been blessed with a second wife—and she was younger than the first.

"So, how did you get to know her?"

"Who?"

"The foreign woman, Georgie."

"I found her."

"What do you mean you found her? How did you find her?"

"Oh, Fawad! So many questions! I was knocking on doors looking for work, and she gave me some. After that she gave me some more, and then she invited us to come. Okay?"

"Okay."

As we marched through the streets, dodging dog shit and potholes, and with my mother now refusing to give any more information as to how we came to be moving toward this sudden freedom, I tried to imagine the mysterious Georgie who had been found by my mother. I pictured a woman with long golden hair and an easy smile standing under a tree in Wazir Akbar Khan, looking lost with her arms full of the dirty clothes she had no idea how to wash. In my head she looked like the woman from *Titanic*. In reality, she looked more Afghan than I did.

Turning left, just before Massoud Circle, we crisscrossed three roads lined with concrete barriers protecting huge houses that peered over high walls with curls of barbed wire fixed on them. Men holding guns stood guard every ten paces, and they eyed us with lazy suspicion as we moved farther into the residential area of the rich. Eventually we came to a standstill in front of a large green metal gate. Another guard wearing a light blue shirt and black trousers came out of a wooden white hut positioned nearby and greeted my mother. He then opened the side door and shouted inside. As we stepped through, a woman came walking toward us with hair as long and dark as my mother's. She wore a white shirt over blue jeans and looked quite beautiful.

"Salaam aleykum, Mariya!" the woman sang, clasping my mother's hand as she did so.

"Waleykum salaam," my mother replied.

"How are you? How is your health? Are you well? How was your trip? No problems?"

As my mother rattled off her replies, I stared at the woman I guessed to be Georgie, surprised to hear her speaking one of our languages and surprised to find that not only was she dressed like a man, she was also as tall as one.

"And this must be your handsome son, Fawad. How are you, Fawad? Welcome to your new home."

I held out my hand, and Georgie shook it. Although I tried to speak, my mouth was a few steps behind my head and I couldn't find the words to answer her.

"Ha! He is a little shy, I think. Please, come in, both of you."

My mother walked farther into the yard, where she felt free to lift the burka back from her face. My first thought was that she looked afraid, which didn't exactly set my mind at rest. But then I realized that, like me, she didn't quite know what to say.

Silently, we followed Georgie to a small building sitting behind and to the right of the gate.

"This will be your place, Fawad. I hope you will be happy here."

Georgie pointed to the building, waving at us to follow her in. So we did.

Inside there were two rooms separated by a small, clean toilet and shower area. As she opened the door to the first room I saw two beds with blankets sitting upon them. They were still in their plastic cases and looked new. In the other room there were three long cushions, a small table, an electric fan, and a television—a real live Samsung television! And it looked like it might even work! All my life I had dreamed of owning a TV, and I felt tears sticking sharp pins in the backs of my eyes at the very sight of it.

"Come," Georgie said with a smile, "leave your things here and I'll show you around."

My first day in the new house was a blur of sights, smells, and sounds. There was our home and a bigger building where Georgie and her friends lived upstairs. There was a kitchen the size of the yard where my mother was told she would do much of her work, and a sitting room with another television (much bigger than ours), a music system, and a pool table. To the back of the house was a massive lawn framed with rosebushes. When I saw them parading their pretty colors in the sun my heart leaped at the thought of my mother once again being surrounded by such beauty.

But then I saw a man standing in the middle of this beauty with his chest as bare as that of Pir the Madman, who played with the dogs in Shahr-e Naw Park, and I began seriously to worry for my mother's reputation. The man was holding a long stick in his hand, a bottle of beer in the other, and he had a cigarette balanced between his teeth. He had been using the stick to hit a small ball into a glass lying on the ground, and not doing very well by the looks of it.

"Hello, I'm James," he shouted, looking up in time to catch us staring at him.

He wandered over to offer his hand to my mother, who, quite rightly, waved but didn't accept it. Georgie said something sharp in what I recognized was English, and the man gave a small easy laugh before reaching for his shirt, which lay close by on the back of a white plastic chair.

"This is James," explained Georgie. "He's a journalist, so please forgive his manners."

After James pulled on his clothes he walked back to us saying something I didn't quite understand before reaching out with his right hand to mess up my hair. I shook my head, knocking him away, and threw him a look to warn that this kind of attention wasn't appreciated, but then he rolled his hand into a fist, knocked me on the chin, and started laughing. Georgie spoke again, and James raised his arms in pretend surrender before putting his right hand to his heart and smiling at me. It was a true smile that made moon-shaped holes around his lips, and I accepted it with one of my own. I knew then that I liked the man James. He was tall and thin, and he had a dark beard. He could easily have passed for an Afghan if he managed to keep his clothes on.

Behind us I heard the gate open, and a woman came striding into the garden. She looked angry and slightly confused, but when Georgie spoke she smiled and waved.

"Our final housemate," explained Georgie. "This is May; she's an engineer."

May greeted us with handshakes. She was short, with yellow hair escaping from a green headscarf. She had spots on her face, and she also looked nothing like the woman from *Titanic*. The man called James gave her his beer, and she seemed happy with this. And although I tried not to look, I could see that under her blue shirt she had the most enormous breasts I'd ever come across. I wondered whether James had seen them.

"We are all quite friendly here and very relaxed, so please treat this place as your home for as long as you need it," said Georgie.

My mother then thanked her and led me back to our rooms—away from the foreigners who had invited us into their home and away from the sight of May's chest.

Over the next few days, as my mother washed and cooked and basically did everything the foreigners seemed incapable of, I kept a careful eye on my new landlords. Although I was glad to be there, I had to protect my mother, and to do that I needed to know just who and what I was dealing with. My main concern was the naked journalist.

Thankfully, the layout of the place gave me the chance to observe pretty much everything, unseen. The passageway behind the house allowed me to watch the garden unnoticed; the big windows gave me a grand view of what was happening downstairs, when it was dark outside and the lights were on; and the high walls and balconies gave me a way in to some of the sights above. Now and again my mother would catch me spying on the foreigners and shake her head, but although her eyes looked puzzled they seemed fairly unconcerned. She'd also taken to laughing more—and mainly when one of the guards, Shir Ahmad, came from his hut to refill his teapot.

I made a mental note to investigate Shir Ahmad as soon as I'd finished with the foreigners.

With so much spying to do, for the first few weeks after we moved to Wazir Akbar Khan I kept away from Chicken Street, despite the almost unbearable ache to tell Jahid about our television, and fill Jamilla's head with the sights and sounds of my new home. Instead, I would return from school, sit in the doorway of the kitchen, chat with my mother as she did her chores, and wait for Georgie, James, and May to come back from wherever they had been.

"How does Georgie know our Dari language?" I asked my mother as she peeled potatoes for that night's dinner.

"From her friends, I think."

"She has Afghan friends?"

"Apparently so. Pass me that pan, will you, Fawad?"

I reached for the metal container, tipped a dead fly out of it, and handed it over.

"So, have you seen these friends?" I asked, settling back onto the kitchen step.

"Once, yes."

"Who are they?"

"Afghans."

"I know *that!*"

My mother laughed, throwing the naked potatoes in the pan as she did so. "They are Pashtuns," she finally offered. "From Jalalabad."

"Oh, she's got some taste then."

"Yes." My mother smiled before adding somewhat mysteriously, "Sort of."

"What do you mean, 'sort of'?"

"They're not . . . how should I put it? They're not the kind of friends I might choose for you."

"Why not?"

"Because you're my boy and I love you. Now that's enough, Fawad. Go and finish your homework."

Dismissed, and left dangling once again by my mother's riddles, I returned to my room to practice the multiplication tables we had been given at school that day. I guessed that in the same way I'd found out about the Taliban shadow, the reason Georgie had sort-of friends would become clear at some later stage of my life. However, I was glad they were Pashtun, like me. If they had been Hazaras, they would have cut off her breasts by now.

As we actually had water connected to the house, I no longer had to make the backbreaking trip to the nearest tap to fight with other kids and dirty dogs for a bucketful of liquid that lasted five minutes, and so after I completed my homework my only real job was to run to the baker's each evening with a handful of afs to collect five hot fresh long breads.

Other than that, my life usually involved waiting for the foreigners.

Georgie was normally the first to arrive home, and quite often she would allow me to sit in the garden with her as she drank her coffee. Although my mother was always invited, she rarely came to join us. She had quickly made friends with a woman across the road who managed a house for the wife of one of the Ministry of Interior's men. Her name was Homeira and she was pretty fat, so I guessed they paid her well. I was happy my mother had found a friend, so I felt no jealousy when she spent much of her time talking to her in our rooms or at the house of Homeira's employer. In fact, I was more than happy; I was amazed. It was as if a hidden key had turned in my mother's head, releasing a river of words that had been locked in there for years.

More amazing, however, was my mother's willingness to let me stay in the house alone and to sit with the Westerners for as long as "they don't become bored." Perhaps she thought it would be good for my English, although James was hardly ever around, May always seemed to be crying, and Georgie and I usually spoke Dari together.

From these little conversations I learned that Georgie came from England, the same country as London. She'd been in Afghanistan for ages and came to live with James and May two years ago because they had become friends and James needed the rent money. She worked for an NGO and combed goats for a living, and because she knew the country and traveled a lot she had made loads of Afghan friends. In that way, and many more, she was different from most foreigners I had met, and I think I fell in love with her instantly. She was gentle and funny, and she seemed to like being with me. She was also very beautiful with thick almost-black hair and dark eyes. I hoped one day to marry her—once she had given up smoking and converted to the one true faith, of course.

The engineer, May, was usually the second one home and tended to disappear into her room as soon as her quick greetings were over. Georgie told me she came from America on a contract with one of the ministries and that she was "a little unhappy right now." She didn't explain further, and I didn't ask more. I liked the mystery it gave to May's tears.

As a rule, James was always the last one home, and at least twice a week he would return very late, bouncing off walls and singing to himself. The more I got to know him, the more I was convinced he was related to Pir the Madman.

"He works very hard," Georgie explained, "and mainly with the ladies."

Georgie laughed at that, and I wondered how these women got permission from their husbands to work so late with a man who freely showed his nipples to the world as if they were medals of war.

"What work does he do with them?" I asked, causing Georgie to laugh even louder. It was a good, strong sound, like thunder in summer.

"Fawad," she finally said, "you'd best ask your mother that question."

And that put a stop to that.

And because that's always the way with adults—they shut you out just as things get interesting—I had no choice but to carry on with my own investigations, investigations my mother might call "snooping."

Through much trying and failing, I found the best time to watch my new friends was at night, when the lights were on, it was dark outside, and everyone thought I was asleep. Luckily, my mother was a great help when it came to my nighttime spying, as she had chosen to sleep in the TV room, meaning I now had a bedroom to myself for the very first time, which gave me complete freedom to explore my surroundings and their strange Godless inhabitants.

Now and again, about an hour after I'd turned out my light, my mother would open the door to my room, which surprised me the first time because I was a breath away from leaving. But it was one of those warm surprises that make your toes tingle and your heart feel like it's bleeding inside, because, thinking I was asleep, she kissed me softly on the cheek before returning to her own room, satisfied I was safely locked up in my dreams. Which of course I wasn't. As a result of that first sweet surprise, I quickly learned to wait a good hour until after my mother's visit before pulling on my shoes and allowing my adventures to begin.

Creeping along walls and crouching in bushes, I listened to magical, mysterious conversations that exploded with laughter as Georgie, James, and May spoke with other white-faced friends around the table in the garden. Of course, I could hardly understand a word they were saying, but this simply meant I now had a code I would have to learn to decipher.

Really, I felt like I'd been plucked from the flames of Hell and placed into Paradise. In those first few weeks I wasn't simply Fawad from Paghman; I was Fawad the secret agent. In those days, Kabul was crawling with spies—British, Pakistani, French, Italian, Russian, Indian, and American men as big as giants who wore their beards long to try to look Afghan. My mission from the president was simple: to discover who in the house was working as a spy, and the identity of their masters.

As I crept and crawled my way through the heavy heat of those Kabul summer nights, I wrapped layers of dreams and heroic tales around my adventures, and I plotted escape routes and hatched complicated plans to avoid detection so that I might hand over my carefully gathered information to my comrades at the palace. I lived in a world of hazy future glories, picturing myself as a national hero thanks to all the good work I had carried out as a mere boy.

"He was so young!" the people would say as they listened to the story of my successes.

"Yes, but he was a true Afghan," President Karzai would tell them, smiling widely because he was the man who had appointed me.

"So brave! So fearless!" they would marvel. "He must have had balls as big as Ahmad Shah Massoud's."

"Bigger!" the president would correct. "The boy was a Pashtun!"

In order to fulfill my mission, I kept a careful record of all the foreigners' movements in a red notebook Georgie had given me to practice my writing. Because James was hardly ever there, and Georgie was too beautiful to work for the enemy, I decided to concentrate on May.

Once my mother had gone to sleep, I would sneak out of my room and shimmy up the wall of the "secret" passageway. From there I could see the door to May's bedroom, on which was hung a long woolen jacket. On the far wall there was a wooden board with a collection of photographs pinned on it. I guessed they were of her family because the people caught in various poses all seemed to be short and yellow, but in my imagination they were part of a terror network supported by the pigs of Pakistan. The ISI, the country's secret service, knew that the Afghan government would never suspect a Western woman from America of carrying out their evil plans. In that way they were as cunning as the devil himself. But they weren't clever enough for Fawad—Afghanistan's silent protector.

Unfortunately, though, May seemed to be going through some kind of trauma. Most of the time she just disappeared to her room. And if she wasn't in her room, she would be shouting into her mobile phone. And if she wasn't shouting into her phone, she would be downstairs picking at the food my mother had spent all day preparing for her, or even worse, she would be crying. Although it's never good to see a woman cry, her face looked angry rather than sad, and I found it confusing. To be honest, I thought May was slightly mental, and by the end of the second week I decided to give up investigating her spying activity for the Pakistanis and dedicate my time to getting a look at her breasts.

Now, there was one small problem with this new mission. I could see only a third of May's bedroom from the wall, and it wasn't the third she undressed in. After thinking about this situation as I waited for my mother's light to snap off, I realized my only option was to jump from the wall onto her balcony. This meant I would have to clear a gap roughly a meter wide and try not to think about the fall below.

After a fortnight of undercover operations I'd discovered that the buzz of the generator, which gave light to the house every second night when the city electricity took a holiday, easily hid any noise I made as I scrambled around, so with no fear of alerting May, even if I fell to my death, I climbed up the wall opposite the edge of her balcony and concentrated on the railings in front of me. Twelve bars across. I just had to jump and reach out for one of them.

Taking five deep breaths, I closed my eyes, offered a prayer to Allah, and pushed my feet from the wall with every bit of strength my legs had in them. Suddenly, almost as if I hadn't yet decided to jump, I felt my head slamming against the railings, and by some miracle my hands had hold of two of the bars.

Dazed and not quite believing I was there, I took a moment to breathe the silence back into my thumping heart. Only one small kick, and I could swing my legs onto the edge, pull myself onto the balcony, and the secrets of May's balloonlike figure would be mine. I'd get to see her breasts, possibly more. If I was really lucky, I might even see her—

"A-hem."

A sound came to worry my ears. It was a sound like a cough, and it seemed to be coming from below.

"A-a-hem."

There it was again.

Slowly, hoping against hope that I was just imagining things, I looked down, a little to the right, and saw James standing there, shaking his head and wagging his finger at me. I looked back at the bright light coming from May's bedroom, then back at James. He hadn't gone anywhere, which would have been the polite thing to do. He was obviously waiting for me to make some kind of move.

"Salaam aleykum." I smiled weakly.

I let go of the bars and fell to his feet, rolling myself into a tight ball as I landed to kill the blow of the soon-to-come assault. After a silence that lasted only seconds but seemed to last at least half of my short life, I heard another cough. I looked up to see James smiling. His eyes were shiny like glass, and he was swaying slightly. He then nodded his head in the direction of the garden and waved at me to follow.

I was in no hurry to go, but I decided it would be better to take a beating as far away from the front of the house—and as far away from the chance of my mother seeing my shame and adding her own style of torture afterward—as possible. So, holding my head high like a man, I followed James to the plastic chairs standing ghostlike in the gloom of the garden.

Without a word he invited me to sit next to him. He then reached down to his side, picked up a bottle of beer from a cardboard box, knocked its metal cap off on the edge of the table, and handed it to me.

It was obviously a trick, but I took it anyway.

James then reached for another bottle, opened it the same way, hit it against the one I held in my hand, and slurred something I didn't understand. His breath smelled of old cheese.

Carefully I watched him, not daring to move, but he tipped his hand to his lips, showing that I should drink. So I did.

At first the beer tasted disgusting, bubbly and bitter like rotten Pepsi, but this was obviously my punishment and it was better than being beaten with a stick, so I took another sip, and then another, and another, and another.

In no time at all, I found my head had gone numb. A warmth, different from heat, breathed through my body, traveling up inside my veins to finish at my cheeks, making my eyes feel starry. Everything around me seemed to be muffled by an invisible blanket, and James was speaking in a language I didn't understand. As I continued to drink, I began to talk to him too. I couldn't help myself; the words were jumping from my mouth as if they were racing down a hill, rolling over and over one another. Neither of us knew what the other was saying, that much was still clear, but it didn't seem to matter. It felt like the best conversation I'd ever had in my life. The fact is, James really seemed to understand me.

By the end of my second bottle I'd told him all about Jahid and Jamilla and my best friend, Spandi. I revealed the secrets of our wages, our trips around the city hanging off the back of trucks, how we once found Pir the Madman asleep in the park and put wet mud in his pants so he'd think he'd shit himself when he woke up.

As the night grew old and the edges of the world blurred, I confessed to spying on May. At the sound of her name, James wiggled his hands in front of his chest, waved his cigarette and beer in big circles, and laughed. I laughed as well, although I wasn't sure why, and soon James was jumping up from his seat, slapping me on the back, crashing his bottle into mine, and rubbing my hair, which I didn't seem to mind anymore.

But then, as quickly as it had started, it all stopped.

Like a street dog caught in headlights, James turned and froze, his hand raised above his head, still holding the bottle of beer. Everything around us seemed to grow still, even the air we were breathing, and I watched mesmerized as the ashy tip of his cigarette floated to the floor and a dark figure emerged in the distance in front of him. It looked something like Georgie.

She was staring at us, and she didn't appear happy.

She was dressed only in a long black T-shirt, her legs were bare, and her dark hair whipped about her head like a mass of angry snakes. She looked more magical than normal, furious and amazing, and I thought my heart would break at the dark, angry beauty of her, but then maybe it was the shock of her arrival, I don't know, or the sight of her naked legs, or the heavy thumping in my chest, or the sudden weight of a thousand camels that had come to drag at my head, but at that exact moment I leaned forward in my chair and threw up on my shoes.

3

THE DAY AFTER I covered my shoes in vomit was possibly the worst day of my life. Well, not the worst. But it was pretty damn bad.

My throat was sore, all dry and swollen; my stomach ached, feeling empty and rotten; my skin was damp and cold; my head had a million steel workers hammering inside it; and my mother had found me a job before noon, even though it was Friday and nobody was working—yet another example of the mysterious magic mothers carry out when their eyes burn with anger. From now on, for two hours after school I would have to play servant to Pir Hederi, a shopkeeper as old as the King's Tomb whose sight had disappeared behind milky white curtains.

I was beyond annoyed.

"If you can't behave, you'll have to earn," my mother stated matter-of-factly. "And from now on you stay away from James. Do you hear me?"

I groaned. It was just like Jahid all over again.

"How am I supposed to do *that*?" I whimpered.

"I don't care how you do it, just do it!"

My mother was impossible. In fact, she was more impossible than all the warlords trying to run this country, and that was pretty much as impossible as you get. Thank God, then, that Georgie informed her only that I'd been drinking beer. If she knew I'd also been trying to sneak a look at May's breasts before I fell to the ground and hit the bottle, I'm certain she would have packed me off to a madrassa, right there and then.

"Drinking alcohol is against Islam," she reminded me. "Now you'll have to pay for your sin in the fires of Hell. You're probably not even ten years old, Fawad. At this rate you'll be burning for eternity along with all the Godless foreigners!"

"I didn't know it was beer!" I shouted back.

"There! That's another ten years in Hell for lying, plus five more for shouting at your mother. I'd shut up now if I was you."

"But—"

"But! But! No more buts! Get out of my sight before I change my mind and beat you!"

I shook my head slowly. It appeared Jahid was right. There was just no reasoning with women, especially when the woman was your mother.

I turned from the kitchen and shuffled toward the garden to escape the fury I didn't feel I strictly deserved. I was a boy after all. What about James? He had made me commit the sin, and he was a man. Would he be forced to work for Hederi the Blind for a handful of afs I could just as easily find in the gutters of Chicken Street? No such luck. And this was the new democratic Afghanistan!

Further evidence of this great injustice appeared as I turned the corner to seek refuge in the garden and saw James, my great undoer, sitting hunched over his laptop wearing dark glasses. His forehead looked like a great weight was hanging above it, pressing deep lines into the skin below.

"Brilliant," I mumbled, and turned back toward my room.

Defeated, I crawled into bed to sleep off the sickness that was crawling over my skin like body lice.

Pir Hederi's shop was on the corner of Street 15, opposite a roundabout and close to the British Embassy. It was a messy place with cans spilling from shelves, boxes piled high on the floor, bleeding cloths, towels, and other cleaning stuff, and crates of fruit that had seen better days but still seemed to sell. During my first day on duty he told me that I'd been hired because he'd sacked his "bastard shit of a nephew" who used to place boxes and chairs in his path just to see him fall. He was also a thief, apparently.

"Don't try anything on, son," he warned me. "I may not have eyes no more, but I can still see."

He pointed his gnarly hand at the doorway, where a dog as big as a small donkey stood guard, watching me as if I was that day's dinner.

"What's his name?" I asked, keeping a careful eye on the beast that threatened to eat me. He was as old and as ugly as his master, with gray stumps for ears, marking him out as a former fighter.

"Whose name?"

"The dog."

"Dog."

"Yes, the dog."

"Dog. His name is Dog."

"Oh."

Despite his appearance, and obvious lack of imagination, I soon found out that Pir Hederi was actually quite funny. And from what I could tell, he didn't need my help at all. If a man came in asking for shaving foam, Pir would move from his seat in front of the cigarette counter, shuffle over to the far right corner, reach out to the second shelf down, and come away with the correct can. If some no-good kids came in and tried to lift any of the stock, Dog would block their way out, growling and snarling, spit hanging from his teeth like slimy string and the hairs on his back standing to attention, until the would-be thieves pissed their pants and cried for their mothers. Pir would then charge them fifty afs for a safe exit.

No, he didn't really need me, but I got the impression that

Pir was a lonely old man looking for someone to talk to. So, the first week, I mainly poured him tea and sat on the Pepsi boxes eating dry chickpeas as he wandered through his thoughts and war memories.

"We lost a lot of good men that day," he said one afternoon after recounting another tale about his time with the mujahideen. I nodded wisely, then grunted after remembering he couldn't actually see me. There had been sixty of them that day, all Pashtuns, "all committed to the cause of freedom," and they were armed to the teeth with Kalashnikovs and rocket launchers. They'd just carried out a daring daylight attack on a Russian base north of Kunar. "Hundreds of enemy soldiers died in the assault," said Pir, "caught unawares by the sheer daring of our raid and knocked senseless by a lifetime of vodka. We'd also battered them with rocket-propelled grenades and a wall of bullets fired by men with nothing to lose and everything to gain." It was a famous victory for the mujahideen, he told me, a triumph that was spun into songs and sung around campfires for years to come. And as quickly as they had appeared, rising from nowhere to unleash hell on the Russians, they melted away again, "like ghosts drifting back into the landscape."

But they hadn't got away with the attack.

As the victorious mujahideen crossed the mountains of Nuristan, marching their way toward secret war camps dug into rock, they were swallowed up by a blizzard that ripped at their clothes and tore at their skin. In the roar of the wind they failed to hear the blades of the helicopter that came whooshing over their heads, dropping brilliant burning light upon their path. As they ran for their lives, the Russian air force tracked them every step of the way, on and on into the night, finally forcing them into a narrow gorge where they were ambushed by five hundred waiting Russian soldiers. The mujahideen didn't stand a chance, but somehow they fought their way out of the valley to split and scatter under the cover of a leafless forest, throwing themselves into icy mountain rivers and burying themselves under a meter of snow.

"Yes, we lost a lot of good men that day," said Pir with a sigh. "We also lost most of our toes . . ."

I looked at Pir's cracked feet. All ten toes peeked out from the leather straps, carrying thick yellow nails.

"So, is that how you came to be blind then? From fighting in the jihad?"

"Mercy, no," he grumbled. "I lost my sight the day I got married. I saw my wife for the first time, and she was that ugly my eyes closed down and refused to work again."

Pir usually finished with me about five thirty in the evening. If I timed it just right, I'd hit the main road about the same time Georgie was being driven home, and I would hitch a ride with her back to the house. Like most foreigners, she had her own driver, Massoud, which I thought was pretty good considering she only combed goats for a living.

"They're not just any old goats," Georgie told me one day as I laughed about her being the richest goat herder in the whole of Afghanistan. "They're cashmere goats."

"So what? A goat's a goat, born to be eaten or dragged around a field by *buzkashi* horsemen! What's so special about some dumb cashmere goat?"

"The wool, sweetie. It's very expensive. Women in the West will practically sell their souls for sweaters and shawls made out of cashmere. And luckily for your country, Afghanistan is home to some of the finest cashmere in the world."

"So why aren't all the goat herders rich then?"

"Well, most goat owners don't realize the value of what they've got, so they let the cashmere drop off, or they shear it off with the rest of the wool and throw it away. You see, it's the soft undercoat of the goat which is the good bit, and it needs to be combed out and separated. In its raw, unwashed state, this can sell for about twenty dollars per kilogram."

"Ho, that's not bad."

"It's not bad, but it's also not that good."

"No?"

"No. Not yet." Georgie smiled and raised her eyebrows as if she was about to tell me some big secret. "Even if the farmers know about the special wool, they will only collect it. It's then shipped off to Iran or Belgium or China, where it's mixed with inferior wool and sometimes reimported, which is pure madness. Now, if we could set up the facilities to treat the wool in Afghanistan and make it as good as good can be, your goat herders would be very rich men indeed. Well, compared to what they are now anyway. It would also create more jobs and develop into a proper industry. And that's why I'm here in your country, to help everyone do just that."

Georgie leaned back into the seat of the car and seemed very pleased with herself.

Personally, as far as secrets went I thought this had to be the worst of the worst. However, I quite liked the idea of her teaching the poor goat herders how to become rich. Most people only come to Afghanistan to help themselves get rich, or richer.

"Will you take me one day?" I asked. "To see the goats?"

"Yes, of course I will, as long as your mother agrees."

"I think it will be okay," I said. "Unless you invite James, and then it might be a bit more complicated."

Georgie laughed. "Yes, I think you're right about that. He's not exactly her favorite person at the moment, is he?"

No, he isn't, I thought. Far from it.

Ever since *that* night, my mother had stopped talking to James. Sometimes she couldn't even bring herself to look at him, which was a bit embarrassing because he'd taken to bringing her flowers every day as some kind of peace offering. Unfortunately for James, this small effort had also landed him in hot water with Shir Ahmad, and I was certain that if the guard wasn't being paid three hundred dollars a month, he would have had James murdered.

I think Shir Ahmad had fallen in love with my mother at some point when I wasn't looking, or maybe when I was looking at someone else. I guess this was because she was still very beautiful, and I felt a little sorry for him—as long as he didn't try to touch her. For my mother's part, she laughed at his jokes, fixed his tea, and cooked his food, but she seemed to prefer the company of Homeira across the road. So that left Shir Ahmad alone to take care of his hopeful heart—and to stare dangerously at James when he came home with yet another unwanted bunch of flowers.

In fact, the only person who was allowed and seemed to want to talk to James these days was May, who had stopped crying and started getting drunk. I didn't know which was worse. Either way her face was still red and puffy.

"What's happened to May?" I asked Georgie one day in the car.

"What do you mean?"

"She's always laughing now."

"Well, that's better than crying, isn't it?"

"I don't know. And I'm not sure James does either."

Georgie smiled and turned to look at me. "Yes, she does seem to spend more time with him these days."

"She wants to be his girlfriend," I stated knowingly, only for Georgie to shake her head and laugh hard.

"I don't think so, Fawad. She's a . . . what do you call it in Dari? She's a woman who likes other women more than she likes men."

My heart skipped a beat at this latest shock of information, and I felt the sticky prickle of sweat break out at the sides of my head.

"What do you mean *likes*?" I whispered, asking about May but thinking of my mother and her many visits across the road.

"Like husbands like wives . . . that kind of like," Georgie explained with a wink, obviously mistaking my concern for surprise.

I nodded my head, as if I didn't care and to show I was a man of the world, but her words bumped around my brain like a death sentence. *Like husbands like wives . . . like husbands like wives . . .* It was unreal. It was unbelievable. That didn't mean just talking. That meant kissing and *everything*.

As the words slowly sank in and I pictured the full horror of my future playing out before my eyes, I realized I'd have to take drastic action, and quick.

I'd have to force my mother to marry Shir Ahmad.

"You're a bit young to be looking for a woman, aren't you?"

Pir Hederi turned his white eyes in my direction. We were sitting side by side, in front of the shop, enjoying the warm breeze that breathed the end of summer on our faces.

"It's not for me," I corrected, a bit disgusted at the thought.

"Who for, then?"

"Just someone—a man."

Since the shock of discovering my mother might be a woman who likes other women, I'd been trying everything I could think of to make her fall in love with Shir Ahmad, but nothing seemed to be working.

The first thing I'd done was to convince James during the rare moments my mother left us alone in the house to hand over his flowers to the guard so that he might pass them on to her. Both men hesitated at first, not liking the idea of giving and receiving flowers from each other, but when I explained using a mixture of hand gestures and pieces of English that my mother might feel more comfortable getting gifts from a foreigner through an Afghan, they both agreed to try it. And although my mother now accepted the flowers, which she arranged in old coffee jars and placed around the windows, she didn't seem to be moving any closer to accepting Shir Ahmad's company beyond quick conversations during the handover of teapots and food plates.

My next tactic involved making Shir appear interesting. "Oh! That Shir! He's a funny man!" I'd laugh, collapse, and shake my head with the hilarity of another made-up story or joke he'd never told, hoping to arouse my mother's curiosity. "Here, listen to this!" I ordered one evening, coming to sit by my mother's side as she washed one of Georgie's white shirts in a bowl of soapy water. "One day, a mental fell asleep by the side of the road. He was wearing a brand-new pair of boots. A man walked up to him and decided to steal the snoring mental's boots. Carefully, the thief removed them and put his old pair of shoes on the crazy man's feet. Not long after, a car came up the road and stopped in front of the mental. The driver woke him and told him, 'Move your feet out of the road so that I may pass by.' The mental then looked at his feet and said, 'Brother, pass by. These feet don't belong to me!'" I slapped my thighs, threw my head back in laughter, and waited for my mother to join in. But she didn't. She simply gave me a look and asked, "Have you been drinking beer again?" before returning her attention to Georgie's wet, soapy shirts.

After the jokes failed to work, I slowly began to gather the threads of Shir Ahmad's life, from the short conversations we shared as I left for and returned from school.

"He used to have a wife," I told my mother after I had collected all the facts and pulled them into something that might show him to be more than a man who just stood at the door.

"Who did?"

"Shir Ahmad."

Mother put down the knife she was using to saw up the fatty flesh of one of Afghanistan's big-bottomed sheep.

"So?" she asked. "What happened to her?"

"It's a sad story, Mother. A very sad story."

"Don't be dramatic, Fawad."

She turned back to the raw meat and carried on hacking.

"Okay," I hurried, worried that I'd lost her so early on in the tale, "but it *is* sad."

I threw her a stern look to remind her that a good Muslim woman should have more sympathy.

"Shir told me that he was married very young to an even younger girl from his village and that he loved her very, very much. Every day he would bring her flowers." I paused, watching my mother as I stressed the word *flowers*, but she didn't even blink. "So, he brought her *flowers* every day, and he would sing to her every night as she prepared their dinner. They didn't have much because Shir only had a small job learning how to file paperwork at the offices of the Department of Agriculture. He was educated, you see. He could read and write; that's how he got the job with the department, where you have to know your numbers. Anyway, Shir and his wife were planning on having a big family. They wanted at least five sons and as many daughters, but when the first child came—he was a boy—he got stuck inside Shir's wife. For two days the women of the village tried to pull the baby from her stomach, and their house became filled with her blood and all of Shir's tears. For those two days he never left his wife's side, staying instead to hold her hand and press cold, wet cloths onto her head. Then finally, in the early hours of the third day, the women pulled the baby from Shir's wife's stomach. The baby boy was already dead, and as the women pulled him free that little dead baby took the last of his mother's breath away with him."

As I finished the story, my mother paused to wipe some strands of her hair away from her face using the back of the hand that still held the knife.

"We have all known suffering," she said quietly. "This is Afghanistan after all."

As she turned back to the meat, my brain finally caught up with my mouth and I felt bad. I suddenly realized I'd reminded her of all those things she was trying so hard to forget. It was a stupid mistake to make, and I kicked myself on the way back to my room. Properly. However, after my story, which was more or less true, my mother smiled at Shir Ahmad a little more kindly whenever she saw him, which was great, but it was hardly the breakthrough I'd been waiting for. And she was still spending too much of her time with the woman working across the road.

I decided to seek advice.

"Money," announced Pir Hederi as he cleaned his teeth with the frayed ends of a twig. "That's the only thing women want or understand. Money, and maybe gold. They seem to like that too."

I thought about this idea for a while, but couldn't imagine Shir Ahmad had a lot of either. He was far too skinny. In Afghanistan, the wealthier a man is, the bigger his belly.

"I think he's more poor than rich," I confessed.

"He's screwed then," Pir grumbled, patting Dog on the head as he did so. Dog thumped his heavy tail on the floor, then got to his feet and walked over to my side, where he nuzzled his face in my hands. After I'd spent a few weeks working at the shop without trying to rob or further cripple his master, me and Dog got on just fine.

At that moment, Georgie's 4×4 pulled up in front of us.

She'd started passing by after work to see if I wanted a lift home, and though it was only a little thing it made my head grow fat with pride. Georgie opened her door but didn't get out.

"Salaam aleykum, Pir Hederi. How are you? Are you well? How's your health? Everything fine? Are you good?"

As Pir answered that he was okay, he was well, his health was strong, everything was fine, and he was good, I picked up my schoolbooks, stroked Dog good-bye, and jumped into the car.

"Don't forget, Fawad!" Pir shouted after me. "Money and gold! Money and gold!" He started cackling the way old people do, then got to his feet and headed back into the shop, Dog padding after him.

"What was that about?" Georgie asked as I settled in beside her.

"Oh, nothing," I lied. "He's crazy." Which was true.

"Fair enough. So how was school today?"

"Pretty good. Our teacher dropped dead from a heart attack."

"You're kidding?"

"No, really, it's true. One minute he was standing in front of us writing Pashto spellings on the board the Americans gave us; the next he was on the ground, completely dead."

"That's awful, Fawad. Are you okay?" Georgie reached for my hand.

"Yes. It was quite interesting really. The teacher hit his head on a table when he fell, and there was blood coming out of a cut by the side of his ear. It made a small picture on the floor. It looked like a map of Afghanistan. Don't you think that's interesting? Have you ever seen anything like that?"

Georgie shook her head. Her hair was covered by a dark brown shawl that matched the color of her eyes, and I thought she looked more beautiful than ever. I realized then that if I was ever going to marry her I'd have to be very, very rich indeed, possibly the richest man in all of Afghanistan.

"Why do women like money so much?" I asked, turning to look out of the window to hide the red heat I felt breaking out on the tops of my cheeks.

"Who told you they do?" Georgie asked.

"Pir Hederi. He said women only like money or gold."

"Oh, that's what he was shouting about." She smiled. "I think that despite his age Pir may still have a lot to learn about women."

"Really?" I almost pleaded, hope coming once again for Shir Ahmad's so-far doomed romance with my mother.

"Yes, really. Although money is useful, there are far more important things in life to wish for, like being healthy or finding true love."

"Are you saying you could love someone who was poor?"

"Of course I could." Georgie laughed, flicking her finished cigarette out of the car window.

"What, even a goat herder?"

"Well, maybe not a goat herder," she confessed. "They tend to be a bit smelly. Like their goats. But really, money isn't that big a deal. Maybe some women might be attracted to money, gold, and power, but many more will find a good character and personality—and a nice smell—far more important qualities to have in the men they choose to marry. Why do you ask?"

"Oh, it's not important," I lied again. "It's just that I was thinking one day you might . . ."

As my thoughts gathered to speak the words I'd been hiding in my heart for so long, Georgie's phone rang.

"Sorry, Fawad jan," she said as she interrupted me to take the call.

"It's okay," I lied yet again.

"Hello?"

I heard a man's voice on the other end of the line. Worse than that, I heard him use the word *jan*.

"Khalid!" Georgie shouted, her face lighting up in a way I'd never seen before. "Where are you? What? No, I'm nearly home. In fact we're just turning into the road now. Hey! I see you!"

As Massoud pulled up, Georgie snapped her mobile phone shut and practically jumped out of the car before the wheels had stopped turning. I leaned forward in my seat to find out who she was running to.

In front of the house I could see three large Land Cruisers surrounded by fifteen or more armed guards. Two of the guards stood on the opposite side of the road facing the house, more stood in front of and behind the vehicles, and the rest were gathered around a tall man dressed in a sky blue *salwar kameez*. He wore a gray waistcoat that matched the color of his *pakol*.

I thought he was about to either be arrested or start a one-man war.

As Georgie walked up to him, quick and easy as a cat, his face creased into a large, friendly smile. He took her hand and covered it with both of his own before leading her into the house. Our house.

I quickly grabbed my books and mumbled my good-byes to Massoud, disturbed that I might be missing something and upset because Georgie hadn't even looked back to make sure I was following her. At the sight of this man she'd forgotten all about me, and I suddenly felt small and childish. Even the army of guards surrounding our house ignored me as I walked past them, talking among themselves and lighting up cigarettes now their boss had gone. It was as if I was so small I didn't even exist. I was a nobody, a tiny little nobody that nobody cared about and nobody saw, which is great if you're a spy, but I wasn't a spy, not really. I was just a boy in love with a woman called Georgie.

I entered the yard and saw that the man still had hold of her hand. I felt daggers hit my heart and an anger creep into my stomach. The man seemed to be apologizing for something.

"You have to take more care of me," I heard Georgie tell him.

"I will. I promise. Just forgive me," he replied.

His voice was deep and low, and it suited his face, which was strong and framed by thick dark hair, a trim black beard, and heavy eyebrows. He looked like an Afghan film star, and I hated him for it.

Slamming the gate behind me, I broke up their embrace, and Georgie held her now-free hands out to introduce me. The man was called Haji Khalid Khan, and I realized from her actions and in spite of her words that she was in love with a man who was not only very rich but also powerful enough to have a lot of enemies, judging by the number of bodyguards now swarming around our house.

4

AUTUMN IS MY favorite season in Kabul. After the burning heat of summer, the air relaxes, allowing a cool wind to travel through the city, carrying the smell of wood fires and smoking kebabs on its back. The night comes early, swallowing up the day before it's barely begun, and a million gas burners and single lightbulbs shine from stores built out of old shipping containers that snake through the city, making it glow like a massive wedding party.

I know most people think of spring as the season of new beginnings, when women chase the winter dirt from their homes, when the plants come out of hiding and the animals give birth to their babies, but for me autumn is the season that whispers fresh promise.

Coming as it did during the holy time of Ramazan, when the adults step closer to Allah through fasting and prayers, it was autumn when the Taliban finally gave up control of Afghanistan. One November night they simply fled from the capital in pickups and stolen cars as the soldiers of the Northern Alliance rumbled in from the Shomali Plain to take Kabul without a fight. At the gate of the city where the hill dips to an easy slope, I watched from Spandi's house as thousands of men dressed in uniforms and *salwar kameez* gathered in groups, leaning lazily on the tanks and jeeps that had brought them there, their guns slung casually over their shoulders. It was like a huge picnic rather than a war as local men came out of their homes to offer what food and water they had to the new conquerors of Afghanistan.

As me, Spandi, and Jahid sat watching at the window—a five-minute walk from where the soldiers were eating, smoking, and laughing—we all confessed to being mightily disappointed at the lack of fighting. For weeks the Taliban had been spitting insults and threats across the radio, vowing to fight the Northern Alliance and their infidel backers to the very last man. But when the time came to stand, the Taliban ran away like frightened dogs, leaving only the Arabs and Pakistanis to carry out their suicidal ideas of war.

"We should go down and welcome them," Jahid suggested as we watched the swarm of figures silhouetted by the headlights of their vehicles.

"Good idea," I said. "Let's do it."

"Not so fast, gentlemen," Spandi ordered, his face a lighter shade of gray than it is today. "You can't know a man's real intentions in only one night."

I looked at Spandi with something close to wonder. It was the wisest thing I'd ever heard anyone say.

Smiling shyly, he added, "My father told me that."

"Your father should be working for the Genius Ministry!" I laughed, because Spandi's father was one hundred percent right.

My mother told me that when the Taliban originally came marching from the south to lay claim to Kabul, they were welcomed like saviors. The capital had become a city of rubble after the Russians left because the victorious mujahideen had turned on one another, fighting like dogs over a piece of meat—and Kabul was that piece of meat. In the chaos and confusion of civil war, crime was everywhere; shops were made to pay special taxes, homes were taken, people were murdered, and their daughters were raped. But when the Taliban came, it all stopped. Order was brought, and the people were grateful. However, as Spandi's father said, you cannot know a man's real intentions in only one night, and over the years the Taliban showed their true colors. They stopped women from working, they wouldn't let girls go to school, they roamed the streets beating people with sticks, they jailed men with short beards, they banned kite flying and music, they chopped off hands, they crushed people under walls, and they shot people in the football stadium. They had freed Afghanistan from war, but they locked up our people in a religion we no longer recognized. And it was only the warm winds of autumn that finally blew them away.

"The Taliban were bastards all right," declared Pir Hederi as I sorted through the crates of fruit and moldering vegetables to see what could be saved for the morning. "Thick as cow shit as well. Most of them were small men from small villages who'd never been taught to read and write. Hell, even their leaders were illiterate."

"Can you read and write?" I asked, scraping the mold off one potato and putting it in the "for sale" box.

"No, Fawad, I'm blind."

"Oh yeah, sorry about that."

"Blame the wife."

"So how did they get to rule Afghanistan then," I asked, "if they were so stupid?"

"Through fear," mumbled Pir as he picked the dry dust from the inside of his nose. "Your mother was right: when they first arrived everybody more or less loved them. The country was being bombed to hell by warlords who worked only to fill their own pockets, and the people were scared and tired of being scared. Suddenly this group of fighters emerged from Kandahar promising order, preaching Islam, and hanging child rapists. Who wouldn't welcome them?"

"Welcome who?" Spandi asked, arriving out of the dark, his can hanging smokeless and hooked on the waistband of his jeans.

"The Taliban," I answered.

"Oh, those bastards."

Pir started cackling. "Exactly, son. Come, take the weight off your feet."

Spandi pulled up a crate and kicked off his shoes. He had become a regular visitor to the shop after finding me throwing rubbish into a ditch at the end of the street a few weeks back. He had been walking to Old Makroyan at the time, the sprawl of flats he and his father had moved to after the fall of the Taliban. In their golden days the blocks of Old Makroyan were the pride of the city, but now they were no more than slum dwellings, a new hole for Kabul's lost to fall into. But they were closer to the city than Khair Khana, which made it easier to find work.

"So, where was I?" Pir asked, magically picking out a can of Pepsi, which he handed to Spandi.

"The people were welcoming the Taliban because they killed child rapists and talked about Islam," I reminded him.

"Oh yes, Islam." He sighed, nodding his head thoughtfully. "Of course, it was a very strict interpretation of sharia law that they preached, and it brought back public executions and floggings. Kites were also banned, as were televisions and music. You couldn't even clap your hands at sporting events anymore—not that I've ever been able to see who was winning anyway. At one point they even put a stop to New Year celebrations. In fact the only thing we were permitted to do was walk to the park and sniff at the flowers. Damn homosexuals. But really it was the women who had it worse than anyone else."

"I know," Spandi interrupted. "My father knew a woman who had all of her fingers cut off by the religious police just because she'd colored her nails."

"See!" Pir shouted. "That's exactly what they were like!"

"But why did they do it?" I asked, unable to understand

why anyone should cut off the fingers of someone's mother just for the sake of some paint.

"They said it was to protect women's honor. In reality it was because they were out-and-out bastards. Why do you think anyone who was anyone tried to escape to Pakistan?"

"The Pakistanis are all bastards too," mumbled Spandi.

"Right again, son," Pir agreed. "But at least they offered people some standard of living. Despite the promises, this place went to shit under the Taliban. There was hardly enough food, minimal clean water, and even fewer jobs. The government was a shambles, and the whole damn machine began to grind to a halt. Then, what do you know? When food prices soared and conditions sank so low we could no longer see the sun, or feel it in my case, the Taliban's planning minister, a man called Qari Din Mohammad, told the world we didn't need international help because 'we Muslims believe God the Almighty will feed everybody one way or another.' Bullshit! God had enough on His plate trying to keep us alive."

God, Afghanistan, and the Taliban were complicated subjects when put together, and difficult to make sense of, especially when you were only a boy, because the bottom line was this: a good Muslim should never question the ways of the Almighty. A good Muslim would trust in God to provide, no matter what, and even if He didn't provide, a good Muslim would trust that the hunger, death, fighting, and disease that came to visit his door were all part of God's plan. And given that knowledge, the Taliban planning minister must have been right and his regime must also have been part of God's plan for Afghanistan. And that's quite an argument when you're taking over a country.

Taliban basically means "religious students," so it must have been easy to convince ordinary Muslims living in the countryside, who couldn't read and write, that the orders they gave came straight from the pages of the Koran. If it says in the Holy Koran that girls should not go to school, who was a farmer to question the Word of God? Of course, my mother said the Holy Koran doesn't say any such thing, although how she knows this, being illiterate herself, I'm not sure, but she seems pretty confident. However, when a Talib tells a man with no schooling that it is written just so, how can he argue against such knowledge and learning, and therefore against God Himself? He has to accept it. And that's why the best weapon the Afghan people have against the Taliban or any other terrible power that may choose to put itself in Afghanistan is education. At least that's what Ismerai told me.

Ismerai was the latest newest person in my life, and he was Haji Khalid Khan's uncle.

"When you can read and write and discover facts for yourself, it is far easier to see God's truth," he explained as he leaned back on the blanket that had been laid on the grass of our garden, sucking deeply from his hands, which were wrapped around an Afghan cigarette. "Education is the key to Afghanistan's successful future, Fawad, because it fights ignorance and intolerance and brings the blessing of opportunity. When a man has knowledge he has power—the power to make informed decisions; the power to distinguish truth from lies; and the power to shape his own destiny in accordance with God's will. He is stronger than the ignorant man, who can do nothing but blindly accept the supposed learning of another. And speaking of the blind . . ." Ismerai paused to force a huge smoke ring from his mouth. "I'd advise your friend Pir Hederi to be a little more careful when speaking about the Taliban in the future. Any man can shave off his beard and swap his turban, but it doesn't mean he is a changed man." Taking another pull on his cigarette, he added mysteriously, "We are not alone."

I nodded slowly, letting the words take shape in my head so that I'd remember them. "Okay, I'll tell Pir Hederi," I promised, because I looked up to Ismerai and I trusted what he had to say. He also smoked drugs, and though my mother disapproved, I thought it made him funny and interesting.

Ismerai and Haji Khalid Khan often visited the house together because, apparently, Georgie was friends with the whole family. She told me she knew his brothers and cousins and even his children, so I realized it was little wonder she'd never found time to learn how to wash her clothes. She was too busy collecting Afghans.

Since the day Haji Khalid Khan had come into my world, with his army of bodyguards and two-hand embraces, my relationship with Georgie had been, at best, polite. We would talk now and again, but I preferred to keep my distance, and Georgie didn't push it. We were growing apart, and though it was all my doing, I couldn't help myself. I felt betrayed. I felt like she'd let me down. Led me on and let me down.

I think Georgie realized I was upset because when she came to pick me up from Pir Hederi's I would make up some excuse or tell her I was busy rather than accept a lift home—and I wouldn't let her hold my hand anymore. "I'm not a child!" I'd shouted at her the last time she'd reached for me, and I knew I'd hurt her feelings because she said very quietly, "Fawad, I have never, ever treated you like a child."

"You told my mother I'd been drinking beer!" I sharply reminded her.

"Okay, apart from that time," she agreed, then walked off, leaving me feeling angry and horrid because it wasn't really her fault and the blame lay completely in my own head.

"She's a good woman, you know," Ismerai scolded me as we sat in the garden passing another hour together as Haji

Khalid Khan took Georgie inside to do God knows what with her.

"I didn't say she wasn't," I snapped.

"No," he admitted, "but your actions talk for you, and it's not a nice way to behave to someone who's a guest in our country and, even more than that, a friend."

And of course he was right. I was jealous without having the right to be jealous. I should have been pleased to see Georgie happy. But it was hard, and I was annoyed by the smile that played on her face now. I hated the fact that she drank her coffee with Haji Khalid Khan in the late afternoon when it used to be me, and I was wild with anger that at least twice a week she would stay away from the house and I knew she was with him.

"Your time will come, child," Ismerai said, "but it won't be with Georgie."

And I realized he'd looked deep into my heart and knew everything.

Despite the hurt that covered my insides like a bad bruise slowly going yellow, it was hard not to like Haji Khalid Khan.

"He's a charmer," my mother admitted as we talked about Georgie's friendship. "He could talk the birds from the trees, that man."

"Shir Ahmad talks to the dogs in the street," I offered.

"It's not quite the same thing," she replied.

"What do you mean, then?"

"You'll find out soon enough, Fawad, because if I'm not mistaken you've got the same gift—although right now you only seem capable of talking the hind legs off a donkey. But it'll come, son. It'll come."

And my mother went back to her chores, leaving me to think about my future talent and my current, previously unknown, ability to cripple donkeys.

However, it wasn't Haji Khalid Khan's way with words that slowly ate away at my anger, although he was funny and strangely gentle in his manners for such a big man. No, my feelings began to slide on the Friday when Spandi came for lunch. It was Georgie's idea to invite him, and I guessed it was mainly for my benefit.

All of us—me, my mother, Georgie, James, May, Ismerai, Spandi, and Haji Khalid Khan—were drinking green tea outside in the garden. Although a cold wind bit at our fingers, we were enjoying the last of the autumn days before another winter closed in and locked us indoors. On a deep-red blanket we sat cross-legged, forming a ragged circle as the adults fired happy stories into the air. Georgie and Haji Khalid Khan acted as translators, which marked them out as different from the rest of us, somehow more worldly and knowledgeable, and brought them together as a couple. Nobody seemed to question this other than me, so I tried to hide my annoyance whenever Georgie rested her hand on Haji Khalid Khan's knee or softly stroked his shoulder as she got to her feet to refill our cups.

For it wasn't just Georgie whose mood changed with the appearance of Haji Khalid Khan; everyone seemed to be different around this elegant man, who dressed like a king and smelled of expensive perfume. His visits dragged everyone away from their different lives, uniting us in shared jokes and happy moments like a family. It wasn't a daily thing, of course, but while Haji Khalid Khan was in Kabul everyone at the house gathered at least once a week, twice if there was a reason to, such as Spandi's invitation to lunch.

That afternoon, after a great spread of sheep kebabs,

curried chicken, *Kabuli pilau*, and warm naan—all of which had appeared with Haji Khalid Khan and Ismerai—we relaxed into the evening, drinking from cups steaming with the green tea my mother had prepared. Although she sat a little back from us, on one of the plastic chairs, my mother was as much a part of the group as any of us on the blanket, listening and laughing to the stories batting from one person to another.

James, who was sharing a cushion with May, and an Afghan cigarette with Ismerai, was taking charge of most of the conversation as he had recently returned from Bamiyan. He said he had seen the huge holes that once housed two giant Buddhas and told us some international companies were now looking at ways to recapture the thousands of years of history that had been blown away by the Taliban.

"Among other things they were talking about was a laser show," he informed us, "the idea being to re-create the Buddhas in 3-D light where they used to stand. A pretty neat idea, but they'd need a bloody big generator." He laughed.

"I think it's a ridiculous waste of money," commented May, wrinkling the top of her nose. "People can hardly feed themselves, yet they want to spend millions on a fancy light show."

"But if this 'fancy light show' brings in tourists, it would create jobs and bring in money and therefore allow people to feed themselves," argued James, who always saw the good in everything, even May.

"Tourism!" she replied. "I don't think Afghanistan's quite ready for that yet. In fact, wasn't the tourism minister murdered by pilgrims on their way to hajj?"

"That was a few years ago," Georgie reminded her.

"And you think the situation is any better now?" May almost shouted. "The Taliban are back, the south has gone to crap, corruption is at an all-time high, and the government's influence barely stretches outside Kabul."

"The Taliban are back?" I asked Georgie, startled at the bit of news I had clearly understood.

I sat next to her, and she gently touched my hand. For the first time in a long while I didn't move away.

"Not really, Fawad," she reassured me. "But yes, they are fighting with government and international troops in some areas. It's nothing to get worried about."

"But why have they come back?"

Georgie looked at Haji Khalid Khan, who leaned in my direction.

"They never really went away," he said. "Some of them hid out in the mountains bordering Pakistan; others simply hid out in their own towns and villages."

"Don't worry too much about the Taliban," Ismerai joined in. "They're not the major concern right now. Afghanistan's main problem is outside interference. People are playing games in our country, and it's making it increasingly hard to tell friend from foe these days."

"What kind of games?" I asked. "Who's playing them?"

Georgie shot Haji Khalid Khan another look she obviously hoped I wouldn't see, and he clapped his hands together.

"Enough, now," he ordered in a soft growl created by years of smoking. "These are questions for politicians, not honest, everyday folk like us."

Ismerai laughed. "True enough, Haji Sahib. Which reminds me of a joke. Georgie, you translate for our foreign guests. Haji might not want to make fun of his friends."

"Do politicians have friends?" she asked, and those of us who spoke Dari all laughed.

"A busload of politicians was traveling down the road," Ismerai began. "Suddenly the bus veered off the road and hit a tree near a village. A farmer who was working on his land nearby came over. When he saw the politicians and the wreckage of the bus, he grabbed his shovel and buried all the politicians. Some days later, a police inspector passed by, and he saw the bus that had crashed into the tree. The policeman asked the farmer, who was working on his land as usual, when the accident had taken place. The farmer replied that the accident had taken place a few days earlier. The policeman then asked him about the identity of the travelers, and the farmer replied that 'all the passengers were politicians' and that he had buried them all. The policeman asked whether any of them had survived the crash. The farmer smiled and answered, 'Maybe. Some of them told me they were alive, but we both know politicians lie a lot.'"

As Ismerai ended, we all applauded the joke; however, it was Spandi who laughed the longest and loudest. He was practically doubled up, and I wondered whether this was from sitting so close to Ismerai's burning cigarette. As my friend tried to take back control of his body, tears sprang from his eyes, forcing him to wipe them away with the back of his hand, which left black smudges on his face.

Suddenly, Haji Khalid Khan stopped to look at him, dark and serious.

"You sell *spand*, I take it?" he asked flatly.

"Yes, Haji, I do," Spandi replied, his shoulders relaxing from the fit that had just passed over him.

"That's hard work, boy," Ismerai admitted, sucking again on his sweet-smelling cigarette before handing it over to Haji Khalid Khan, who took it and nodded.

The big man then leaned over to his uncle and whispered something in his ear. Ismerai smiled, got to his feet, and walked out of the garden and through the gate without another word. None of us asked where he was going because in

Afghanistan you don't ask. In the company of men, a boy is merely expected to sit, watch, and learn. There are many rules in our country, but the rule of not asking is learned pretty quickly.

About thirty minutes later, after James and even May had shared their own jokes with us—some of which I found hard to find funny because they didn't mention mentals or donkeys—Ismerai came back with a long chain of cards. They were held together by plastic wrapping and advertised companies like Roshan, AWCC, and Areeba. Haji Khalid Khan handed over the chain and a small bag to Spandi. Inside were dozens of the cards that people bought in order to make calls on their mobile phones. They each had a special number that you had to scratch from the back and then dial into your phone. This was big business in Afghanistan because even if you didn't own the clothes on your back you sure as hell owned a phone.

"These are for you," Haji Khalid Khan informed my friend. "From now on, you sell these cards, and for every card you sell you get to keep one dollar. The rest belongs to me. Okay?"

Spandi looked at the cards lying in the bag beside him, his red eyes wide and amazed, and nodded his head.

"Thank you," he said quietly.

"My pleasure, son," replied Haji Khalid Khan, and Georgie placed her hand gently on his knee and smiled. In fact all of us smiled, and I saw in that one act something of the man she had fallen in love with, because giving Spandi the means to work away from his can was probably the greatest kindness I'd ever witnessed, but never thought of. If I had, maybe I could have convinced Georgie to find Spandi a different job, something away from the poison smoke that clogged his lungs and stung his eyes. But it was Haji Khalid Khan who looked through the black and saw the boy. He had thrown him a second chance, and I felt ashamed of myself for having ignored what was so obvious. Even so, I also felt some small pride in having been the one to introduce Spandi to his new boss.

And that's when I felt my anger start to slip away from me.

A little after eight, when all the adults had gone their separate ways—James and May to one of Kabul's many bars, my mother to her room to watch the latest episode of a hysterical Indian soap opera on Tolo TV, and Georgie to Haji Khalid Khan's house with Ismerai—Spandi and I walked to the dump that wafted bad smells and disease across Massoud Circle. Without a word, I watched him unhook the can from the waist of his trousers, give it one last look, then throw it as far into the heap as his thin arms could manage. As we stood side by side, our eyes followed the can as it bounced off the top of an old gas bottle before disappearing into the fleshy mess of rotten food and waste.

I glanced over at Spandi and saw his lips move with no sound. Suddenly, he turned to me and asked, "You know who your girlfriend's boyfriend is, don't you?"

"She's not my girlfriend." I laughed, pushing him hard in the stomach, the spell of the ceremony now broken.

"Whatever you say," Spandi said, pushing me back. "Your *friend's* boyfriend, then."

"If you are referring to Haji Khalid Khan, then yes, I do know who he is."

"Who?" Spandi challenged.

"He's a businessman from Jalalabad. He imports diesel and ghee oil from Pakistan and Toyota car parts from Japan."

"Of course he does." Spandi laughed, slapping me on the back. "For God's sake, Fawad! It's Haji Khan! *The* Haji

Khan—the scourge of the Taliban, the son of one of Afghanistan's most famous mujahideen, and now one of the country's biggest drug dealers. He's Haji Khan, Fawad! I recognized him the moment I saw him. And he's drinking tea at your house and sleeping with your girlfriend!"

5

A FGHANISTAN IS FAMOUS for two things: fighting and growing poppies. And despite the best efforts of the international community to put a stop to both, we seem to be better than ever at these two occupations.

After the Taliban fled in 2001, the air was filled with talk about "democracy," and within a couple of years everyone had the right to vote; women were allowed in Parliament; laws were written to protect the innocent; girls were allowed back in school; and all the wrongs done by our past leaders were apparently put right. But in the middle of all the excitement, everyone seemed to forget that Afghanistan already had a set of rules, a justice system going back thousands of years that was as much a part of our lives as the Hindu Kush mountains, and even though it was generally agreed that "democracy" was a good thing, the fact remained that if a man committed murder, then he was going to get it. Some blood feuds have gone on for generations in Afghanistan, with families carrying out so many killings nobody knows who started them anymore.

And even though the government has ordered everyone to give up their weapons for the greater good of the country, no one seems to be in a hurry to do so because things change so fast here. Therefore, the big men in the north and the west still fight over territory and power; army commanders in the east continue to shoot at Pakistanis who creep onto our soil uninvited; the Taliban fight goes on in the south against

Afghans and foreigners; and in the streets the adults beat boys, the boys beat smaller boys, and everyone beats donkeys and dogs.

Meanwhile, the opium crops continue to grow, and grow, and grow, and the newspapers say that this year there was a record harvest, making Afghanistan the biggest opium producer in the world. Although my mother says everyone should work to be the best at something, I don't think she has this in mind when she says it. I think she means math or religious studies.

And though I don't know much, I do know that fighting is bad because people die, they lose body parts, and it makes the women cry; and I know it's wrong to grow poppies because the West says it is and therefore so does President Karzai. So I don't think I'm being childish or selfish when I say that Haji Khalid Khan, or Haji Khan as I now know him to be, is probably not the right man for an Englishwoman in Kabul who combs goats for a living, having, as he does, a history of violence and opium money in his pocket.

Although how I should convince Georgie of this is anyone's guess. As my mother once said, and as Pir Hederi found to his cost, love is blind.

"Doesn't Haji Khan come from Shinwar, not Jalalabad?" I asked Georgie as she drank her coffee on the steps of the house. It was cold now, and she was wrapped in a soft gray *patu*, a parting gift from her lover before he left for the east.

"Yes, he does," she admitted. "But he has a house in Jalalabad and tends to spend most of his time there. Why do you ask?"

"Oh, nothing," I mumbled, wrapping my arms around my body and coming to sit by her side.

"Here, get under this." Georgie shuffled closer, placing the *patu* around my back and over my shoulder. It carried the heat of her body and the smell of her perfume. "Better?"

"Yes, thanks. It's cold, isn't it?"

"Yes, it is," she agreed, and I bit at my bottom lip, not sure where to begin, and even less sure about whether Georgie would take the *patu* away once I did begin.

"What's the matter?" she finally asked after we'd sat there in silence for the best part of a minute. "You look serious."

"Do I? Well, yes, maybe I am," I admitted. "It's just that, well, I heard that there are a lot of poppy crops in Shinwar."

"Not at the moment there aren't; it's winter." She laughed.

"I know that," I joined in, happy to have got the subject going at last. "But usually there are. Shinwar is famous for poppy."

"Yes, I suppose it is," Georgie agreed. "And your point is?"

"Nothing." I shrugged. "I just thought I'd mention it."

"Why? Because you think Khalid is involved in poppy?"

Georgie turned her head to look at me. To my gigantic relief she didn't seem angry, but I still thought it best to ignore the question.

"Look," she continued. "I know a lot of people think Khalid is involved in drugs because he's a rich man, but he isn't— isn't involved in drugs, that is; of course he's a rich man. Khalid hates drugs. He says they trap people in poverty, they damage the reputation of the country, and they pay for the insurgency that is threatening to wreck Afghanistan once again. He hates them, Fawad, absolutely hates them."

"But how can you be sure he's telling the truth?" I asked.

Georgie reached for the packet of cigarettes lying by her feet, removed one from the box, and lit it.

"Well, there are a number of reasons," she explained, releasing a line of smoke through her lips. "I know he has several projects running in the east helping farmers find work away

from poppy growing, like providing them with fruit and olive trees and seeds for wheat and perfume flowers. But mainly
I know he's telling the truth because I trust him."

Georgie looked away, sipped her coffee, and sucked heavily on her cigarette. I turned my face to my feet and watched
from the corner of my eye as she slowly dragged a pale hand
through her hair, stroking it away from her face. Against the
near-black of her hair and the gray of the *patu*, her skin looked
frosty white, and dark circles hung beneath her eyes.

"Are you tired?" I asked.

"A little, yes," she replied, a small smile thinning her lips.

I nodded. "I am too," I said, which wasn't true, but I didn't
want her to feel alone. Haji Khan had been gone a week, disappearing from our lives as suddenly as he had appeared,
and I guessed she was missing him.

"I've known Khalid for three years," Georgie stated, almost as if she had read my thoughts. "I would know if he
was lying to me."

"I didn't say he was lying."

"No. Well, not in so many words you didn't, so, thank you."

I shuffled my feet and let the softness of the *patu* cover
them.

"But . . . how can you really be sure that he's not?"

"How?" she asked, shrugging her shoulders in a very Afghan way that marked her out as nearly one of us. "Because
I am."

After a few seconds' pause, during which a crease appeared
in the middle of her eyebrows as if she was thinking hard,
she added, "It's like when a man, or a woman, says they love
you. How can you be sure they aren't just saying the words
and they really mean it? Well, you look into their eyes. I mean
really look, look hard, and you will feel it in your heart if they
are telling you the truth. I love Khalid. He wouldn't lie to me.
Now"—Georgie breathed a small laugh that sounded empty,

like the sound of trying—"he may not be the best boyfriend in the world—he disappears on a whim, and sometimes he doesn't call me for weeks, and no matter how hard I try to find him I can't—but even so, I still know he loves me, and in the same way that I know that, I know he isn't involved in poppies. There, does that set your mind at rest?"

Not really, I thought, but I nodded my head anyway. And inside I felt my heart hurt. I hadn't heard Georgie's excited chatter for several days now. She looked tired, the light had dimmed in her eyes, and I guessed Haji Khan had disappeared on something called "a whim" again, without bothering to call.

It probably wasn't the right time to ask if he'd left on account of his drug business.

Maybe Georgie was right and Haji Khan wasn't smuggling drugs out of the country, but she was also a woman in love and she couldn't be relied on to think straight. "Love makes fools of all of us," Shir Ahmad once said as we watched my mother scamper across the street to visit Homeira. Considering love was also blind, I wondered why anyone would bother wasting so much energy chasing it. However, it was facts I needed right now, not poetry.

My first thought was to talk to James as he was a journalist and was bound to know who was doing what in the country, but my English, which was getting pretty good, wasn't strong enough to deal with the subject, and James's Dari had barely progressed beyond "salaam aleykum." I didn't feel I could talk to May, because we hadn't really become friends and I got the impression that as well as not liking men she didn't like boys much either—maybe because one day, if Allah willed it, we would grow up to become men. And Pir Hederi, although blind, was maybe not as wise as a blind man ought to be. I guessed that he colored his stories to make up for the darkness he lived in.

I decided to speak to Spandi. After all, he was the one who first suggested Haji Khan was a drug lord, and he must have got his information from somewhere. So, for the first time in over four months I left Wazir Akbar Khan and crossed the city to return to Chicken Street.

There is something quite wonderful about Chicken Street, but I'm not sure what it is. I've never been able to put my finger on it. Perhaps it's the noise and confusion of the place that breathe life into me—the playful demands of shopkeepers battling for attention over the irritated beeps of drivers; the mass of people that clog the road along with the cars and push-carts; the explosions of anger as vehicles ignore the one-way system; the chatter of kids terrorizing the tourists; the smell of kebabs wafting in from Cinema Park—or simply the great, glorious mess of it all that makes this small corner of Kabul come alive like a massive wriggling beast.

If Parliament is the brains of the capital—God help us— then Chicken Street is its heart.

However, there's one thing that's even better than Chicken Street, and that's Chicken Street during the run-up to Christmas, the time when the foreigners celebrate the birthday of their prophet, Jesus. For three weeks something almost holy comes over the place. Money exchanges hands more freely; beggars get their share of crumpled afs before they even have time to mention their sick, dying baby; shops glow bright in the early darkness; bags of shopping hang in the arms of people thinking about their families; angry outbursts are quickly softened by happy smiles; and laughter bounces from pavements and doorways as the swarm hides from sudden snowstorms or tries to pick its way across the deep lines of rubbish on either side of the road. This is Chicken Street at its most heavenly, and it felt good to be back. It was like coming home.

"Fawad!"

Jamilla came running up to me, grabbing me in a huge embrace that in a few years' time she would no longer be able to do without ending up in the prison for wayward girls. Her face was pinched red by the cold, and her eyes shone bright.

"Where have you been? We've missed you!"

"I've missed you too," I shouted back over the clash of noises filling the air, a racket of shouting, beeping, and growling generators.

And it was true, I had missed her. Okay, my thoughts had been kept busy with the events of my new life and the unexpected problems that came with it, but a true Afghan never forgets his past. That's what makes us so good at holding grudges.

"I've so much to tell you, Jamilla!"

"I know some of it." She smiled. "Spandi has been keeping me informed. Apparently you work for a blind man now; that's why you have deserted us!"

"I haven't deserted you," I protested, "I've just been busy!"

"I know, Fawad, relax, I'm just joking with you. I'm happy for you, really I am."

Jamilla took my hand and weaved me through the legs of the adults, taking me to the archway leading to a small shopping court where we used to gather to swap stories, information, and scraps of food.

"Fawad, you dirty little bastard!"

As we ducked into the alcove, Jahid rose from a crouch and came over to embrace me.

"I've got a television!" I told him.

"Fuck off, you liar!"

"No, it's true! And there's a girl in my house with breasts as big as the dome on top of Abdul Rahman Mosque!"

"No way!" he screamed, slapping his forehead. "There's no justice in this world. Here I am, fully equipped to show the ladies a good time, and Allah in all his wisdom brings the best tits in the city to a fucking homosexual like you!"

Jahid punched me in the arm, but it was a playful punch and so we wrestled for a bit, falling into the display of scarves coloring the walls around us as we did so and earning us a not-so-playful slap around the head from the seller.

It felt fantastic to be back, tasting the fun and the violence of the street. I hadn't realized how much I'd missed it and everyone in it—even Jahid.

As we moved farther into the courtyard, away from the scarf seller, to sit on dirty steps leading to a closed trinket shop, Jahid told me that his mother seemed depressed now that we'd gone and she no longer had anyone to shout with. He also revealed he would be getting out of Chicken Street soon: his father had called in a favor from someone who owed him one, and they'd found Jahid a job in the municipality offices, on account of his reading and writing. They were going to train him to do something useful, they said—once he'd mastered the art of tea making.

"It's a good job," he declared, sitting up straighter than I remembered him doing before. "It's a good opportunity for me."

"I know," I told him, genuinely pleased. "Congratulations, Jahid. I really mean it."

"Yeah." Jahid nodded. "Yeah, thanks." And he punched me on the arm again.

Unfortunately, Jamilla hadn't done so well since I'd been gone. I noticed an old bruise under her left eye, and she told me that one of the beggar women had elbowed her in the face during the usual crushes to get to a foreigner's wallet.

"It's starting to change here," she said. "It's like the mafia now. You have to be part of their family, or you're done for. I'm only here today because it's Christmastime and there's enough for everyone—and because Jahid and Spandi are here."

I looked carefully at Jamilla and saw for the first time the color of fun washed from her cheeks, like she was suddenly older and more tired. I decided to ask Pir Hederi to find a job for her at the store.

"So, where is Spandi?" I asked.

"At the other end of the street selling his cards," Jamilla revealed. "He's looking so much better now that your friend Haji Khan took away his can."

"Yeah, fuck me, Fawad," Jahid joined in. "Haji Khan. You're playing with the big boys now."

"Do you know him?" I asked.

"Yeah . . . well, no, not personally, but I've heard of him. He's a real Afghan hero!"

"Not a drug dealer, then?"

Jahid shrugged. "Show me a rich man in Afghanistan who isn't mixed up in drugs. It doesn't make him a bad man, does it? This 'stop growing poppy' shit is the West's problem, not ours. It's all their people who are injecting the stuff and catching AIDS off each other. We're just trying to get by."

"So, how do you know Haji Khan is into drugs?" I asked Spandi as we walked back home from Chicken Street.

"It's just something I heard."

Spandi was counting his dollars as we walked, separating his money from Haji Khan's and placing the notes in different pockets. He did look better, cleaner and younger. If only his face hadn't been chewed away by the sand flies disease, he might even have been called handsome now.

"My father has some contacts in the east, some truck drivers who bring diesel over the border. They spend quite a bit of time in Jalalabad, and I've heard them mention Haji Khan once or twice."

"And they say he's a drug dealer?"

"So they say, but it's only a rumor. He's never been arrested or anything."

"And what do you think?"

"Me?" Spandi shrugged. "I think it's hard to arrest a man who's fought for his country—and lost his family doing so."

"What do you mean?"

"My father says Haji Khan used to be married to quite a woman, but the ISI killed her and their eldest daughter, shot them both as they lay in bed sleeping."

"No!" A twist of guilt pulled at my body as I pictured Haji Khan leaning over what was left of his wife and daughter, darkness and death drowning him in tears. "Why would they do that?"

"He was fighting the Taliban, Fawad. It was probably a warning to him, but if that's what they intended they fucked up badly because he fought like a madman after that. My father says some of his missions from Peshawar into Afghanistan were legendary because they were largely suicidal, but I guess Haji Khan didn't care about dying after what happened. I don't suppose he cared about anything."

I said good-bye to Spandi at the corner of the British Embassy in Wazir and popped by Pir Hederi's shop to beg for a job for Jamilla. He told me he'd think about it, despite all women, no matter how young they are, being a curse to every Afghan man of sound mind, and I thanked him for his consideration, knowing full well he would help her, because otherwise he would have just said no.

As I walked the long way home, past the large homes of

NGO workers, ministers, and businessmen and the laughter-filled grounds of the Lebanese and Indian restaurants, I thought of Jamilla and how happy she would be when I told her about Pir Hederi's job. And as I got closer to my house I thought of how utterly destroyed Haji Khan must have been when he returned to his own home to find his family asleep forever, their bodies wet with blood.

His pain was real to me. I could almost taste it.

Amazingly, when foreigners visit this country, they can't help but go on about its "breathtaking beauty" and how "noble and courageous" its people are, but this is the reality of Afghanistan: pain and death. There's not one of us who hasn't been touched by them in one way or another. From the Russians to the mujahideen to the Taliban, war has stolen our fathers and brothers; the leftovers of war continue to take our children; and the results of war have left us poor as beggars. So the foreigners can keep their talk of beautiful scenery and traditional goodness because all of us would swap it in a heartbeat for just one moment's peace, and it's high time the sorrow that came to plant itself in our soil just packed up and went away to terrorize someone else.

When I got to the house, all the lights were on and I could see James and May through the back window fixing colored paper to the walls. A strong smell of alcohol was coming from the kitchen, and when I went in to investigate I found my mother there stirring a large pot of oranges and herbs swimming in hot red liquid. The radio was belting out a Hindi love song, and she was dancing as she worked.

"Is that alcohol?" I demanded, startling my mother into a halt.

"It's only forbidden to drink it, Fawad, not stir it."

She started laughing, and I wondered whether she was

suffering from its fumes, in the same way Spandi had been knocked senseless by the smoke of Ismerai's cigarettes.

"Fawad, my boy!" James came bounding into the kitchen. He had glitter in his hair. "Come, help!" he ordered.

I followed him into the large living room, which was now a mess of tattered paper hanging from the walls and ceiling. A small plastic tree had been placed in the corner, and candles covered every spare space on the window ledges, tabletops, and cupboards. May was now sitting on the floor next to the wood-burning *bukhari*, keeping warm as she glued lines of paper together. She smiled when I came in, which confirmed what I already knew: everyone had gone mad.

"Where is Georgie?" I asked James before he could get me involved.

He pointed upstairs and brought the corners of his mouth down, pretending to look sad. I nodded and left the room. I needed to show her that I was on her side now. And Haji Khan's.

Although I'd never been to the top of the house before— well, not from the inside—I climbed the stairs and walked straight to Georgie's door because my bearings were good and in my first few weeks I'd made a plan of the house in the notebook she'd given me.

I knocked gently and waited.

"Who is it?" she yelled from behind the closed door.

"Fawad!" I yelled back.

From inside the room I could hear some drawers being opened and closed again. Then, after a few seconds' pause, the door opened, and Georgie stood there looking like she'd just woken up. Her hair was all over the place, she had no makeup on, and her sweater was on backward.

"Fawad," she said, flatly surprised to see me.

"Sorry to disturb you, Georgie."

She shrugged and opened the door wider for me to come

inside. As she did so, I saw a large photo of Haji Khan sitting on a table by her bed.

I shook my head to tell her I wasn't coming in. Carefully, I reached for her hand, which hung like a dead thing at her side, and told her, "Don't worry, Georgie. He'll call you."

I then turned and walked back downstairs to help James with his decorations.

6

THE BIRTHDAY OF Prophet Muhammad (Peace Be Upon Him) is called Mawlid al-Nabi, and we celebrate the day on the twelfth of the lunar month of Rabi al-Awwal, although the Shia celebrate it five days later. During this day, rice is cooked, and milk and butter are collected. We then visit our neighbors to share what we have, even with those we don't like. If we manage to find someone poorer than us, we share food with them as well. During the afternoon, the men and the older boys walk to the mosque to offer up prayers, while all the cars remain parked and the television and radio sets stand silent. As this is also the day the Prophet died, we neither laugh nor cry because we are happy that he came and sad that he went. Therefore we mostly spend the day just remembering him.

What we don't do, however, is drink alcohol from the moment we get up until the moment we fall into bed—or, in James's case, on the stairs. And after attending my first celebration of Jesus's birthday, I now understand why everybody needs two days off work to recover.

Jesus—or, as we call him, Isa—is one of the most important prophets, but he is not the Son of God as the foreigners believe; he was one of His messengers. Although it is true that Isa performed many miracles with the permission of God, like raising the dead, creating a bird from clay, and talking as an infant, he did not die on a cross. Instead, he was raised up to God so that he could return to the earth one day to fight evil.

74 as Andrea Busfield

As a Muslim I respect the foreigners' Jesus, and I like the fact that they celebrate his birthday even if they have got their facts muddled. However, it was hard to believe that for such a big day in their calendar I never once heard my friends mention Jesus's name. Although James shouted "Christ" when he slipped on the stairs, I don't think that strictly counts as remembering.

At ten in the morning on the day called "Christmas," Georgie came knocking at our door to insist that my mother and I move away from the television and come into the living room in her part of the house. She was dressed in loose patchwork green pyjamas, which I thought were more suitable than many of her normal clothes, and her hair was pulled up in a rough ponytail. Her cheeks were red.

"Happy Christmas!" she loudly greeted us in English, hugging both me and my mother fondly.

"Happy Christmas!" I shouted back as my mother gave a shy giggle and reached for a chador to cover her loose black hair so that we could dutifully follow Georgie into the house.

As we shuffled through the door of the front room we were met by a wall of noise coming from the stereo, and we found James and May sitting on the floor close to the *bukhari* surrounded by half-opened presents. They waved at us to sit with them. James was wearing dirty jeans and a bright red sweater, and May was wrapped in a bed blanket. In front of them were cartons of orange juice and a bottle of champagne—a celebratory drink that James told me came from France. Georgie filled two slim glasses with juice for me and my mother and mixed her own with the fizzing liquid from the champagne bottle.

"Happy Christmas!" James said, smiling and raising his glass. Everyone else did the same, so my mother and I followed suit, passing giggly looks to each other as we did so.

"Oh, that's gorgeous," squealed May in the middle of our

embarrassment, holding up a heavy necklace made of ragged chunks of deep-red stone.

"I thought it would match your eyes," James joked, causing May to jump forward and grab him in a headlock. As she wrestled him to the floor she accidentally showed a thigh of dimpled white flesh, and I quickly looked away, almost relieved I'd never got to see her breasts. Skin can be a frightening thing on the wrong body.

"And this is for you, Mariya."

Georgie handed over a parcel wrapped in *Sada-e Azadi* newspaper. As my mother worked the package loose, slowly and carefully as if the paper itself was worth a month's wages (which I knew it wasn't because it was handed out free by international soldiers every two weeks), the most beautiful golden shawl appeared, woven with swirls of silver thread.

"Thank you," my mother said shyly in English. She removed her own worn chador and placed the sparkle of colors over her hair. I thought she looked amazing, like every imagined picture I'd ever formed in my head of the days when my father was here to praise her looks and help her walk life's path. It's sometimes easy to forget your mother's beauty when surrounded by the exotic colors and smells of foreign women, but the fact remained she was incredibly beautiful, with olive-colored skin, deep-green eyes, and hair you could wrap yourself in. In another time and another place she could have been a famous actress or a singer.

"And this is for you, Fawad . . ."

Georgie stood up, took me by the hand, and led me to the kitchen. As we walked out of the room the others followed, including my mother, and a tickle of sickness played in my stomach at suddenly being the center of attention.

Standing by the kitchen door, Georgie released my hand and nodded at me to go in. When I passed her I found myself looking at the pale, plucked ass of a massive chicken, staring me right in the face from the work surface. I turned to express my confused gratitude, thinking a dead bird might be something of an honor to receive on the Prophet Jesus's birthday, but then I saw something else; something glinting promised freedom at me near a cupboard and leaning against the wall. It was a bicycle, a brand-new bicycle.

I couldn't believe my eyes, and though half of me wanted to run up and touch it and wheel it into the yard and cycle off to show all my friends, I didn't dare think that this could be a gift for me. It was just too good to be true. But as I looked back at Georgie she nodded her head with such an exaggerated grin I knew it was mine.

I owned my own bike!

"Happy Christmas!" James shouted behind Georgie, raising his glass to his lips.

"Yes, happy Christmas, Fawad," repeated Georgie, and at her side I could see happy tears in my mother's eyes.

I self-consciously walked over to "my bike," my eyes spinning at the very sight of it. It was amazing; it was fantastic; it was shiny as new money, red as blood—and, on closer inspection, fitted with five gears.

"Thank you, Georgie," I stammered. "Thank you. Thank you so very, very much."

"My pleasure, Fawad. It's a gift from all of us—even May," she added with a wink.

"Give us a feel then." Pir Hederi moved out of his seat to run his hands over the handlebars, humming, cooing, and nodding his head in appreciation as he did so. "That's a fine machine, Fawad, congratulations."

"Thanks," I replied, moving the bike away from Dog as he sniffed around the wheels and positioned himself to celebrate its arrival by pissing all over it. "So, I've been thinking . . ."

"Careful, lad," Pir rasped. "Thinking's one of the most dangerous pastimes a man can have in Afghanistan!"

"Yeah, yeah. Listen. I've been thinking that now I've got a bike we can set up some kind of delivery service. You know, take orders and stuff, and then I can take the food or whatever to the customers' houses."

"A delivery service, eh?" Pir shrugged, wrapping the idea around his head and licking the possibilities of the proposal along his dry lips. "With all these foreigners around here it might just work, you know."

"Of course," I added, a little more quietly, "that would mean I might not be around the shop so much and . . . well, you might need . . ."

"A little extra help?" Pir finished for me. "Such as a little slip of a girl you might know?"

"As I told you, Jamilla can read and she can write, and if people start calling up she can take orders for you. She can also make tea and clean the place up a bit and—"

"Okay," Pir said, stopping me short with a wave of his hand, "she can come."

"Brilliant!"

"On one condition: you give me a go on that bicycle."

"But you're blind!" I protested.

"Good!" He laughed. "I won't see the danger coming!"

For thirty minutes I had to deal with the sight of Pir Hederi threatening to wreck my new bicycle as he bumbled up and down the road supported by the local shoe-shine boy and a money exchanger from across the road, all the while accompanied by the claps and cheers of a small crowd and the confused, excited barks of Dog. Only when he was finally upended by a particularly vicious pothole did he give up, laughing like a mental and wiping the sweat and grit from his forehead.

I tried to laugh with the rest of the crowd, but to be honest, I was annoyed.

I lifted my bike off the road and checked it for damage. There was a slight scratch on the main frame that angered my eyes, but I guessed it was a small price to pay to stop Jamilla from getting beaten up by gypsies. And when I raced into Chicken Street twenty minutes later, the smile that appeared on her face when I told her the news was worth a dozen scratches.

"You're joking me!" she screamed as I grandly revealed I'd found her a job at Pir Hederi's shop.

"No, it's true. The money's not great, not like the riches here, but at least in Wazir you'll be away from the gypsies."

"You're my hero, Fawad!"

Jamilla flung her arms around me and planted a kiss on my cheek, which I thought was kind of wrong, but not too bad. Saying that, at some point in the future I knew I would have to make it clear that we weren't now engaged or anything.

You have to be careful with girls.

With Jamilla on the seat of my bike, we hurried toward Old Makroyan to pick up Spandi. Georgie had ordered me to bring my friends back to the house for Christmas lunch, and I wanted them to arrive before the foreigners got too drunk. When I'd left they were finishing off a second bottle of champagne, and there was another one waiting in the fridge.

After fifteen minutes of hard pedaling, through Shahr-e Naw, over the Jalalabad roundabout, across the bridge spanning Kabul's muddy river, and narrowly avoiding death a million times under the wheels of yellow Corolla taxis, we bumped our way into the broken lanes separating a dozen blocks of battered flats. The air was thick with chatter, and from most of the trees that were still standing after escaping another winter as firewood hung a mess of old ropes tied to balconies that paraded wet blankets, *salwar kameez*, bright-colored T-shirts, and dresses grown stiff in the cold.

Coming to a halt at the entrance of Block 4, we found Spandi huddled in the doorway, apparently closing some sort of deal with a boy a little younger than him. When he saw us, he patted the boy's shoulder and came to greet us with a shy shrug.

"He's working for me," he explained, jerking his head in the direction of the boy. "I give him a handful of phone cards, and he gets to keep fifty cents for every one he sells."

"Ooh, look at the big businessman!" Jamilla laughed.

"You've got to start somewhere." Spandi smiled. "For every card he sells I get half a dollar and the rest goes to Haji Khan. This means that I not only make money from my own cards but also from those I don't even sell. And I can get rid of more too. Honestly, you wouldn't believe it; these things sell like hot *bolani*. I made fifty dollars last week."

"How do you know the boy won't run off with the cards and keep the money for himself?" I asked, impressed but ever suspicious—as any right-thinking Afghan would be.

"He's my aunt's son," Spandi explained. "And besides, I told him Haji Khan would rip his head off if he turned us over."

By the time we arrived back at the house—me and Jamilla wheeling up to the gate on our horse of steel as Spandi ran beside us, a feat that was pretty impressive given how much *spand* he'd breathed in during his life—I realized we had visitors. This wasn't some kind of psychic revelation or anything; the three armored Land Cruisers and the posse of guards cluttering our street gave it away.

Kicking our shoes off, we pushed through the front door to find it embarrassingly obvious that not only was the house now in chaos but most of its occupants were out of control; James, Ismerai, and Haji Khan were lost in a cloud of hashish, shouting jokes about Kandaharis and donkeys over the noise of the stereo belting out the same songs I'd heard that morning; and May and Georgie were drunk in the kitchen, giggling uncontrollably as my mother carved into the giant chicken, looking increasingly distressed. Whereas a few hours ago the bird had been a raw slab of white pitted flesh, it was now burned black on the outside and colored pink in the middle. According to the women, this was not a good sign.

"It probably needs another hour," May suggested.

"It doesn't need another hour; it needs a bloody funeral!" Georgie replied.

Turning her head in our direction, she welcomed Spandi and Jamilla to the house and wished them a happy Christmas.

"Fawad, I'm so sorry," she added, turning her attention to me. "I really wanted to give your mother the day off, but it's quite clear that cooking isn't my thing."

My mother laughed—a good, honest, deep chuckle the likes of which I'd never heard before. "I'm fairly sure Haji Khan isn't that interested in your cooking skills," she stated.

"Mother!" I shouted, mortified by what she was so obviously suggesting, and in front of my friends too. If I didn't know any better, I'd have thought she was drunk.

Not that anyone else seemed to share my concern. Everyone was laughing at her joke, even May, whose Dari was passable and whose sense of humor had obviously been helped by the growing number of empty champagne bottles and beer cans cluttering the house.

"Oh well," Georgie exclaimed, sticking a large knife into the breast of the two-tone bird. "There's nothing to be done. Khalid! You need to make a trip to Afghan Fried Chicken!"

A few days before Christmas, Georgie had looked wretched— pale and unhappy and constantly attached to a mobile phone that never rang. Now her skin was glowing, her eyes were bright, and a smile that was almost stupid was stuck to her face.

Throughout the afternoon and deep into the evening, Haji Khan was more often than not glued to her side, being funny and affectionate, and though I welcomed his return along with everyone else, I was amazed to see how just a few minutes' tenderness was enough to make up for weeks of disinterest. It seemed a pretty good deal if you were the man in the relationship. Still, I'd been told that this was the way of love, that it was all-forgiving. And I guessed it must be true. You only have to look at our beloved Afghanistan, the country that's brought us nothing but death and misery, yet we cry over her beauty and spin songs around her cruelty like lovesick teenagers. We forgive her anything, and I guess for Georgie, Haji Khan was her Afghanistan.

Of course, love isn't a disease suffered only by women; one look at Shir Ahmad told you that. He had been invited into the house along with our other guard, Abdul, to share food and drinks while Haji Khan's men turned the house into a fortress. Shir was sitting diagonally across from my mother, and I could see it was difficult for him not to allow his eyes to keep wandering in her direction. For my mother's part, she was coldly separate, hardly noticing his presence in the room beyond the first greeting. Even so, I noticed she was sitting with her back a little straighter than usual and she had stopped laughing with the other women. And when Ismerai and Haji Khan began reciting poetry, her cheeks colored a little.

Our love of poetry is one of the craziest things about Afghans. Men will shoot someone in the head without a second thought, families will sell their daughters into marriage for a bucket of sand, and everyone will shit on the dead body of their enemy given half the chance; but at the sound of a well-written verse an Afghan man will become weak as a woman. When a poem ends he shakes his head and sits still for at least five minutes, staring far away, deep into the floor, as if seeing his own heart ripped open by the words, baring its shame and pain to the world.

One of the most famous Pashtun poets was Rahman Baba, otherwise known as the Nightingale of Afghanistan. He is as famous and respected as ever an Afghan was, and though he's been dead for more than three hundred years, people still remember him and hold ceremonies in his honor, and every school has at least one of his poems stuck to a wall. Legend says that he used to scratch his poems in the mud of the Bara River, which must have helped people love him more because he was poor like us.

But the reason I think Afghans adore poetry so much is that it lets them believe in love and its power to change everything—like the way it transformed Georgie's tears into smiles and Shir Ahmad's blood into water.

Not long ago, school sent me home with a poem to learn. Me and Spandi discussed it for a while, but even though we looked in every way to find a reason to love poetry as much as the men we knew, we decided it was rubbish and written by homos. We hated homos. We also hated poetry, especially poetry written by homos.

Ismerai and Haji Khan, though, who seemed to know an awful lot of homo poetry for tough men, practically had the women fainting over their words as they took center stage at our Christmas party—and there was only my mother among them who spoke Pashto. But that's the magic of our language: you could recite a poem about a rotting cat's ass, and it would sound like warm honey.

Of course the foreigners were also drunk, which probably helped, and they were feeling the heat of recent good fortune after licking their fingers clean from the grease of AFC's fried chicken to accept the presents Haji Khan had brought for them. To James he had given a bottle of whiskey, which the journalist had been cradling in his arms ever since; May was now out of her blanket and wearing a deep-blue velvet *kuchi* dress; and Georgie was revealing a flash of gold around her neck and a flower-shaped ring on her finger. Surprisingly, given it wasn't strictly our celebration, Haji Khan didn't forget the Muslims in the house. He generously presented my mother with a fine red carpet for her room, handed over new boots to Shir Ahmad and Abdul, and gave envelopes of money to Jamilla, Spandi, and me, which was as horrible as it was exciting because, as all the adults mooned over one another, these packages burned holes in our pockets and all we could think of doing was escaping and finding out how much he'd given us.

In the end, the party finished in a mess of broken adults as the clock struck ten: May bolted upstairs to vomit in the bathroom; James fell down, and asleep, on the stairs; and Georgie, Spandi, and Jamilla disappeared out the door with Ismerai and Haji Khan. As my mother cleared up, and covered a very loud, snoring James with a blanket, I sneaked out into the yard to take a last look at my bike and count the dollars in my pocket. Haji Khan had placed one hundred dollars in ten-dollar bills in the envelope—more money than the National Police earn in one month! And even though I went to bed still no nearer to understanding the foreigners' relationship with Jesus, I really hoped they would be around for his next birthday.

As I lay in my room, I looked back on the day with all of its color and surprises—a day when the rich sat with the poor, the Godless with the believers, the foreigners with Afghans, the men with women, and the children with adults. It was how a perfect world might be if people didn't keep strangling one another in rules and laws and fear. Were we really so different from one another? If you give a boy a bike, he is going to be happy whether he is a Muslim, a Christian, or a Jew. And if you love someone truly, it doesn't matter if he or she is Afghan or British.

But life isn't straightforward, and just as sudden happiness can appear to brighten your day, sadness is usually only a heartbeat away. The day after Christmas my mother went to visit her sister, and my aunt repaid this kindness by trying to kill her.

7

I<small>T WAS THICK</small> dark in my bed when I heard a heavy thud come from the bathroom of our house. I listened hard, trying to work out the cause, but there was nothing more. Yet I must have sensed there was something wrong because I swung my legs out of the blanket's warmth, put on my plastic slippers, and left my room.

Standing outside the bathroom door, I could clearly hear the sound of retching, violent and frightening, followed by heavy, tearful groans.

"Mother?" I knocked gently. "Mother? It's me, Fawad."

I heard my mother trying to get to her feet, but a whimper came with the effort and she slid down again with another dull thud.

"Mother, please!"

I turned the handle. The door opened just enough for me to see her on the floor, slumped across the hole of our toilet, cradling her stomach. Her dress was clearly soiled, and the stench of vomit and diarrhea hit me like a wall.

"No, Fawad!"

Her voice was harsh and broken, and I closed the door quickly at the terrible sound of it, trapped by the need to save her and a son's wish to protect his mother's shame.

"I'm going for help!" I cried, and ran into the main house to get Georgie.

Without knocking, I ran into her room and dragged at the blankets that hid her.

"Please, Georgie, please," I begged, "it's my mother! Get up!"

The words left my mouth with a scream, and Georgie sat upright, quickly kicking away the covers. In two strides she reached the bedroom door and pulled on the long dressing gown that hung there.

"What is it? What's the matter with your mother?" she asked as she grabbed me by the hand and pulled me out of the door.

"I don't know, but she's very sick. Oh Georgie, I think she's dying!"

I started to cry. I didn't mean to, but it was all too much, just really too damn much. Seeing her lying on the floor, her pretty face turned white, her clothes black and filthy. I couldn't lose my mother like this, not her as well. I loved her too much. She was all I had left in the world.

"May!" Georgie shouted as we ran down the stairs. "May, we need you!"

Both May and James jumped out from their rooms, looking sleepy and worried. James had hold of a long piece of wood.

"It's Mariya, she's sick," Georgie explained.

"Fuck. Okay, I'm coming," May answered.

"Me too, I'll just get some clothes on," added James.

"No! You can't see Mariya like this," Georgie barked at him, turning abruptly to face him. "Get dressed and take care of Fawad."

"I want to come with you," I protested, but Georgie was already at the bottom of the stairs and heading outside.

Quickly running after her, I caught up in time to see her push open the door of our bathroom. She paused for a moment, taking in the twisted mess that was my mother's body.

"Oh God, Mariya . . ."

"Georgie, please," my mother begged, trying to lift herself from the floor before falling back defeated. "Please, the boy, don't let my boy see me like this."

My mother was crying, and her body, which looked tiny as a doll's in the half-light of the coming day, was shaking with retches and sobs. I held out my hands to her.

"Please, Mother, please stop . . ."

Georgie moved me back from the door and gently pushed me into the arms of James, who had by now come out of the main house. May was with him, and she carried a small black bag with her.

"Your mother will be fine, Fawad," May said in English. "We'll sort this out, don't worry."

May kissed me on the cheek and went to join Georgie, who by now had torn a strip of cloth from the bottom of her long sleeping shirt and was soaking it in cold water from the sink to wipe the sweat from my mother's head.

For the next two hours, Georgie and May ran back and forth from our house to their own, fixing ways to keep my mother from slipping into death. They had taken my mother's clothes, placed them in the metal trash can in the yard, and given James orders to burn them. They then sent him out for bottles of mineral water after finishing their own supplies. May had used them in the kitchen, mixing the clean water with salt and sugar, creating gallons and gallons of salty, sugary liquid, all for my mother to drink.

"Your mother needs a lot of water to replace all the fluid she has lost," May explained, filling yet another glass.

"What's the matter with her?" I asked, now mixing up the concoction myself after May had shown me how—half a spoon of salt and four spoons of sugar to every glass.

"I'm not sure, Fawad, but I guess she may have cholera. I've seen it once before in Badakhshan, and your mother's symptoms seem to be very similar."

"What's chol . . . chol . . ."

"Cholera," May repeated.

"What's cholera?" I tried again, not liking the hardness of its sound in my mouth.

"It's a disease caused by bacteria—germs," explained May. "If I'm right, your mother will be fine, Fawad, but we need to rehydrate her and get her to a hospital as soon as possible. Georgie has called Massoud, and he's on his way."

"She's not going to die, is she?"

"No, Fawad." May bent down to take my face in her hands. "Your mother won't die, I promise you that, but she is very, very sick and you have to be a strong little boy right now. Okay?"

"Okay."

There are a million and one things in this country that can kill you—people and weapons are just the tip of a very large mountain—and one of these things is cholera.

After my mother was laid on the backseat of Massoud's car and driven to a German hospital in the west of the city with Georgie and May, James tried to take my mind off my worries in the only way he knew how—by filling my head with knowledge about the disease. He opened up his laptop computer, logged on to something called Wikipedia, and typed in the word *cholera*. A whole page of words in blue letters arrived, and James slowly read them.

The basic diagnosis was that cholera sounded awful, and I cursed my mother's misfortune, asking Allah to visit a million illnesses on my aunt, who must surely have been the one to infect my mother, being as dirty as an outhouse herself. I knew they didn't like each other, but to kill her with food was unforgivable.

According to Wikipedia, cholera was quite commonplace in countries like Afghanistan, and the symptoms included terrible muscle and stomach cramps, vomiting, and fever. "At some stage," read James, translating the words into a language I understood, "the watery shit of the sufferer turns almost clear with flecks of white, like rice. If it's very bad a person's skin can turn blue-black, the eyes become sunken, and their lips also turn blue."

I remembered my mother's face, and although it had lost its gentle brown color it hadn't turned blue, which gave me some kind of hope. Of course, I hadn't been able to examine her shit, though.

"In general," continued James, "to save someone you have to make them drink as much water as they lose."

That explained why May had given my mother enough fluid to drown a camel, and as I listened to James reading from the screen of his computer, I developed a newfound respect for the yellow-haired man hater, because May had basically saved my mother's life. I owed her now.

8

" S O, YOU'RE A lesbian, are you?"

As I spoke, May choked on her coffee, breathing in as she spluttered and releasing milky brown liquid through her nose soon after.

It wasn't a good look.

"Jeez, you're not shy in coming forward, are you?"

She coughed out the question, then wiped her nose with the sleeve of her tunic. Her cheeks had burst pink, and I looked at her blankly.

"I mean to say, you're not afraid to speak about what's on your mind," she explained, seeing my confusion through the small tears that had collected in the lines hanging around her eyes.

I shrugged. "If I don't ask, how am I going to learn?" I asked.

"Yeah," snorted May, "you've got a point."

She shuffled the papers she'd been reading at the desk by the front window, then carefully placed them in a pile before moving in her seat to give me her full attention. I was sitting on the floor trying to place the words of the new national anthem in my head—one of the tasks we had been set at school before it closed for the winter. As it was as long as the Koran, this was no easy task.

"In answer to your question, yes, I am a lesbian," May admitted.

Her words were carefully spaced, and she eyed me warily.

I nodded my head, thoughtfully, and returned to the note-book in front of me.

"Why?" I asked some seconds later.

May shook her head and blinked. "I don't know why; I just am. It's not something you decide; you just are, or you're not. And from a very early age I knew I was."

"But how will you find a husband if you only love women?"

"Fawad, I will never find a husband."

"You're not that bad-looking."

"I beg your pardon?"

May looked shocked, and I felt a similar stab of surprise that she was shocked because I'd seen her look in the mirror James always checked himself in, the one that hung in the hallway and made your face look longer than it really was, so she must have known.

"I mean, you're not beautiful like Georgie," I explained. "But not every man is as beautiful as Haji Khan."

"My looks aren't really the issue, Fawad. The issue, the point," she added quickly as I visibly struggled with another new word, "is I don't *want* to find a husband."

"Then how will you ever have children if you don't get married?"

"You don't have to have a husband to have children," she stated, shaking her head.

"May," I replied gently, now shaking my own head, "I think you're very clever and you know a lot of things, like how you knew how to save my mother's life, but really, this is one of the most stupid things I have ever heard you, or anyone, say."

May laughed. It brought to her face a whisper of pretti-ness that was usually missing.

"Things are very different in our culture, young man. In

America I can adopt children—take unwanted babies and bring them to my home, where I can love them and raise them. So you see, having a husband is not that necessary."

"But every woman wants to get married," I protested.

"Do they now?" May paused slightly to wipe spilled coffee from the desktop before slowly admitting, "Well, maybe you're right. Actually, Fawad, I'll let you in on a little secret: I was hoping to get married later this year, but sadly it didn't work out."

"Really?"

"Yes, really." May leaned over the desk, and it caused her breasts to spread on the polished surface like broken cushions. They looked soft and wonderful. "You may remember when you first came here I was a little unhappy. Well, that was because the woman I loved had just told me she no longer wanted to marry me. She had found someone else in America, apparently. A man, as it turned out."

"I'm sorry . . ."

"That's okay," said May.

"No, I mean, I'm sorry, I don't understand. You said you wanted to marry a *woman*. How is that even possible?"

"Oh," May replied with a smile, "actually it's very possible. In some places in America men are free to marry men and women are free to marry women." She rose from her seat to take her coffee cup to the kitchen and playfully pushed my head as she passed by. "That is one of the wonderful things about democracy," she added, laughing. Then she left the room, leaving me speechless.

I always knew the West was filled with crazy ideas, like scientists believing we all come from monkeys, but this was just incredible. I decided that as soon as I'd finished remembering the national anthem I'd write to President Karzai to warn him. There could be such a thing as too much democracy, and he should be made aware of that fact.

At the German hospital, the doctors in white coats confirmed May's suspicions that my mother had cholera. They
also confirmed that she would be fine. Because of the special
water my mother had drunk she hadn't gone into shock,
which I was told was the biggest danger she had faced. However, the doctors insisted that she stay overnight in order to
recover from her ordeal.

During that terrible twenty-four hours it was also agreed
that when my mother came out she would go to live with
Homeira and her family for a week in Qala-e Fatullah. Homeira's employer, across the road from us, had also been kind,
giving her the week off to look after my mother—although
James said this had nothing to do with niceness and everything to do with not wanting to catch diseases from poor
people.

"My home is only a ten-minute drive away, so come and
visit anytime," Homeira told me when she came to pick up
some of my mother's clothes. "My children would love to meet
you."

"Okay," I agreed, although I was in no mood to make
new friends and felt better staying with the friends I already had.

Georgie said that at the hospital my mother had been
very against the idea of leaving me behind—right up to the
point where she fell asleep, exhausted. However, both Georgie and May said they would look after me, and they promised my mother that not only would they guarantee I washed,
said my prayers, and did my school assignments, they would
also keep an eye on James and ban him from the house if
need be.

I felt a bit sorry for James, who seemed genuinely hurt
that no one thought he could be trusted to look after a boy,

but if he hadn't agreed to such supervision I was in no doubt that I would have been packed off to my aunt's house—where I'm certain she would have tried to kill me too.

So that afternoon, after my mother had been hospitalized and May had admitted to her own sickness, my bed was temporarily moved into James's room and placed at a right angle to his.

At first, the place was an absolute mess, filled as it was with piles of newspapers, dirty clothes, and books taking up every bit of space. A board similar to the one May had in her bedroom hung on the wall, now over my bed, but unlike May's there were no family photographs pinned to it, just scraps of paper that seemed mostly to hold telephone numbers. A large knife was also stabbed into the board. I had seen James use it to clean the dirt from his nails.

As Georgie and James struggled to fit my bed into the corner of his room, I tried to help by shoving the other one closer to the far wall. As I did so a magazine escaped from the tangled mass of bedclothes, falling to the floor and opening at the center. The pages showed a blond-haired woman with soapy bubbles covering huge naked breasts.

Georgie and James looked at the magazine as if someone had just tossed a grenade into the room. For at least three seconds they stood in stunned silence, first looking at the naked woman, then at each other, then at me, then back at the magazine. I stooped to pick it up, but this seemed to knock the sense back into both of them, and as Georgie ordered "No!" James quickly swooped, beating me to it and snatching away the flapping pages, which he tucked into the belt of his trousers, under his sweater.

"Research, Fawad, research," he explained.

"For all the work you do with the ladies?" I asked, remembering Georgie's words and suddenly fitting them into place.

Most afternoons, after Georgie had finished with her job and Pir Hederi had finished with me, we would drive to Homeira's house to spend an hour or so with my mother. The first visit we made was awkward and shy, but because I was relieved to see her alive I cried when she reached out to hold me, and because she was my mother she matched my tears with her own.

Although my mother looked better than the last time I'd seen her, and a lot cleaner, her face still shone pale and she looked fragile compared to her friend, who was as fat as Ibrar the Baker from Flower Street. However, despite my natural suspicion of anyone fat, which I think came from living with my aunt for so long, I liked Homeira. She was large and funny and smiled easily, in the way most people do when their stomachs are full. I was also mesmerized by her hands, which appeared to be holding prisoner a large number of rings—like small hills of flesh laying siege to valleys of gold on her fingers. There was no way they could possibly be removed, so I guessed they'd have to stay there until the day she died or until someone cut off her fingers—maybe the Taliban, if they came back.

Homeira's husband was also quite fascinating in his fatness. If I squinted, closing my eyes half shut as if I was looking into the sun, I could clearly see the shape of his thin face battling to come out of the folds. It was like watching a man drowning in skin.

Not surprisingly, Homeira and her husband had made six plump children together—a collection of bellies waddling around the house on pudgy legs. They were friendly kids who shared their toys easily, and I was massively comforted to see my mother surrounded by such a large family, living in a house that was busy and alive and full of cheerful conversation. I was also relieved to know she'd be in no danger of starving.

What was surprising, however, was the discovery that Georgie and I weren't my mother's only visitors. Twice in five days I caught Shir Ahmad leaving the house, shyly waving at me as we passed each other on the street.

I guessed we'd soon have to have a talk, man to man.

But even though I was happy to see my mother being looked after for once in her life, I found it really difficult to be without her. I didn't say anything because May had told me to be strong, so after my first tears at seeing her alive I didn't cry again. But the truth was, she was my mother and I missed her so much that I now had a constant ache pounding at my insides. In all my years I had never been without my mother. When I went to bed at night, I placed her chador and her smell over my pillow, praying to Allah that she missed me just as much as I missed her and that she wouldn't decide to stay with Homeira's happy fat family.

As I struggled to get used to this new loneliness, I also sensed the same feeling in Georgie. The day after Christmas, Haji Khan had left for Dubai, telling her he had to sort out "some business" and promising to call. As usual Georgie spent the following days without him, holding her mobile phone and waiting for him to keep his promise.

Therefore, because God always provides, we now clung to each other's company in the new-winter evenings, tied together because we were one and the same.

And it wasn't only me and Georgie who missed the presence of my mother and Haji Khan; both James and May were also struggling to cope. Our family, which was made up of the motherless, husbandless, and, in two cases, wifeless, was dining pretty much every night on something called noodles—stringy lines of pasta that came from a package and were flavored with powdered water. It was okay at first, but after four nights I knew this wasn't what our teachers would call a "well-balanced diet."

Therefore it came as a blessed relief when Georgie in-formed me we would be hosting a party at our house to cel-ebrate New Year's Eve—the foreigners' one, not mine. As you would expect in a place recently visited by near-death, when we sat on the long cushions in the front room to discuss the matter, everyone agreed it should be a quiet affair. As we went through the options it was almost as if we were holding a mini Shura, a council of elders—without all the beards, of course—and it made me feel impossibly grown-up. Georgie explained she'd prefer something quiet because she "wasn't feeling up to a big one"; May revealed she "hated half the fuck-ers left here over the holidays anyway"; and James went along with the plan simply because he was outnumbered by the women—and, I think, trying to prove he could be a respon-sible adult. "Yes, quite right," he muttered. "We've got the boy to think about." Therefore with no one up for "a big one," it was agreed that one guest each would be invited by those that could be bothered and the food would be ordered in from the Lebanese restaurant down the road.

The evening of New Year's Eve, we placed a large board over the pool table and decorated it with candles. May and Georgie also brought six chairs from their offices, which they carried home in the back of a Toyota pickup Massoud had borrowed from his brother.

As Georgie lit the eight candles on our new "table" and James mixed a bowl of alcohol that he called "punch," the first of our guests arrived. His name was Philippe, and he was a friend of May's. He was thin as a pencil with tufts of beard that didn't connect and struggled to cover his sharp face. He was dressed in the Afghan *salwar kameez* and wore a *pakol*. When he entered the house, James rolled his eyes.

"He's only been in Afghanistan two months, and he's

French," he whispered to me as I giggled at the man's too-short trousers and badly rolled hat.

Philippe ignored the comment, as well as James, and came over to shake my hand.

"Salaam aleykum. How you are? What the name is it you are having?" He spoke to me in Dari.

"I speak English," I told him, in English.

James laughed out loud, although I wasn't making a joke. I was trying to be helpful, as the man was a guest in our house. "That's my boy!" he shouted, then grabbed me in a headlock as May led her friend into the living room, spitting the word *kids* behind her.

About twenty minutes later our next guest turned up, a friend of James's who—it came as no surprise to anyone—was a woman. Unlike the Frenchman, who'd brought nothing to the party, she carried with her a bottle of wine and a tin of chocolate biscuits, which she handed over to Georgie. Her name was Rachel, and she came from a place called Ireland. She may have been pretty, but it was hard to tell because for some reason she had hidden her face under a mask of makeup that would have put an Afghan bride to shame.

"You look, erm, stunning," James said as he greeted her, kissing her on the cheek, which left his beard shining with glitter.

"Really?" Rachel asked. "I was having a dreadful time of it before I came out. The electricity went off, and the generator ran out of fuel. I had to use candlelight! Can you believe it?"

"Yes," admitted May, coming into the kitchen to refill Philippe's already empty glass with more punch.

Rachel giggled but sounded scared. "You know, I just wanted to make some sort of effort—look a bit festive and all that?"

"Well, you look divine," James assured her.

"She looks like Ziggy freakin' Stardust," May muttered under her breath.

"Ziggy who?" I whispered to Georgie.

"Shhh," she said, passing me an orange juice. "May's just being mean."

For the foreigners' New Year's Eve I had been declared Georgie's guest of honor, although as I also lived in the house she could just as easily have been mine, and as the night wore on it became increasingly obvious that we were the only two people who actually appeared to get on with everyone.

Everything began fairly well thanks to the food from Taverne du Liban, which was a great success. Within an hour we had demolished all the *fatoush*, the tabbouleh, eight small pastries filled with potato and spinach, a plate of meat patties that came with yogurt, side dishes of hummus, twelve skewers of chicken and lamb kebabs, as well as a small mountain of fluffy white pita breads. By the end of it all I was fit to burst and imagined this must be how Homeira's family ate every night.

Philippe and Rachel, however, didn't eat half as much as those of us who lived in the house, though they probably hadn't been living on watery noodles for the best part of a week. The Frenchman made excuses for his lack of appetite, saying he had a stomach upset. I didn't believe him. He hadn't run to the toilet even once during the meal, so I decided it had more to do with his mouth being busy with all the free alcohol my friends had provided, and the fact that he never shut up.

Rachel also spent much of the evening picking at her food, but I sensed this was because she was nervous, as she kept playing with her hair. I also noticed that her eyes grew big as saucers every time she looked at James. I liked her because of that, and I really hoped James liked her too. Her makeup looked a lot prettier in the candlelight of the room rather than the bright, generator-made light of the kitchen, and her voice sounded soft like summer rain whenever she spoke, which wasn't often because the Frenchman was pretty much holding us hostage with talk about himself.

As Philippe went on and on and on, I saw James getting more and more irritated. It was easy to tell when he was annoyed because he'd constantly grab the back of his neck as if some pain needed to be rubbed away, and he'd flick the ash of his cigarette with sharp, quick taps of his first finger.

"I mean, it's just so impossible to get anything done quickly here," said Phillipe. "These people are so lazy."

"Like Fawad, you mean?" James asked, cocking his head and raising his left eyebrow, which made him look surprised, and also a little dangerous.

"Well, no, he is obviously just a boy."

"Oh. His mother then, the woman who works for us sixteen hours a day? Or perhaps the guards who protect our lives for a month's wages that wouldn't even pay for the fancy dress you're wearing?"

"That's enough, James," May warned him quietly.

James took the comment with an angry look, then ignored her.

"Or perhaps you mean the bread guys who work from dawn to dusk in the blistering heat of their baking houses, or the shoe-shine boys who stand on our corner every day hoping to make a few afs, or the metal welders with their scarred skin and scorched eyes, or—"

"That's enough, I said!" May hit the table with her fist, causing us all to jump, Rachel most of all.

"Well," James said, lifting his voice and arms in surrender, "maybe when Philippe has been here for longer than eight weeks he might just be in a position to talk about another nation's defects."

As James finished we all sat in embarrassed silence, even me, because although he had been sticking up for Afghans like me he had been rude to a guest, and in our culture that was as bad as calling someone's mother a whore, or, worse still, using her as one.

"I've been here ten weeks actually," Philippe eventually said.

As we all looked at him, not sure if he was making a joke or not, Georgie started laughing, then slowly the rest of us joined in, even James, who nodded his head and lifted his glass to knock it against the Frenchman's.

After finishing our meal, and after Philippe had pretty much drunk his own body weight in alcohol, all six of us moved from the table to settle on the long cushions in the other half of the room. James brought with him two bottles of red wine and sat close to Rachel, who looked as pleased as a boy who'd just been given a bike for Christmas. Georgie and May placed themselves on either side of me, like bodyguards. Georgie was just being Georgie, but May, I think, saw me differently now and I wondered whether she would have tried to adopt me if my mother hadn't survived.

For the next half hour the Frenchman continued to bore us with stories about himself, but unlike at the dinner table, James didn't seem to mind anymore, nodding now and again as he leaned back on the cushions, slumping closer to Rachel's side. I thought they looked nice together.

When Philippe began a new story about his time in a place called Sudan, Rachel took the chance to escape. Getting to her feet, she apologized for the interruption and asked for directions to the toilet. As she left, Philippe continued with his talk about something called solar energy. I really had no idea what he was going on about, and I had no interest in trying to find out either. As nobody else interrupted him, I guessed they felt the same way.

When Rachel didn't return from the bathroom for a full ten minutes, Georgie also took the chance to get away from

Philippe and went to look for her—and that's when the party pretty much ended.

"Rachel's leaving," Georgie said quietly, having popped her head around the door a few seconds later. James got to his feet, and we followed him.

In the clear light of the hallway we found Rachel pulling on her coat. The mask of makeup that had hidden her face had been washed away, leaving her skin pink. It looked like she had been crying. I looked at Georgie, not sure what was going on, and she pointed to the light and the mirror and made a face full of shock. I remembered then about Rachel getting ready in the dark and realized it must have been the first time she had seen her made-up face properly when she went to the bathroom. I felt quite sorry for her. She hadn't looked that bad in the candlelight.

Pulling her gloves on, Rachel hurriedly thanked Georgie and May for inviting her to the party, pretending she needed to go because she didn't feel well.

"Rachel, stay a while longer, you may feel better in a minute or two," James tried, but as he spoke she hardly looked at him, her eyes darting quickly to the door as if she couldn't run away fast enough.

"No, really, I must go," she insisted, and as her gaze finally met his, her cheeks turned from pink to red and small tears came to blur her eyes.

Georgie gave her a hug, and before James walked her to the gate May also moved to embrace her. As she headed back into the living room, I could tell from May's face that she felt ashamed about the jokes she'd made earlier.

Once Rachel had left the house and jumped into the front seat of the car that was waiting for her, nobody seemed to be in the mood to party anymore, only to drink. And as another bottle of wine was magically brought out from the kitchen, this was my cue, apparently, to go to bed. Taking me by the hand, Georgie led me upstairs and into James's room.

"Well, that was a bit of a disaster, wasn't it?" she said, coming over to sit on my bed.

"The food was good," I stated, wanting to rescue something from the night to make her feel better.

"Yes, the food was good, you're right. As always."

Leaning forward, Georgie placed a kiss on my cheek before whispering, "Happy New Year, Fawad. I hope all your wishes come true this year." Then she got up and switched off the light.

As she closed the door behind her I offered a quick prayer to my God, asking Him to help make Georgie's dreams come true too.

In my head, behind my eyes, there was a storm of color; ugly rips breaking up the sky I saw there, flashing clouds of black and red, fighting for space in giant, greedy swirls. I felt the anger of the world wrap itself around the wind and I ran for a bush to take cover, but I struggled to reach it in time and the night tore it away before I got there, so I ran from the hill, tumbling through the long grass as I lost my feet, rolling through blades grown black in the dark. I knew I had to get away, but my hands were caught and I couldn't free them until the light came to carry me away to the valley.

High in the sky I saw eagles circling above me, swooping in pairs to a pocket of brown lying on the ground. I got to my feet and saw I was wearing Rachel's gloves.

Slowly I walked toward the brown, and as I drew close I recognized it as a dead thing. I thought it was a sheep at first, but as I walked nearer I realized it was too large, and now there was Georgie knelt near, holding the goat comb she carried. She was stroking the dead thing's hair and smiling, so I smiled back.

"You want to help?" she asked.

"Okay." I smiled.

But as I leaned closer to comb the dead thing I saw long black hair covering its back and I grew afraid.

"Go on," Georgie encouraged, so I leaned forward and parted the hair. It covered a woman's face, and it was the face of my mother.

Throwing the comb to the floor, I backed away.

"Don't leave me, son," she cried.

She was crawling toward me on her hands and knees. Her fingers reached for me, but they were rotten and black and the buzz of flies hung around them, feeding off her sickness. She jumped for me, and I screamed.

It was pitch-black in the room, and I could hear James snoring in the dark beside me. The lights were off, and the generator stood silent.

I needed water, but I was too scared to get out of bed. My mother's face was still strong in my mind, and it was so cold I could see my own breath. My eyes felt sticky with sleep, and my throat had turned tight as if my body was trying to strangle me.

I needed water.

"James?" My voice sounded weak, as if it was traveling from another place. "James?"

When he gave no answer I grabbed the knife that was stuck in the board on my side of the wall and slipped out from under the blanket. I put on my plastic slippers and walked to the door.

Outside our room everything was covered in night, creating fuzzy black shapes that knew I was afraid. I reached out with my feet, found the stairs, and moved slowly toward the kitchen, now helped by a faint light that broke through the blackness and came from the candles still burning in the living room. The tiny flames turned the air red where the light crept through the sides of the door. It was a flickering, dancing light that pulsed with the sound of voices coming from the other side. And as I half listened my heart quickened because I knew it was wrong.

I watched my hands reach out and push the door open.

"No, you drunken idiot. I told you, not here!"

She was struggling, and he was on top of her, holding her down, his hands too strong, his body too heavy. It was crushing her.

"Come on, stop fucking around; you said you wanted this."

The voice was thick, heavy, but I heard it, like I'd heard it before, and I saw him pressing her arms into the cushions as the flames danced around them, turning them both orange; him fighting to control her, his body on top of hers, light licking at his feet and revealing the terrible black of his eyes and the white of hers as they both turned to look.

Around me, the air turned to screams. It sounded like hell in my ears as it pushed through the hate and the fear, burning like fire in my blood. Then the anger burst from my mouth with the howl of a million animals, and because I couldn't let it happen again, not a second time, not this time, I ran forward and raised my hand, feeling the knife sink into softness as I slammed myself hard against him.

Still the screams kept coming, tearing at my head.

I kicked my legs at the air around me, trying to break free of the noise and the fear, but now there were more screams and they were different from mine, and I saw the flames laughing and the shape of a thousand terrors surrounded me and then she was upon me and she forced the fire to leave, bringing her arms to catch me, smothering me in her smell.

In the chaos of my mind I recognized Georgie and I melted into her flesh as she took my head into her body and I let her breathe her love into me. She was telling me not to worry, and I felt the warmth of her hands press on my hair, and it felt good, but in the distance somewhere around us I heard a man shouting.

"He stabbed me in the ass! The little shit stabbed me in the fucking ass!"

The accent was French.

9

I DON'T THINK I'm particularly special. I'm not amazingly beautiful, but I'm not Jahid-ugly either. I'm not the biggest brain in my class, but neither am I dumb as a donkey. I'm not the fastest runner; I don't tell the best jokes; I'm not the best fighter; and though I know I've seen things that maybe a boy my age shouldn't have seen, even that doesn't make me particularly special.

My father was killed, my brothers are dead, and my sister is missing. But in Afghanistan, that's a big "so what?"

Spandi's mother died in childbirth, the sister she was trying to deliver died with her, and from the age of two Spandi never felt his mother's warmth again or the comfort of her love. He doesn't even have a photograph to remember her by, just a picture in his head that fades with every year he grows taller.

Jamilla's parents are both alive, but their house has become terrorized by drugs. Sometime in the past her dad went to work with the poppy, and he fell under its spell as he licked the resin from his fingers during the harvest. Now he is hungry for the drug, day and night, while the rest of his family just remains hungry. And even though he stays away from the home for days on end, he always returns eventually, looking for money; and when he can't find any money he visits his fists on the head of his wife as well as Jamilla and her two older sisters.

Meanwhile the orphanages of Kabul are filled with children whose parents have been lost and killed.

So none of us is particularly special. We just carry with us different versions of the same story.

However, when I woke up the morning after the night came to haunt me, I opened my eyes to see May and Georgie sharing the bed next to me while James was wrapped in a blanket snoring on the floor by my side, and I did at last feel in some way special.

So I was really sorry when seconds later I touched the mattress under me and realized I'd wet the bed.

IO

JALALABAD IS THE capital of Nangarhar Province in the east of Afghanistan, and for more years than anyone can remember Kabul's rich have come to this city to escape the biting cold of winter.

Georgie and I, however, had simply come to escape.

With my mother's illness still keeping her at Homeira's house and my recent attack on Philippe, it was decided I needed a break.

"He was only play-fighting with May," Georgie explained as we worked our way through the seven sisters, the snow-topped mountains that took us away from the capital and into the warm valleys of the east. "He wasn't really trying to hurt her."

"Are you sure of that?"

"Yes, Fawad, I am."

Although the pictures in my head told me a different story, everything was so muddy in there right now I couldn't be clear of anything anymore, and if Georgie said it was so, then I guess it must have been.

"I'm sorry," I mumbled. "I didn't realize."

"There's no need to apologize," she continued, ruffling my hair. "How could you have known? Philippe had drunk far too much, and so had May. But I promise you, they are really very good friends, and they would never hurt each other. And maybe May and James and I are all to blame for what happened, not you. We should have been more sensible with you,

Fawad, what with your mother being away. So, we're sorry too. We didn't think."

Georgie pulled me into her side, which felt a little bony, and held me there for as long as the journey allowed. The rest of the time we were thrown around the back of the car like two bees in a jar as the city road crumbled and turned into rocks.

The journey from Kabul to Jalalabad was pretty interesting, and if my thoughts hadn't been so busy with miseries pouring in from the night before, and if my head hadn't kept smacking against the window with the force of the drive, I guess I would have enjoyed it tremendously because it took us through the pictures of a million painters and a million more stories. For four hours we traveled beyond the giant mountains that guarded the Kabul River; past the command post where the warlord Zardad kept a soldier chained up as a dog, feeding him on the testicles of his enemies; over the small bridge where four foreign journalists were murdered in 2001; down into Surobi and past its shimmering lake; along gentle bends hugged by brilliant green fields, overtaking *kuchis* and camels and dark clouds of fat-bottomed sheep; back along the river toward the fish restaurants of Durunta; and through the Russian-built tunnel that skirted a dam and led us to Jalalabad.

It was my first proper trip out of Kabul—holidays not being that common among people who can hardly feed themselves—and the ever-changing views were more than amazing, but I was simply too upset to take any pleasure in them. The fact was, I felt truly sorry and deeply ashamed about what I'd done to Philippe, and I knew that his view of Afghan hospitality would have changed quite a lot now that one of us had stabbed him in the ass.

It was unforgivable, really.

May had told me the next day that Philippe had gone

to see the surgeons at the Italian Emergency Hospital in Shahr-e Naw, where they had sewed a row of stitches into the wound. He also had to have something called "a tetanus jab."

James, on the other hand, had spent much of the day laughing.

When we arrived in Jalalabad it was late afternoon, and we drove straight into the heart of the city, which, unlike the winter gray of Kabul, was still glowing yellow in dusty sunshine. There were more donkeys and carts crowding the streets than in the capital, and the place crawled with tiny *tuk-tuks*, Pakistani-style buggies painted blue and decorated with wildly colorful pictures of flowers and women's eyes.

Beeping and pushing our way through the traffic, we eventually slipped into a side road, a beaten track leading to the front doors of about ten high-walled houses. Halfway down we stopped at Haji Khan's place, a large white mansion set in a garden of green that could easily have been home to King Mohammad Zahir Shah, if he still had any money.

As our Land Cruiser pulled into the drive, we found Ismerai already waiting for us on the steps of the house. He was talking into a mobile phone that he clicked shut as we jumped out of our vehicle, and after greeting us with warm handshakes and big smiles he took us inside.

The sight that filled my eyes almost blinded me. Through two large wooden doors, outside of which waited a number of sandals, a massive hall appeared with eight white leather sofas facing one another in rows of four. Georgie sat on one of them and pulled off her boots. I'd kicked my own shoes away at the door, which was the proper thing to do, but Georgie's boots were complicated. At the back of the hallway a giant staircase grew from the ground, going off in two directions to meet up again on the top floor. Upstairs, beyond a fence of wooden balconies, I could see a number of doors leading to a number of rooms. A small man no bigger than a child grabbed our bags and disappeared up there. Back downstairs, to the left of the hallway was a raised floor glinting with a golden carpet and long lapis-blue cushions. Relaxing on them were four brown men in brown *pakols* and brown *patus*. They were watching a wide-screen television and seemed quite at home.

As we entered the house and made our way to the TV area, all the men stood up and offered their hands to Georgie in welcome. She obviously knew them, and they seemed happy to see her, gently scolding her for having stayed away too long. They then waved at her to sit down, offering her the position of honored guest on the cushion farthest from the door. I followed her to the end of the room and sat down nearby, but not too close because I wasn't a baby and I wanted the men to see that.

As green tea arrived, joined by glass plates of green raisins, pistachios, almonds, and papered sweets, Ismerai came to sit with us. The other guests settled closer to the television, even though the sound had now gone.

Away from our house and the protection of its walls, Ismerai acted differently with Georgie, much more formally. I knew this was largely due to the other men being in the room. Despite all the years Georgie and Ismerai had been friends, they were friends in Afghanistan and therefore there were rules to follow, which mainly involved not being too friendly with women, foreign or not. The fact was, laughing and joking with women didn't look good, it looked weak, and it was probably only one step away from finding pleasure in the bracelet-jangling swirls of Afghanistan's dancing boys.

But although I wasn't that surprised by Ismerai's behavior— he was a Pashtun after all—I was a little amazed to see the change in Georgie. She was terrible for teasing Ismerai when he came to our house, but now she was quiet and respectful, and she didn't speak again with the other men unless they looked over to invite her into their conversation, which they didn't really.

In our culture, a woman is usually permitted to sit only with the men she is related to. Georgie's presence was tolerated only because she was a foreigner. If she hadn't come from England, she'd have been hidden in the back of the house with the rest of the women.

Haji Khan was in Shinwar, Ismerai told us. "The signal doesn't work well in the mountains." He apologized to Georgie with a shy smile, looking at her silent mobile phone as he did so.

Georgie shrugged as if she didn't care, and I almost believed her. "I'm just grateful you invited us over," she replied, "especially at such short notice."

As she spoke I suddenly realized she must have called Ismerai that morning when I wasn't listening, and the knowledge of it made my cheeks burn with added shame because now everyone must know what I'd done, even my friends living half a world away in Jalalabad.

Therefore, when our dinner was laid out for us and Ismerai joked that the household help had "better keep the knives away from the boy," I didn't laugh.

"So, do you want to talk about it?"

Georgie stopped to light a cigarette after beating me for the fifth time at *carambul*, a wooden board game imported from India where two players fight with their fingers, flicking bright-colored disks into four holes drilled into the corners. She was impossibly good at it for a girl.

"I don't know," I answered truthfully, sensing that Georgie was looking for reasons for my behavior. "Maybe."

"Sometimes it helps to talk about things, especially difficult things," Georgie pushed gently, fiddling as she did so with a box of matches showing the Khyber Pass on the front. "It's a way of chasing the bad spirits out from your head."

"I guess," I said, even though I was certain the devils that lived there were too strong for the magic of talk. "Okay. I'll try."

Long before I was born my mother was married to my father, and together they made Bilal. He was my oldest brother. Three years later, when the Russians packed up to begin their long journey home, rolling out of Afghanistan in the tanks they had brought with them, my parents celebrated by bringing Mina into the family. In Pashto, her name means "love." Some years after that Yosef, my other brother, arrived, and then finally, after all of them had taken up most of the space in our house, I was born.

This was my family, as complete and happy as it would ever be.

Then, one by one, like leaves falling from a tree, they began to die.

First to go was Yosef, who stopped eating the day after he was bitten by a dog. I was a baby, so he was lost to us before I could remember him, but my mother says I'm a little like him and that Allah took him away because He needed more sunshine in Paradise.

A year after Yosef died, my father also left us. He was a teacher, but he laid down his schoolbooks and picked up a gun to fight alongside the soldiers of the Northern Alliance with a group of other men from our village. Mother says his heart became furious as his eyes watched the Taliban change our ways, and because he was a man of honor and courage he felt it was his duty to stop them, being as he was a son of Afghanistan. Unfortunately for my father, it turned out that he was better suited to schooling than fighting, and he died in a battle near Mazar-e Sharif in the north of the country.

That left my mother a widow, a widow with a baby and two young children. But because of her tears she clung to our home, as it still held the smell of my father and the ghostly laughter of my brother, even though everyone said she would be better off living with her sister.

Of course, this being Afghanistan, things then went from bad to worse than bad.

Sometime after my father died, and at the time when my head began to save the pictures of my life, the Taliban came to Paghman. By now I was no longer a baby—I was walking and talking—and I heard the fear in my mother's voice when one night she shook me awake to pull me into her arms and carry me from my bed to the corner of the kitchen where my sister and brother were waiting. I remember it clearly now: my mother was trembling through her clothes, and outside I could hear the sound of heavy trucks filling the street with the noise of their engines.

"What is it?" I asked.

"Please, Fawad, please be quiet," my mother begged. She was crying, and, outside, shouts and screams invaded the stillness of the night as the light coming in through our window burned the color of flames.

As we hid in the corner, the sound of panic and pain grew closer, steadily creeping upon us, looking to find us. All this time my mother whispered to Allah under her breath, quick and quiet as she rocked on her legs, holding on to all three of her children. Her prayer was broken by a sharp intake of breath as the door cracked open at the front of our house and the barks of men we didn't know began to fill our home.

It wasn't a big house, and it didn't take long for them to discover us—five black shadows jumping on our huddle to snatch my sister's arm away from our mother and shout their hate into our faces. As my mother leaped to her feet, one of the Taliban soldiers threw her to the floor, slamming his boot onto her head to keep her in place. My brother Bilal, who had the heart of a lion, immediately sprang from the ground, raining blows on the man's back and kicking at his legs. Another of the men then grabbed my brother as if he were a toy. He smashed his fist into Bilal's face and threw him across the kitchen, his head bouncing off the corner of a cupboard.

As my brother slipped to the floor, no longer awake and no longer able to help us, my mother screamed into the Talib's boot and pushed with all her power to reach her eldest child. As she threw herself at Bilal, the man who had hurt her came on her again and pulled her back to the ground. But this time it wasn't the boot he laid on top of her; it was his body. I saw his hands ripping at her clothes while, from somewhere behind us, the smell of burning began to fill our noses.

"Run, Fawad, run!" she shouted.

The man hit my mother in the face, but as he did so another shadow came running into the room. His black eyes caught me first, and he stared at me for a moment that seemed to last forever. When I remember it now, I think I saw sadness written there. Releasing me from his gaze, he turned toward the man on top of my mother and pulled him from her, shouting something angry and hard.

"Run, Fawad!" my mother shouted again.

Because I was scared and I didn't know what to do, and because my brother was asleep, and because one of the men had my sister's arm, and because my mother had told me to, I did. I ran as fast as I could from the back of the house and found a place in the bushes near our home.

Crouching low into the prickles, I watched the whole world catch fire. As the houses of my neighbors spat out flames, the screams of fear filling my ears gradually turned into howls of mourning as the men dressed in black ripped apart our lives, beating the old people with sticks and stealing the young from their arms. In the orange light of that night I watched those men drag my terrified sister onto the back of a truck, along with twenty other girls from our village, and drive her away.

As the engines faded into the distance and the air died around us, leaving only the sound of fire and tears, I saw my mother come from the house, carrying my brother over her shoulder. Her face was pale, and blood poured from a cut by her mouth.

"Fawad?" she shouted. "Fawad?"

I stood up, and she saw me. The light of relief flickered in her eyes before she fell to her knees and opened her mouth to let go of a scream that would have frozen the blood of the devil himself.

With our house now a broken shell of black and our neighbors just as broken, my mother, Bilal, and I walked from our home in Paghman to arrive at the place of my aunt. I remember nothing of the journey, so I guess I must have slept, my mother carrying me for most of it. I also can't remember any discussion once we got to my aunt's house, but I can clearly see the look in my mother's eyes. It was one of death, and the blankness that went with it was mirrored in the eyes of Bilal.

All I knew for certain was that my mother had been hurt by the Taliban; my sister, who was only eleven or twelve years old, had been taken by the Taliban; and my brother was now lost to the Afghan obsession with revenge.

· After waking from his sleep, Bilal had been greeted by the battered face of our mother and the hole in our family that used to be filled by our sister. Giant tears of anger came falling from his eyes, spilling onto the dirt that used to be our garden. Because Bilal had become the man of the house after my father was killed, he made himself crazy with thoughts that he should have done more to protect us. But he was only a boy—a boy up against an army of black turbaned devils. There was nothing more he could have done for any of us. Even so, for the next few weeks Bilal covered himself in silence, hardly able to speak through his own shame and dishonor, until one day his place simply stood empty. My only living brother had left our aunt's house to join the Northern Alliance.

He was fourteen years old at the time, an age when he should have been moving closer to God, as he was now old enough to deliver his prayers at the mosque and fast with the adults at the time of Ramazan. Instead, he gave himself up to war and revenge, and we never saw him again.

Once the Americans had bombed the Taliban out of our lives, I wondered whether Bilal would return, but when the Northern Alliance marched into Kabul he still stayed away. Though neither my mother nor I said anything, we both knew he was dead.

II

IT WAS NIGHT when the lights woke me, the time of night when you're stuck between yesterday and today and everything's so quiet and deaf with sleep there's no sign of the morning coming to get you. It was the time of night that calls for a stretch and a smile.

And it was this time of night that Haji Khan chose to return home.

It started with the sound of metal on concrete as the gates were pulled open and three Land Cruisers with blacked-out windows roared into the driveway, spilling guards from the doors and Haji Khan from the front seat. As two men with guns pulled the gates shut behind him, another man jumped into the seat he'd abandoned and the cars facing the house now turned in circles on the grass to point at the exit instead.

Watching this dance of headlights from my window, I saw Haji Khan lead a group of men into the house. His face looked fierce, and I wondered whether he'd just found out that Ismerai had let Georgie and me come to stay.

I tiptoed toward the bedroom door and pulled it ajar, blinking at the sudden light that shone from the floor below. Rising from the ground, a mumble of voices came to my ears, low man sounds it took me a few seconds to catch properly. Then, above them all, I heard Haji Khan's words filling the air like coming thunder.

I opened the door a little farther and leaned into the crack, which allowed me to see what was going on through the wooden pillars of the balcony. Haji Khan was now standing by the door, with five men nearby holding quiet conversations with one another. I didn't recognize any of them, but they looked pretty rich, dressed as they were in pressed *salwar kameez* with large, heavy watches hanging off their wrists.

Haji Khan was talking to the small man who had taken my bags upstairs when I arrived. The man nodded upward to the side of the house where Georgie was sleeping, just along the corridor from where I should have been sleeping, and Haji Khan's gaze briefly followed the man's head, causing me to catch my breath and fall a little farther into the darkness of my room.

If he didn't know we were here before he arrived, he certainly did now.

After a few seconds, and when no sound of footsteps came to throw us out of our beds, I inched forward again.

Haji Khan was now sitting on one of the sofas, his *pakol* balanced on his knee and a cup of green tea in his hand. As he reached for the sugared almonds that had been placed on a table before him, a man approached holding a mobile phone. Haji Khan put it to his ear, and though he never shouted, his voice echoed loudly around the room, causing the other men to stop their conversations and eye one another from beneath bowed heads and heavy eyebrows.

"I don't care how you do it, just do it," Haji Khan ordered. "I want him out by the morning."

He clicked the phone shut and handed it back to the man who had given it to him, and I wondered if this was the reason Haji Khan never called Georgie: he'd lost his phone and had to keep borrowing someone else's.

In the morning I went downstairs looking for breakfast and found the hall empty of the big men who had filled it the night before and busy with three small ones armed with cleaning cloths and a vacuum cleaner. A boy a little older than me was playing *carambul* by himself on the platform floor close to the TV.

"Salaam," I said, going over to join him. "I'm Fawad."

The boy looked up from his game.

"Salaam," he replied. "Ahmad."

He then carried on playing, and with nothing else to do, I sat on a long cushion and watched him. He was very good, flicking the disks effortlessly into the holes opposite him. He also looked very clean, new even. But although his skin had the look of the rich about it—a soft creamy brown—his eyes held an old man's stare within them.

We were the only children in the room, but the boy called Ahmad didn't seem in a rush to talk, so I was glad when my breakfast arrived because it at least gave me something to do. I was also starving, which was strange, because I never usually had much of an appetite. "You eat like a bird," my mother once remarked, and I immediately wondered how worms tasted.

After I'd finished my eggs and a cup of sweet tea, Ahmad knocked the *carambul* board in my direction and jerked his head upward, inviting me to play. As I shuffled toward him to take up the challenge, he set the pieces in place and let me go first.

"You came with Georgie, didn't you?" he finally asked.

"Yes," I admitted, badly missing the cluster of disks I had to break. The boy waved as if he didn't care and let me take the shot again, which I thought showed very good manners.

"I saw you last night," he said as I carefully lined up my shot, "spying on my father."

The disks clattered around the board as I hit them, and Ahmad reached for the large one to take his turn.

"I saw you across the hall," he continued as he casually

flicked a blue piece into the far right hole. "My bedroom is opposite the one you're staying in."

"And your dad is?"

"Haji Khalid Khan. Who else?"

I looked up, surprised. Although I knew Haji Khan had children by his dead wife, I was a little shocked to find one of them sitting opposite me because Georgie had told me they stayed with his sister.

"I thought you lived somewhere else," I said.

"I do. I sleep at my aunt's place usually, but the noise is a nightmare. Too many women in the house, that's the problem. Here, your turn."

I took the disk and managed to slide one of my whites close to a hole.

"Not bad," Ahmad said. "Of course, you seriously need to practice."

"I only started playing yesterday."

"Yes, and you seriously need to practice."

Ahmad laughed, and as he did so I saw some of Haji Khan in his face.

"Your father seemed a bit angry last night," I mentioned, watching Ahmad steadily demolish the board in front of me.

"Ha! He was pissed all right."

"Is it because of us?"

"Who?" Ahmad looked up from the game, genuinely puzzled.

"Me and Georgie," I explained. "Is he angry because we turned up uninvited?"

"No, of course not." Ahmad shook his head. "Georgie has always been welcome here. This is her home, that's what my father says."

"Oh."

"No, if you must know, he's pissed about some family business, but it'll soon be sorted because it always is."

About three hours after I'd finished my breakfast, and about two hours after Ahmad had disappeared back to the house full of women in one of his father's Land Cruisers, Georgie appeared downstairs looking fed up. "Come on, Fawad, it's time to see a man about some goats," she said, and we grabbed our boots, jumped into another of Haji Khan's cars, and roared out of Jalalabad.

It was a beautiful day with brilliant skies that carried none of the dust and car-fog hanging above Kabul, and an Indian love song played from a cassette. As well as me and Georgie there was a driver and a guard with a gun placed between his legs in the front seat. He didn't belong to us, so I guessed he must belong to Haji Khan.

Driving out of the city toward Pakistan, we passed a large portrait of the martyr Haji Abdul Qadir, the former vice president who was murdered eight months after the Taliban fled. Jalalabad had been his home, and I thought the people must have really loved him to place his picture there.

Climbing out of the city, we drove higher, through a mud village and on to a large flat space of brown before dipping back into green, passing rows of olives trees, and into a tunnel of giant trees that seemed to be leaning over the road in an effort to hug their friends on the other side. As we came to another village, we turned right off the main road, through a small bazaar and onto a rough track taking us to Shinwar. This was where we would find a man and his goats, apparently.

As we drove farther into the countryside, we passed scores and scores of old poppy fields. I'd recently seen photographs of them printed in one of the Kabul newspapers Pir Hederi had me read to him. The poppies shone bright and pretty from the pages, and I remember thinking at the time that if they tasted as good as they looked it was no wonder people became addicted.

As we passed an old man with a donkey laden with twigs, Georgie rolled down her window, and after saying her hellos and asking after his family, she asked where we could find a man called Baba Gul Rahman. The old man lifted his hand and revealed that we could find him at the hut over the next field under the hill. "If he still has a hut," he grumbled. Georgie said thank you, looked at me, and shrugged, and then we all set off toward the hill over the next field to see if Baba Gul still had his hut.

When we arrived at the foot of the hill we were relieved to find Baba Gul's hut was still standing, but annoyingly for us there was no Baba Gul in it. One of the children we assumed to be his went running off to the next village in search of him.

Sitting on the grass, watching a herd of goats eating and playing, we passed the time drinking tea given to us by a girl who was about my age or a little older. She was Baba Gul's oldest daughter, revealed Georgie, who had met her before. Her name was Mulallah, and she had the prettiest green eyes I'd ever seen.

"How are you doing?" Georgie asked as she came to sit with us. "Your goats look well."

"Yes, the goats are good," she replied, roughly wiping the hair from her face and frowning.

"Something wrong, Mulallah?"

The girl shrugged. "This is Afghanistan, Khanum Georgie. Sometimes, life is not so easy. You know this better than us."

Georgie nodded, but I saw the questions sitting in her eyes.

As I didn't know what to say, I kept my mouth shut.

"My father's playing at the cards again," the girl finally explained as we sat there in silence. "And when he loses we pay for it. It must be Allah's punishment for the sin he's committing. I mean, just look where we're living now." The girl waved her hands at the hut, which was more of a tent really, a flimsy house of wood covered in plastic sheeting bearing the initials of something called UNICEF.

As the girl spoke, her mother approached. She was a tiny woman with a face that could have been carved out of the mountains behind us. She greeted Georgie affectionately but didn't hang around. After nodding her head at her daughter, they both left to round up the goats, but as she turned away I caught the look on her face, and it was one of deep shame. I understood then that the lifelong humiliation she had suffered at the hands of her husband had been the cause of the ugly lines cut into her skin. And now that the girl was speaking of the family's dishonor to virtual strangers, there wasn't any use in pretending life was anything different.

Sometimes, when you possess nothing at all, the only thing you can do is hang on to your dignity. But even simple words can take that away from you if you're not careful.

"Was Haji Khan happy to see you?" I asked Georgie as we continued to await Baba Gul's arrival.

"He was tired, but yes, I think so," she answered, fiddling with the frayed ends of her jeans as we sat on the grass.

"You *think* so?"

"Yes."

"You don't *know*?"

"Well . . ." Georgie breathed in deeply and then out again. "No, I don't really."

I shook my head in disbelief. As far as lovers' reunions went, this didn't really sound up there with Laila and Majnun.

Theirs was a story Jamilla had told me one day in Chicken Street after her mother had told it to her one night to take the sting out of her father's fists. In the legend, Laila was a beautiful girl born to a rich family. Of course, when she grew up her family wanted her to marry a rich man, but instead she fell in love with Majnun, a very poor man. When everyone found out, there was hell to pay, and Laila and Majnun were banned from seeing each other ever again. Laila's parents then forced her to marry a man of great wealth, and he took her away from the area. But even though she had a beautiful home, her love for Majnun stayed strong, and one day when she couldn't stand being apart from him any longer, she killed herself. When Majnun heard of Laila's death he went mad-crazy with grief, and in the end he died on her grave.

In no part of the story did I hear that Majnun was a little tired and might or might not have been happy to see Laila.

"Were you pleased to see him, then?" I asked.

"Fawad, I'm always pleased to see Khalid, but life is complicated, you know."

"No, I don't know actually. I'm only a boy; I've still got a lot to learn."

Georgie smiled.

"Sorry, Fawad, sometimes I forget your age because you're so wonderfully grown-up! But you're right, there are complications in life you won't know about just yet. So, yes, I was happy to see him, of course I was, but then we argued a little and there were a lot of hot words said, and that doesn't really make me very happy at all."

"What did you argue about?"

"I don't know really . . . the usual. We never used to fight like this, not back when we first met. In those days everything used to be quite lovely. But things change, don't they?"

"Yes, I guess they do," I replied. Then, bowing my head to look at her from the side of my eyes, I asked, "Do you want to talk about it? I mean, sometimes it helps to talk. It chases the bad spirits out from your head."

"Well, that serves me right, doesn't it." Georgie laughed, recognizing her own words from the day before. "Okay. I'll try.

"When I first met Haji Khalid Khan I was working on your country's first ever elections. It was an exciting time, a moment of real hope and opportunity, and walking into all this crazy expectation came the most beautiful man I had ever set eyes upon. Up to that point I'd never believed in love at first sight, and it's not something you can easily explain, but it's a state of the mind and heart that makes your body feel alive and makes each morning that comes worth waking up for.

"So there we were, me and a group of other internationals and a team of Afghans who had arrived in Shinwar to prepare for the elections. In those days Shinwar was said to be a pretty dangerous place, filled with hiding Taliban and bloodthirsty bandits, so Khalid offered our party a place to stay and also his protection.

"Coming from London, it was all terribly exciting—we don't have men with Kalashnikovs driving us around there. And your country was just amazing to me right from the start: the incredible scenery; the beautiful call to prayer that would drift into my dreams at five in the morning; the people we met who had lived such hard, broken lives yet retained the most wonderful spirit. You know, one day I went to visit a refugee camp to speak about the coming elections, and the people I found there were so horrendously poor that they were saving animal dung to burn for the winter, yet when we turned up they immediately offered us tea and what little bread they had because we were guests. To me that was really very humbling, and I began to feel something really special for this country.

"Of course, not every Afghan I met was that poor, and even in those days Khalid was a rich man. But it wasn't his money that brought me to him, no matter what your friend

Pir Hederi likes to think; it was his attitude, his warm humor, and his tenderness. He was really kind, Fawad, and in those days he taught me so much about this country and about your ways without me even realizing it. I'd never met a man like him before, and looking back on it, I think I fell in love with him almost immediately.

"Although my colleagues and I stayed in his house, which wasn't as big as the one in Jalalabad, we rarely saw him throughout the day, as we were all busy with our jobs and he was always locked in talks with various elders, politicians, and military men. However, sometimes when we used to return to the house he would be sitting in the garden amid a circle of men dressed in turbans and lavish robes, and when we passed by to go to our rooms I would glance in his direction and our eyes would meet and I would see a small smile play on his lips.

"Once the sun had gone down and the guests had gone home, Khalid would come to our rooms to sit and talk with us for a while, joking with the men and charming the ladies, and I think every one of us fell in love with him—even the boys! But even though the room was full of people, it felt like we were alone. Of course, I didn't know for sure at that time that he was really interested in me; it was just a feeling I had. But for my part, I spent the days desperate to be back in his company, and most nights his face filled my dreams.

"Then one day, while I was visiting a village some thirty kilometers away from his home, a convoy of cars pulled up and Haji Khan stepped into the sun. All the villagers we were talking to immediately ran to greet him, treating him like a king and leading him to the elder's home for sweet tea. I kept a discreet distance, but as he passed by me he stopped to shake my hand and said under his breath, 'See what you are making me do just to get one look at you?' I nearly fainted with the heat of his words, Fawad, and I knew then that there was something between us and it wasn't only in my head.

"That day, after drinking himself full of tea, Khalid said thank you to everyone as his driver handed out money, and then he offered me a lift home in his car. I remember looking at my driver, not sure if that was really allowed, as we hadn't even finished half of our work in the village, but then Khalid spoke to him. I didn't know Pashto or even Dari in those days. My driver just shrugged and nodded his head, so I left with Khalid. He immediately jumped into the front seat in order to drive, and the door was opened for me by a guard so that I could take my place in the back. Then, as we pulled out of the village I noticed Khalid adjust his mirror so he could see me. Every time I found the courage to meet his gaze, his eyes were so dark and intense that I felt like my skin was on fire. I wanted that journey to last forever. But of course that would have been impossible.

"Anyway, when we got back to the house I was relieved to find that my colleagues hadn't come home yet, and Khalid and I took the opportunity to drink tea in the garden together— we obviously couldn't sit in the house alone, so we had to sit outside where everyone could see. Still, the guards kept their distance, and we were able to talk for once without everybody else wanting to join in.

"As we sat there talking and picking at our biscuits, Khalid revealed a little of his life to me: about how he had fought the Russians alongside his father as soon as he was man enough to do so; about how his family had moved to Pakistan in fury and disbelief as freedom turned into civil war; about how he had returned to fight again when the Taliban took control; and about how he had been captured trying to creep back into Pakistan one night. You know, Fawad, he spent six long months locked inside a Taliban prison in Kandahar, where he was whipped almost daily with electric cables on the soles of his feet. Even now he suffers from those beatings. His legs cramp with a pain so bad he can barely walk.

"Khalid eventually escaped thanks to a sympathetic guard and a healthy bribe, and he fled to Iran with another man, who lost his life when their vehicle hit a land mine. Amazingly, Khalid escaped with only cuts and bruises. After that he traveled to Uzbekistan and met up with some leading members of the Northern Alliance. He agreed to join their war, bringing what he could to the effort via his contacts in Pakistan. Unfortunately, this is probably the reason that his wife and daughter were murdered.

"After their deaths, Khalid said he was almost numb with grief, but he had one more daughter and a son to think about. You see, Khalid loved his wife very much. They were cousins, but because they had grown up together and the adults saw it was a love match they were allowed to marry—something pretty rare in Afghanistan. And then there was his daughter, his first child. Khalid was so proud of her because she was such a clever little girl.

"Well, as you can imagine, after they were killed, Khalid went wild with rage, and he sneaked back into Afghanistan on a regular basis to fight to the death if need be. When the Taliban finally fled and ran into the mountains of Tora Bora, he even followed them there. By then the war was all but over, and when the trail of the Taliban and al-Qaeda grew cold he returned home to the land he loved, satisfied that he had honored the memory of his wife and his daughter.

"As he spoke, Fawad, I was spellbound. Khalid had done so much in his life compared to me; he had seen so many things that usually come only from the pages of storybooks in my country. I thought he was incredibly brave and honorable, and as this man opened up before my eyes, laying his history in my lap for me to wonder at, he suddenly, out of nowhere, told me he loved me.

"I laughed in his face at first, which wasn't the reaction he was expecting, and I told him that it was impossible; that we had only known each other for five minutes and that was far too quick for anyone to sensibly fall in love. But he answered me by saying, 'I'm not joking, Georgie. I know my heart, and my heart is telling me I love you.' And that's when I knew I wanted to spend the rest of my life with this man.

"After that conversation it became almost unbearable to be in his company with so many people watching us, to be unable to do anything but touch with our eyes. But as the weeks went on everyone seemed to notice, and we were given space to spend more and more time alone, until I was certain that his words weren't just words and that they came from his heart.

"It was a magical time, full of late nights talking amid the buzz of the gaslight or sitting under the stars on the flat of his roof. Everything was so beautiful: the brilliance of the stars; the giant moon that hung in the sky; and, of course, Khalid. 'You see how close the star comes to the moon?' he asked me one night. 'Well, you are like that star and I am like that moon, but soon that star will begin to fall away from the moon and slowly that star will disappear into the darkness and become lost to the moon.'

"We both sat silently on the carpet that had been laid out on the rooftop for us, and he gently reached for my hand— brave now because only the tea boy remained with us, to fill our cups when needed, and the boy needed the money too much to tell anyone.

"It was a very sweet moment, but it was also a very sad one because we both knew the story of the star and the moon was true. I did have to leave soon because my job was coming to an end. And even though we tried to treasure every moment we had left together, we felt the days slipping away from us like sand through our fingers.

"Eventually, and because the world does keep on turning and there's nothing you can do to stop it, the day came when I had to return to Kabul, and then to London. Khalid traveled with us, and we were able to steal a few more days together in the capital before I left. We even went to your district one night.

"As soon as I saw Paghman, driving past the old golf course and over the bridge, I was amazed by how pretty it was. It felt like I could have been visiting somewhere in the Mediterranean, which is a warm place where people from my country go on their holidays. And it was in Paghman, as we sat on a stone wall in front of the lake, that Khalid looked at me and whispered that he loved me with all his heart. For the first time I told him that I loved him too, but then his eyes turned sad and, staring hard at me, he said, 'Thank you for that, but I know I love you more. You are my world, Georgie.' It was a beautiful thing to say, because I suppose that's all anybody ever wants in life—to find someone who thinks the world of them.

"Then, as we carried on talking, he said there may be times in the future when I wouldn't hear from him and that I shouldn't become 'hungry for other men' when that happened. I laughed at that because I thought he'd said 'angry for other men,' but as I did he looked at me and said, 'I'm serious, Georgie. You are my woman now. If you leave me, I will kill you.' And of course I laughed again, but although he smiled I couldn't be sure that his eyes were doing the same. In fact I still can't be sure that he was joking, even today.

"Anyway, after I returned to London my life felt pretty empty. No one talks about the moon and stars in my country, and everything seemed so dull and ordinary compared to Afghanistan. I think I became a little obsessed, and I began to fill my time with everything Afghan: watching every documentary about your country, reading every book, helping out at a local community center for asylum seekers, even learning Dari. I chose Dari because it was a lot easier than Pashto, and besides, Pashtuns are so clever they know both languages. But I was waiting, you see, waiting and killing time until I found another job to take me back to Khalid and this country I had so quickly fallen in love with.

"Although it was almost like torture in those first months away, Khalid would call me maybe twice a week, staying on the phone for hours at a time, and we would playfully discuss the future and how he wanted to have at least five children with me and how we would spend our days drinking pomegranate juice in the Shinwar sun.

"Needless to say, within six months I couldn't stand the separation any longer, and I returned to Afghanistan just for a holiday. For two weeks I stayed at Khalid's home in Shinwar and his new house in Jalalabad. We spent the days traveling around, visiting old friends and making new ones. I came to know his family, and he showed me all the projects he was working on. We walked through giant fields filled with tiny ankle-tall saplings that would one day become fruit trees, olive trees, and perfume bushes. Everything was just as I had left it, and more, and I felt the pull even more strongly to return to him once and for all.

"When I flew back home again I applied for every job going, and in the meantime Khalid kept up his calls, whispering his love over satellite phone lines. But then, as the months dragged on, Khalid's calls began to fade, first to once a week, then to once a month, until, by the time a job offer did eventually arrive and I'd packed my bags for Afghanistan, I hadn't spoken to him for three months. I was livid with him, but I couldn't allow myself to believe that everything he had told me was lies, so I carried on with my plan and returned to the country, without even telling him.

"For that first month, I lived in Kabul under a cloud and

cried tears like you wouldn't believe, wondering what I'd done and thinking it was all one big giant mistake. Then one day the doorbell rang at the house I was staying at, and it was Ismerai. I'd first met him in Shinwar and had seen him again during my holiday. Even so, I was pretty shocked, although overjoyed, to see him. He told me that Khalid had sent him to track me down after one of their friends had spotted me on the street one day waiting for my car. 'Kabul is a big city,' Ismerai told me, 'but if we want to find you we can.'

"However, even though Ismerai had dutifully found me, Khalid still didn't call. It was two weeks later that I was summoned to Jalalabad and brought to his house like a naughty schoolgirl.

"When I arrived, Khalid's hall was full of guests so our talk was careful and polite, but when the men finally grew tired of their curiosity and left for their own homes, Khalid turned to look at me as the doors banged shut and his eyes burned bright with fury. 'You come into my country, and you don't even tell me?' he shouted. 'I know you are angry because I didn't call you, and I know what I did was unacceptable, but what you have done is even more unacceptable to me! If I came to your country, the first thing I would do is come to your door.'

"He was right, of course, and I felt ashamed. I tried to argue back, but Khalid was so concentrated on the offense I'd caused him and his own sense of outrage that he wouldn't budge.

"Thankfully, the next morning he was calmer, and the day after that he was calmer still, until we were laughing and joking and talking of our love in the way we used to. Even so, I sensed he was different in some way I couldn't yet understand; not quite the man he used to be. But I ignored the feeling and let my love continue to grow for him until it was the only thing left holding my life together.

"But maybe I should have listened to that little noise in my head rather than the love in my heart, because nearly three years later he still doesn't phone as often as I would like, as often as I need to hear him, and no matter how many times he tells me he's sorry and how many promises he makes to try harder, within two weeks he does exactly the same again. And that's why I'm not sure he was all that happy to see me last night because I told him that if he continued to treat me like this he would push me away forever. I would leave him.

"I love Khalid, and when I'm with him and I look into his eyes I know he loves me too, but sometimes that love seems so far away and almost impossible to hold on to."

Georgie lit a cigarette and stared over at the goats filling their bellies with dry grass.

"Why don't you just get married?" I asked, thinking this might be the ideal solution for everyone because Haji Khan would have to come home at least once a week on "ladies' night," the Thursday before the Friday holiday when the men return from their compounds to spend time with their families.

Georgie turned to me, tears burning her eyes red.

"I'm a Godless *kafir*, Fawad. Khalid's a Muslim. How is that even possible in today's Afghanistan?"

12

LIKE THE RAINS of spring that come to wash away the gray of winter, once Georgie had cried her tears, the world around us brightened.

Baba Gul, who was as thin as a stick and seemed to laugh a lot for a man on the fast track to Hell, eventually arrived before the sun dropped, and before the guard in charge of our lives grew fidgety to leave for Jalalabad. Disappearing into the hut that might or might not be his by the time Georgie visited again, Baba Gul was shown some paperwork, which he might or might not have been able to read, and my friend talked to him about his goats while I spent the last of the day in the fields with Mulallah, who seemed a lot happier once her father returned without having lost anything else they owned to a game of cards.

As we chased the goats around the field, it soon became clear that Mulallah wasn't like other girls I knew—not that I knew that many. She was strong in her eyes and hard in her talk, and, more amazingly for a girl, she was a very fast runner, which is a good talent to have in Afghanistan. As she raced through the fields with her red scarf floating from her neck, I thought she looked like a firework.

I really hoped to see Mulallah again when Georgie returned to talk to her father once the winter had left us, and I don't know why, but I decided under that hill as we tumbled in the grass and she helped me clean the goat shit off my knees that I wouldn't tell Jamilla about her.

"You and Mulallah looked like you were having fun," Georgie remarked when we were back in the car.

I saw the twinkle in her eyes and knew she was trying to tease me.

"Yeah," I admitted. "She's actually quite good fun—for a girl."

"Ooooh," Georgie sang, "you lurve her. You want to kiss her, hold her, and marry her."

"Georgie," I said, shaking my head, "sometimes for a woman as old as my mother you are very immature."

Once we got back to the big house, Haji Khan also seemed to be in a better mood than I was expecting, given Georgie's talk of hot words the night before, and after kicking off our shoes and pulling off our boots we spent the evening filling our bellies with food so pretty it could have come from a painting. It was a massive feast of chopped green and red salad, bowls of creamy white yogurt, fried chicken coated with orange-colored spices, rice and meat, dark green spinach, and warm naan bread followed by fizzing Pepsi and plates piled high with yellow bananas, red apples, and pink pomegranate seeds.

After the meal—when we were all able to sit straight again after all the food we had eaten—we took turns playing *carambul*, with Georgie coming out the clear winner after Haji Khan missed a couple of easy shots because she was a guest and he didn't want "to give her another reason to complain." We then slouched on the cushions wrapped in furry blankets to watch a comedy show on Tolo TV, and I drank so much green tea my stomach grew round as a ball.

But though I laughed with everyone else at the jokes on the television, under my blanket with its red swirls and bright yellow flowers my heart was breaking because every time

Georgie's words came running back into my brain I felt them trickle down my throat to tear at my insides, as if I'd eaten broken glass for dinner.

It was bad enough that she drank alcohol and smoked like a National Army soldier, and that she had come to my country in search of a moon that spent its days hiding in the sun, but it had never even crossed my mind that she had no God. I'd always thought she was a follower of the prophet Jesus. But to have nothing, nothing at all—not to believe in anything—well, this was the worst thing she could have possibly told me.

Georgie was my friend and I loved her as much as I'd ever loved anyone, but she was going to Hell for all eternity, that was for sure. And in Hell a single day feels like a million years. My mother once described it as a place of terrible grief and sadness where the flames had been fanned for a thousand years until everything burned red. After that, Hell was fanned for another thousand years until it grew white-hot, and then it was fanned for a thousand years more until it became nothing but black. As Georgie's words kept rushing back into my mind, I couldn't stop the sight of her pretty face screaming in pain, the fire eating at her skin, and her mouth full of the fruit of the thorny tree that would boil like oil in her belly, bringing unimaginable agony.

It's true that pretty much all of us would be spending at least some time in Hell unless we were the best of all mullahs, because there are a lot of rules in Islam and not all of them are that easy to follow. But Allah is merciful, so even though Ismerai would go to Hell for his smoking, Baba Gul for his gambling, me for my drinking and thieving, and Haji Khan for falling in love with a woman who wasn't his wife, as well as for his possible drug empire, all of us would get out eventually and find our way to Paradise because we were Muslims. But Georgie had no chance. She had no God, and therefore she had no one willing or able to save her. And she couldn't even climb out to the light, because if you throw a rock into Hell it takes seventy years to hit the bottom. Hell is so big it will never become full with all the world's sinners, and you can never escape from it. Even worse than that, Georgie would have to suffer alone because all her friends would eventually leave her. Even the warlord Zardad and his testicle-eating man-dog would get to Paradise in the end.

And when you know all this, as I do, it's hard to look into the eyes of the person you love and not see her death looking back at you.

"I'm praying for you," I whispered to Georgie the next morning over breakfast after a night of terrible worrying.

She looked up from her eggs and smiled. "That's nice, Fawad, thank you."

I shook my head. She so didn't get it.

Also joining us for breakfast that morning was Haji Khan, who walked down from his bedroom looking like he'd just got off a film set. His face was relaxed and handsome, and his light gray *salwar kameez* was covered by a darker gray sweater that looked as soft as clouds.

I watched him carefully, looking for signs of more hot words during the night, but if he was worried about losing Georgie he appeared to be putting a brave face on it—although I did notice he was teasing her a little more than usual, as well as kissing her ass with compliments that made her cheeks red, and holding eyes with her more than was strictly allowed in our society.

As I watched, I prayed inside my head that Haji Khan would try to change his ways, as he was always promising to do, because I was sure that if he really tried, and if he could charm the birds from the trees like my mother said, he could easily make Georgie take Islam to her heart. He just had to love her enough—and phone her more often.

After breakfast, two cups of tea, and four cigarettes, Haji Khan disappeared from the house in a cloud of dust thrown up by his three Land Cruisers, and Georgie headed back upstairs to take a shower, so I passed the rest of the morning in the garden with Ahmad, who had arrived shortly before his father left. Together we teased the fighting birds that sat in little wooden cages around the edges of the lawn as Ismerai watched us, smoking.

I was itching to talk to Ahmad about Georgie and his father, but I couldn't. Although we all knew what the two of them were up to, it couldn't ever be a matter for discussion because that would be like accepting it, which we couldn't really, because we were all trying to be good Muslims and, more than that, pretending our friends were good Muslims too. And I couldn't talk about Georgie being a total unbeliever because it was too shameful for her and I had at least to try to protect her from the bad thoughts everyone would surely have of her if they knew the full horrible truth. So we basically talked about all the creatures we had burned using the force of the sun and broken glass.

As Ahmad was telling me about the time he had seen a scorpion commit suicide—someone had placed it on a metal dish set on top of a fire, and realizing it had no chance of escape, it turned its tail on itself and stabbed poison into its body—a car horn beeped outside the tall gates, which were quickly opened to allow a black Land Cruiser with an eagle painted on the back window into the driveway.

"Ah, my uncle returns," Ahmad said by way of explanation, getting to his feet.

As the car doors opened, a man much smaller than Haji Khan got out of the front seat and moved toward Ismerai, who was nearest to him. He took his hand, smiling wide and revealing a dark hole where one of his bottom teeth had once sat.

"Welcome back, Haji Jawid," Ismerai greeted him.

"Thank you. Is my brother here?" Haji Jawid's face was clean-shaven and pinched at the cheeks, as if he was sucking in.

"No, he's out," Ismerai told him, "taking care of some business."

"I see."

Haji Jawid's eyes, which were as hollow as his cheeks, moved to the steps at the front of the house where a smiling Georgie had appeared. He returned her smile, but because I was standing close to him when he turned I clearly heard him mutter to Ismerai, "I see my brother is still busy with his whore, then." Ismerai quickly looked in my direction, his face closing in a frown, but he said nothing so I moved forward in anger.

Ahmad caught me by the hand before my foot was even able to take one step. "Leave it," he whispered as Haji Jawid moved across to the house, where Georgie held out her hands in welcome. And I did. But I heard polite laughter come from their direction as they touched, and it made me even angrier because Georgie would never have talked to him if she knew what he really thought of her.

"I'm sorry about that," Ahmad said, letting go of my arm. "He didn't know you were a friend of Georgie's. He probably thought you were a friend of mine."

"That's hardly the point, is it?" I asked.

"No," Ahmad admitted. "What he said was unacceptable, but what can I do? He is my uncle."

"And does he talk of Georgie like that to Haji Khan?"

"No, of course not," Ahmad replied, shocked. "He wouldn't dare."

After Haji Jawid arrived we all gathered to sit in the warmth of the house because the cold wind of Kabul had now drifted over to Jalalabad and it covered our bones with an unhappy feel that came with Haji Khan's brother. As the adults talked in the raised room, I watched from the sides on one of the white sofas with Ahmad, who, I was happy to find out, didn't seem to be a fan of his uncle.

"He's the reason my father was in a bad mood," he explained. "The police had him for most of yesterday."

"Why? What had he done?"

"Who knows? But whatever it was, I heard it cost my father a lot of money to get him out."

I nodded at the information and felt the warmth of new friendship rush in my blood because of it. It was unusual to hear someone speak of their relatives in such a way to a complete stranger and I guessed Ahmad must really hate his uncle—which was good, because I did too.

"By rights, my uncle should be the head of the family," Ahmad continued. "He's older, you see. But he didn't fight against the Russians or the Taliban, and he was in a Pakistani jail for years for killing a man. He brought a lot of bad things to our family's door, so when my grandfather passed away it was my father who stepped into his shoes. Haji Jawid hates that, you can see it in his face, but there's nothing he can do about it because it's my father who has the support of the family and the respect of the community, it's my father who is called on to fix disputes, and it's him, not Haji Jawid, who keeps the family together and helps the poor. All Haji Jawid does is spend the money my father gives him."

As the adults sat chatting, a line of men with large stomachs ballooning under their clothes drifted in and out of the house to slap Haji Jawid on the back and laugh together in quiet corners of the room; but although the buzz of easy conversation filled the hall, it felt like we were all waiting for something. And when the metal gates screamed outside and the Land Cruisers roared into the drive to begin their dance on the grass, I realized what it was. Haji Khan.

As he swept into his house, everything went still, as if the very room was holding its breath. I watched as his brother got to his feet. The laziness instantly slipped from his smile, and his eyes moved nervously around him as he watched Haji Khan greet the guests who had arrived at the house to swap talk with Haji Jawid. After greeting Georgie with a formal handshake because of the number of men now in the room, Haji Khan turned to his brother and nodded his head toward a room across the hallway. Haji Jawid dropped his eyes in respect and allowed his brother to lead him away from the group. We all watched as the door closed behind them.

By the look on Haji Khan's face, his brother wouldn't be cracking any more jokes tonight.

13

T HE DAY AFTER Haji Khan's brother turned up, Georgie and I left for Kabul, where the snow had arrived in giant flakes. On the streets there were more men carrying shovels than guns as everyone spent the day clearing flat rooftops to stop them from collapsing. It was always amazing to me how something so light it tickles your nose as it falls can grow into something so heavy it can bring the whole world crashing down upon your head. But I loved the winter—especially as I now had socks to wear thanks to the wages my mother was earning at Georgie's house—and because everything looked so different from when I'd left it, all white and clean and new, it seemed like a million years since cholera hit my mother in the stomach and moved her to Homeira's house.

And when I walked through the door of our home, I could have burst my insides open with happiness as I saw my mother run toward me to gather me into her arms and smother me in her huge love.

"I told your mother I was taking you to Jalalabad for a little holiday," Georgie had explained as we weaved our way through the mountains back to Kabul. "She probably doesn't need to know the full details of why we went . . ."

"Yes, quite right," I'd agreed.

But when my mother wrapped me in her arms and I felt her heartbeat next to mine and she asked what I had been up to, I plain forgot.

"We went to Jalalabad because I needed a break after I stabbed a Frenchman in the ass," I told her.

I saw the look of shock appear on my mother's face, and I quickly moved to calm her.

"Oh it's okay, don't worry. I thought he was attacking May, but Georgie says they are really very good friends and it was only because he was really, really drunk that he was fighting on top of her, and although he needed stitches he didn't call the police."

Behind me I heard a groan, and I turned to see James doubled up and holding the top of his head with both hands.

After my outburst, my mother, Georgie, James, and May all disappeared into the main house to have what James later described as a "peace summit." So, with nothing else to do, I walked to Pir Hederi's, where I found him sitting in front of the cigarette counter by the *bukhari* with Jamilla snuggled up against the warm fur of Dog. She was holding a mobile phone.

"Ah, good, you're back!" Pir shouted as I struggled to greet them while trying to stop Dog from sniffing at my boy's place. "What do you think?" he added, grabbing a long piece of paper from behind the desk and unrolling it. "It's a sign for the window. I had it made in Shahr-e Naw to bring in the foreigners."

As Pir Hederi rolled out the plastic paper, big blue letters appeared in English. They read "Free Delivry Survice for foods stuffs. Call 0793 267 82224. We Also Sell Cak."

"What's 'cak'?" I asked.

"Sweets, biscuits, you know. Eid is coming. I thought it might be a selling point."

"Oh, you mean 'cake.'"

"Cake, cak, what's the difference?"

"Nothing, I suppose."

"Good. Here, help me glue it to the window."

Despite our sign offering free delivery and cak to the nation, our new business plan got off to quite a slow start, and Jamilla and I spent most of the day looking at the mobile phone, which stubbornly refused to ring.

I was now properly beginning to understand why Georgie got so annoyed.

"We need to advertise," Pir Hederi stated as we closed up early because the snow was trapping even our regular customers inside and we'd run out of wood for the *bukhari*. It seemed he was turning into quite the businessman now he had a phone in the shop.

"Advertise? Like on the television?" I asked, excited by the thought of TV men coming to film us.

"Not on the television. Who do you think I am? President Hamid Karzai? I'm not made of money, you know."

"Then how?"

"Don't worry, I have an idea," he said with a wink, which looked pretty creepy coming from his milky eyes.

The next day I found out what Pir Hederi's great idea was as he placed two wooden boards connected with string over my shoulders. On the front he had written in paint "Free Delivry" and our phone number; on the back it read "We Sell Cak."

"Are you joking me?" I asked.

"Do you see me laughing?" he answered before practically shoving me out the door to walk the freezing streets of Wazir Akbar Khan.

As I trudged through the snow I had to accept that this was probably the most humiliating experience of my life. My cheeks burned even hotter than the time when Jahid told Jamilla I'd pissed my pants after we'd had a competition to see who could drink the most water without going to the toilet. With every tenth step I took, another guard would appear from inside his hut to make some crack about my new costume and whether I might also be hired as a table, and the whole shameful experience wasn't helped in the slightest by James, who passed me on the way back from wherever he had been and started laughing so hard he nearly wet his own pants.

"Well, at least you won't be contravening any codes of the Advertising Standards Authority," he shouted as I carried on walking.

I had no idea what he was talking about. "Yeah, yeah," I replied, and wandered off in the opposite direction toward the part of Wazir where the only Westerners trawling the streets were the ones looking for Chinese whores.

Thankfully, the next day I was unexpectedly relieved of my new job as Pir Hederi turned up grumbling that he'd had "a devil of a night."

"It was past midnight, and the mobile phone wouldn't stop ringing," he moaned. "Every time I answered it there was some damn foreigner on the other end asking for 'cak.' I switched it off in the end."

"I think I know why," I offered, coming over to sit by Jamilla close to the warmth of the fire. "James told me last night that when you read the sign out loud it sounds like the English word *cack*."

"And what does that mean?" Pir Hederi asked, wiping at his nose with a dirty handkerchief.

"It means we sell shit," I replied.

14

SEVENTY DAYS AFTER the end of Ramazan, a couple of weeks after the foreigners' New Year, and the day after the pilgrims return from hajj, coloring the roads in cars decorated with glittering tinsel and flowers, Afghanistan celebrates Eid-e Qorban. This is one of our favorite festivals, and Muslims celebrate it in memory of Ibrahim's willingness to sacrifice his son for Allah. For three days our country of tears and war becomes a place of fun, beauty, and full bellies, with everyone dressing in their finest clothes and those who can afford it slaughtering their best sheep, cows, or goats as a symbol of Ibrahim's sacrifice. As it is written in the Koran, a large portion of the meat is given to the poor while the rest is served up for the family meal, to which friends and other relatives are invited.

And even though Eid is always brilliant, this year was better than I ever remembered it being because it brought an armful of surprises into our lives that made the celebration come and go quicker than usual.

First of all, Georgie announced she had given up smoking.

"A New Year's resolution," she explained.

"Bit late, isn't it?" remarked James.

"I had to get used to the idea," Georgie snapped back, hitting him on the head with the empty pen she was now spending her days sucking on.

Personally, I didn't care whether her "resolution" was late or not. I took it as a sign from God that my prayers were working and that Georgie was finally moving in the right direction and away from the flames of Hell that were waiting to eat her.

The next surprise was the fat-bottomed sheep that suddenly turned up in our yard, along with a local butcher to perform the halal act of slaughter. As we all gathered to watch him pronounce the name of God and slit the animal's throat, May turned her back on the river of blood that quickly turned the snow red.

"Christ, it's enough to make you vegetarian," she muttered.

"I thought all you lesbians were anyway," James joked, earning himself a kick in the shins.

It appeared that in the West, if you were annoyed by just about anything you simply beat the nearest man to you.

My next happy surprise was Haji Khan's phone call to Georgie, which sent her running up to her room. She emerged thirty minutes later with the stupid grin covering her face that she seemed to save especially for these occasions.

Then Rachel arrived at the house looking fresh and pretty and bringing a similar stupid look to James's face.

That afternoon Massoud also turned up, and I went with him to take cuts of freshly hacked meat to the homes of Jamilla and Spandi, whose families filled my hands with sugared almonds and papered sweets to take back to the foreigners.

One of the biggest surprises came on the second day of Eid when my aunt arrived at our house with her husband, my cousin Jahid, and their two other kids trailing behind. Although it is expected that Muslims should use the festival to visit their relations, I wasn't sure this applied to relatives you had recently tried to kill. So, naturally, I was shocked when my mother's family turned up out of the blue, though this was nothing compared to the shock of seeing my aunt again because it looked like someone had stuck a pin in her skin, letting all the air out and leaving her a shriveled copy of her old self.

At the sight of my aunt, my mother started crying and immediately took her into her arms, which was a lot easier now she was half the size she used to be. Then my aunt started crying too, which set off May and Georgie, and pretty soon all four of the women were reaching for handkerchiefs hidden up the sleeves of their sweaters and coats while all the men, including James, coughed a bit and stood around looking embarrassed.

Apparently, my aunt had also been struck down with the cholera—and by the looks of it she had come off a lot worse than my mother.

In other ways, though, getting cholera was probably the best thing that could have happened to her because as well as sucking the fat from her body the disease had also sucked the ugliness out of her mind. The words that used to fall from her mouth to torment my mother were gone. Now my aunt was not only smaller but quieter than she used to be, and as she sat in my mother's room holding her hand gently in the palm of her own, I felt a bit sorry for wishing death upon her.

"Fuck, it was awful," Jahid explained. "Shit everywhere. If I hadn't seen it with my own eyes, I wouldn't have believed it. You wouldn't have thought one person could make so much shit."

"Well, at least she survived. It's a pretty bad thing to get over," I replied, trying to block the image of my aunt shitting out half her body weight in the small house we all used to share.

"True," replied Jahid. "Two of our neighbors died actually, two of the older men, Haji Rashid and Haji Habib."

"That's too bad," I said, thinking of these two old men who had managed to survive the Russian occupation, the civil war, and the Taliban years only to die in their own shit.

Sometimes, even during Eid, it's hard to understand God's plan for us.

As the lights of our festival began to fade and we readied ourselves for normal life again, the final and best surprise of all came.

Taking me by the hand, Georgie led me upstairs to her room, pressing her finger to her lips so I wouldn't talk. We were obviously on some kind of secret mission, which was kind of exciting on its own. We positioned ourselves on the floor, and she reached for a small radio with a wind-up handle. As it whirred into action, she placed it in front of us.

The soft, low sound of a man speaking in Dari came to my ears; he was introducing phone calls from other Afghans and repeating a list of telephone numbers. The calls were all short and sometimes hard to hear over the crackle of a bad connection, but they all had one thing in common: the face-less voices were asking for lost family members and friends to get in touch.

It was all quite sad, and as I sat there I wondered why Georgie would want me to listen to such misery at the end of such a beautiful Eid. Then the man introduced another load of callers, and I heard Georgie's voice come dancing into my ears. Her message simply said, "If anyone knows the where-abouts of Mina from Paghman, daughter of Mariya and brother to Fawad, please contact me. Your family is well and happy, and they would love to see you again."

15

IT WAS AGREED that neither Georgie nor I should tell my mother about the radio show because we didn't want to get her hopes up. As Georgie said, the chances of finding my sister were smaller than finding an honest man in government; but at least a tiny hole of light had now opened in our lives, and it shone twice a week on Radio Free Europe's *In Search of the Lost* program.

In the meantime, as I secretly waited for Mina's return, the world crawled its way through winter, forcing us indoors and turning our noses red. Like summer, winter brings great joy when it comes, but then—maybe because we celebrate it too much at the start—it goes on and on and on, outstaying its welcome until you spend every waking minute praying for it to end.

The freezing cold seemed to be good for Pir Hederi's business, though. We were now getting up to five calls a day from houses wanting their shopping delivered. What it wasn't so good for was my toes. After being soaked to the bone in the snow and warmed up again by the *bukhari* in the shop, I returned home one night to find them swollen and blue. I remembered Pir Hederi's story about the doomed mujahideen in the mountains and cried myself to sleep worrying that I'd wake up and find ten rotten holes where my toes used to be. My mother went mental when she saw the state of them the next morning and immediately stomped around to Pir Hederi's to warn him that she would visit a million curses on him unless he took proper care of me. The next day Pir

Hederi sent me off on my deliveries with two plastic bags tied to my feet. "Don't tell your mother," he said, and handed me a chocolate bar to pay for my silence.

Back at the house, the long gray of winter was also starting to creep into our lives. After a promising start, Haji Khan's telephone calls had slowly drifted away with the sunshine, and Georgie was becoming increasingly angry, losing her temper every five minutes as she battled with the cigarettes and Haji Khan's silence. James wasn't really helping the situation because he was still smoking like a *bukhari*, but one evening he left the house with a rucksack slung over his shoulder and he explained that because he was really quite a good friend to Georgie he was choosing to spend the next few nights at Rachel's place in Qala-e Fatullah, which I thought was nice of him. However, I wasn't as stupid as he obviously thought I was. I guessed the real reason he had gone was that he had already made Rachel his girlfriend.

A few days after he moved out, James actually left Kabul altogether—to chase the sunshine and bombers in Kandahar for a couple of weeks, he said. It was sometimes easy to forget that James actually worked for a living. In fact I think he also forgot this quite a lot, until his newspaper rang to remind him.

Throughout the month of February, May also spent more than a few evenings away from the house, even though she didn't smoke. I later learned this was because she was visiting Philippe. When I was told this, I wondered whether the Frenchman was staying away from our house because he was scared of me or scared of coming face-to-face with my mother.

So that left pretty much only my mother and me to take care of Georgie's sadness.

"Haji Khan is probably stuck in the mountains," I said to

Georgie one evening as we both ate with her in the big house to stop her from feeling lonely.

Georgie smiled, but I caught the look she swapped with my mother and it didn't match.

When James finally returned to the house he didn't do much to brighten anyone's mood as he filled our heads with talk of rocket attacks and fighting in the south.

"The insurgency is starting to gain momentum," he told Georgie as she made herself a sandwich in the kitchen, and though I didn't know what *momentum* meant, I didn't think it sounded good. "By the way, Georgie, a second on the lips, a lifetime on the hips," he added, which again I didn't understand.

"Oh fuck off, James," snapped Georgie, which I understood perfectly well.

Two weeks after James returned to tell us about the troubles he had seen, a massive bomb blew five people to smithereens and wounded thirty-two more in Kandahar city, which added some power to Pir Hederi's opinion that the country was "once again going to shit."

"But why are the Taliban bombing Afghans?" I asked as I read the story out loud from the *Kabul Times*.

"Because they're all bloody Pakistanis," Pir Hederi replied, which I knew wasn't true because, for one, they were led by Mullah Omar, and though he had only one eye he was still an Afghan.

"They're not all from Pakistan," I corrected.

"Okay, maybe not," Pir accepted with a grumble, "but the bastard suicide bombers are. Afghans don't go blowing themselves up. It's not the way we do things here. This is something brought in from the outside. In my time we fought because we wanted to see victory, not to watch our legs fly past our bloody ears."

"It's a combination of things—a lot of little things coming together all at once," James explained as we walked home together after he had come to the shop to buy some cigarettes for himself and a package of biscuits, a Twix chocolate bar, and some Happy Cow cheese for Georgie. "First of all, the coalition—those are the Western troops, Fawad—never finished off either the Taliban or al-Qaeda in 2001, giving them the chance to disappear for a while and regroup, to come back together again. Then, the reconstruction that was promised has been slow to make an impact—to be seen—especially in places where it is more dangerous, like in the south and east. And then there is growing resentment—anger—about the government. The Pashtuns think there are too many members of the Northern Alliance in top jobs, the Northern Alliance feel they have been sidelined—had power taken away from them—even though they credit themselves—give themselves a pat on the back—for winning the war. Then there is the corruption problem, with money talking loudest in government departments, offices, and on the streets with all the *bakhsheesh*-taking policemen. When you add it all up, people are bound—are sure—to get pissed off. Then along comes the new Taliban, and the fighting starts again and people begin to question—ask—where all the security and promises went until pretty much everyone is spoiling—everyone is ready—for war again."

"That doesn't sound good," I admitted.

"No, it doesn't especially, does it?"

James flicked his cigarette into the thawing alley of waste and rubbish that lined the road back to our house.

"Why doesn't President Karzai fix it and stop all the corruption, and then the people will be happy with him?"

"I guess it's not that easy, Fawad. He has so many powerful men here and abroad to keep happy, and he needs support from all of them if he is going to make your country peaceful again."

"Then why don't the army and the Western soldiers just go and kill the Taliban properly?"

"Well, that's not so easy either. They keep bloody hiding!"

With that, James swooped down, grabbed me by the legs, and raised me to the sky on his shoulders, catching me by surprise and nearly losing me down his back as he stood up again.

"Come on, Fawad! Maybe we should go to the south and fight jihad against the bad guys!"

"Yeah!" I laughed. "Let's go and kick Mullah Omar in the ass!"

"Why don't you stab him there instead? That's usually your modus operandi, isn't it?"

Although I didn't quite get the words, I understood James's meaning and I laughed out loud because for once my attack on Philippe seemed quite funny. Then together we galloped toward the house, just like the Afghan warriors from my country's past, except I was on the shoulders of an Englishman instead of trying to kill him.

As we ran to the gate, Shir Ahmad saw us coming and saluted as he opened the metal side door, swinging it wide as we rushed inside. James came to a stop with a stamp of his feet and a lip-splitting neigh.

"James?"

Georgie's voice rang out from behind the door.

"James?"

"God, she's impatient for her biscuits, isn't she?" James laughed. "Coming, dear!"

But before he could get to the door it opened in front of us and Georgie fell into our path, holding her stomach. There was blood on her skirt, and it covered her hands where she'd touched it.

"James?" she cried, holding her hands out to him.

"Oh Jesus, darling. Jesus. No."

Part Two

16

W HEN GEORGIE LOST her baby, it was as if a little
something inside all of us died, even those of us
who didn't know a baby was coming in the first
place.

But because Allah is merciful, even to unbelievers like
Georgie, he took away her baby and gave her Dr. Hugo instead.

Of course, it took Georgie a long time to see the good doctor because her eyes were clouded by tears and bad dreams
for weeks after the baby left her. She was like a ghost living
in our house, a white space of sadness that ate all the happiness from our lives—and for a while I was convinced she
would leave us too.

After James brought Georgie back from the hospital, he
walked her to her bed and gathered the rest of us in the front
room downstairs to tell us she had suffered something called
a "miscarriage." James explained that although there was nothing wrong with her body and that a miscarriage was quite
normal for women whose babies are still so tiny in their
stomachs, Georgie's mind would be broken for a while and
she would need all of our help to make it better again.

So for the next few weeks that's what we all tried to do.

James spoke to Georgie's boss at the goat-combing company, and she was allowed to stay at home and still get paid.
May forgot about the Frenchman and stayed by her friend's
side in the evenings, reading to her and trying to get her dressed.
During the day my mother took on the job of sitting by her

bed as May went out to do her engineering. She spent most of her hours up there just stroking Georgie's hair and begging her to eat. But Georgie's mouth was too full of grief to make room for food, and it was a daily battle even to get her to eat some Happy Cow cheese, and she used to love Happy Cow.

In the meantime—in between school, which had started again, and working at Pir Hederi's shop—I stood at the door-way or sat on the floor of Georgie's bedroom, watching the woman who had given me and my mother a new life get thinner and thinner until her pale face collapsed and her arms and legs became twigs under her clothes.

Finally, when it looked like a small breeze might be enough to snap her in two, James fetched Dr. Hugo to our house, who seemed to be a friend of his and who he said could help, although I had my doubts. Tall and a little thin himself with dark hair that was short but somehow messy and eyes as blue as sky, Hugo arrived dressed in jeans and a big coat that wasn't even white. I'd seen the health advertisements on television; I knew what doctors were supposed to look like. Hugo didn't even come close. However, James and May seemed a lot happier when a little later he came back downstairs and revealed that he had given Georgie "something to help her sleep." I would have preferred it if he had given her "something to help her eat," but what did I know? I was just a kid.

"She just needs time," my mother said as we sat in the kitchen preparing chicken soup for Georgie. 'She is very sad, and sadness doesn't just disappear overnight. Georgie loved her baby very much because it offered her hope, and now she needs time to get used to the idea that her baby has gone and that her hope may have gone with it."

"What do you mean 'hope'?" I asked, carefully ladling the hot soup into a bowl.

My mother sighed, took the spoon from my fingers, and knelt down to take my face in her hands.

. "I suppose Georgie hoped that the baby would mean the father would be in her life forever, Fawad. It is the kind of hope that nests in the heart of a woman very much in love. I pray that when you are older, if you ever see this hope in the eyes of a woman close to you, you take the very best care of it that you can because this hope is the most precious thing and the greatest gift God can give to a man. It means you are truly loved, son."

Although we all knew who the father of Georgie's baby was, we never talked about it in the house. It was as if the baby had been made by magic and taken by God, because it was wrong. There were rules to follow, and, although it doesn't happen often in Afghanistan, if you break those rules you must be punished.

And Georgie was being punished: she had lost her baby, she had lost her hope, and she had lost her appetite. I was convinced that very soon we would lose her too—our punishment for having guarded Georgie and Haji Khan's secret.

"What's the matter with you?" Pir Hederi stopped loading the plastic bags on the counter to turn, almost, in my direction. "You speak less than a mute these days."

"It's nothing," I replied. "I'm just feeling quiet, that's all."

"I may be blind, Fawad, but I'm not stupid," he answered back. Then, moving to the doorway to hand me the bags of shopping, he slipped one hundred afs into the pocket of my coat. "Cheer up, boy. Here's a bonus for all the delivery stuff."

"Great," I joked. "All of two dollars. I'll go right ahead and retire then."

"You ungrateful donkey!"

Pir playfully reached out to hit me on the shoulder, but as

I'd started getting onto my bike he punched me in the head instead—a hazard of the job, I guess, when you work for a blind man.

It had been a long time since I'd made any kind of joke, and although it felt good to let the air of one into my brain, the guilt soon followed. I wondered how I could be such a bad friend to Georgie when I could return home at any time and find her stretched out on her bed, cold dead.

Despite all of her ways, Georgie wasn't an Afghan like me and my mother, and therefore she wasn't as strong as us. Just this one death of a baby that didn't even have a name could be the end of her. And I couldn't speak of my fears to anyone outside our house because it would have been wrong in so many ways. Georgie wasn't married, and she was going to have a baby. Women used to get stoned for that kind of behavior in my country; in some parts they still do. And it wouldn't only be Haji Jawid calling her a whore for not taking care of her body and for having sex with a man before marriage. So I couldn't explain my bad mood, and I couldn't hide it. For once in my life, I sort of wished I was a girl because girls are experts at hiding things, and as they never speak straight you hardly ever know what they're thinking.

"Well, I'm glad you had such a good time," Jamilla huffed one day after I accidentally told her about chasing Baba Gul's goats with Mulallah. Despite her words, she didn't look at all glad, and I realized something was up when she hardly spoke to me for the rest of the day. If I asked her a question, she would simply say, "Why don't you go and ask Mulallah?"

My mother was exactly the same. Even though I felt she was beginning to like Shir Ahmad because he was now reading books about computers and going to a special class in the afternoons, whenever I asked her about it she would say, "My only wish is for your happiness, Fawad," which I knew wasn't strictly true because she had started wearing makeup on her eyes and taking better care of her clothes, and I wasn't really bothered by what she looked like.

In fact, Georgie was the only woman I knew who seemed to talk real. After all, she had told me about her love for Haji Khan, and also that May was a lesbian. So to think she might just fade away into nothing was unbearable, especially as giving up smoking wasn't really enough to get her out of Hell.

Therefore, when I'd dropped off the last bag of shopping close to a house by the hospital and saw him standing there in the street—as clear as day, laughing with a fat man and surrounded by all of his guards—a hot redness colored my sight, and suddenly I was off my bike and on top of him.

"You bastard! You lying fucking bastard! You're killing her!"

My fists pounded at his chest and I felt his body tense at the blows, but he didn't move, not one muscle, so I kicked and I beat him even harder, using all of my heart and all of my hate and letting it explode on top of him.

"She's dying, and you're laughing!" I screamed. "You're killing her, and you don't even care, you ugly bastard whore-fucking camel cock! You're killing her!"

And I shoved myself away from him and ran.

17

I RAN FROM WAZIR Akbar Khan, stumbling through the chaos of people and cars, over the bridge covering the river, and into the dark of Old Makroyan. I didn't know where I was running to until I arrived there, and it was the house of Spandi.

"You did what?"

"I beat up Haji Khan," I repeated.

Spandi was sitting on the steps of his block, fiddling with a mobile phone he had recently bought. It played a Bollywood love song when it rang, it had a camera fixed into it, and it was pretty impressive, but he put it down when I burst into his sight gulping for breath with tears covering my face.

"You beat up Haji Khan, and you've still got your legs?"

"Looks like it . . ."

Spandi let out a soft whistle between his teeth.

"Ho, that's crazy. Why did you do it?"

"Because he . . ." As I began to explain, the picture of what I was about to say came running into my head: Georgie on her bed, the baby dead on her skirt, the promises that lay broken all around her, and I knew I couldn't betray her, not even to Spandi, who knew at least half the story. "Because he was joking with someone," I stated finally, knowing how stupid it sounded even as I said it.

"Shit," replied my friend. "It must have been a hell of a bad joke."

"Yeah, it was," I admitted.

For the next three hours Spandi and I talked about the possibility of me being a dead man walking and whether my attack on his boss would be bad for Spandi's business. We both agreed, with black hearts, that I should look for somewhere new to live and Spandi should find another job.

"There are some empty flats around here that we could hide you in, and I can bring you food once or twice a day while I look for something more permanent," Spandi suggested, warming to the idea after his initial shock and despair at the thought of having to find a new can of herbs. "You'll need a gun as well."

"I don't know how to use a gun," I said, frightened but excited by the thought.

"How hard can it be? We're Afghans; it probably comes more naturally than riding a bike."

"My bike!" I shouted, suddenly remembering I'd left it with its wheels spinning somewhere in Wazir as I launched my attack. "I forgot it when I ran off."

"Damn shame," Spandi sympathized, patting me on the shoulder. "That was a fine bike."

"Maybe I should go back and look for it."

Spandi shrugged. "You'll need wheels," he admitted.

"I should also say good-bye to my mother," I added, thinking of her for the first time since I'd punched Haji Khan in public and imagining her sadness as the last of her children left her.

"Haji Khan might be watching the house," Spandi warned. "Maybe you should wait until it is dark . . . and we've got you a gun."

"And how long will that take?"

"I don't know," Spandi admitted. "I've never tried to get a gun before."

"No, I'll have to risk it," I decided, getting to my feet, my mother's face now the only picture in my mind.

"Do you want me to come with you?" Spandi asked, which I thought was kind of him.

"No," I told him after thinking about it a short while. "I'll move faster alone. Besides, Haji Khan might be looking for you too because you're a friend of mine."

"Shit! I never thought of that." Spandi got to his feet. "Do you think I should hide too?"

I shrugged my shoulders. "It might be a good idea."

It was practically dark when I made my way back to Wazir Akbar Khan. Now that I was alone, my bravery had disappeared, so I walked home frightened to the point of one hundred percent scared—ducking into the shadows every time a Land Cruiser came into view, thinking one of them might belong to Haji Khan and imagining it pulling up close to me with its window rolled down so that someone could shoot me in the head.

As I turned the corner into our street, the fear that had been itching at the surface of my skin took on the life of a giant when I saw his three Land Cruisers parked outside the house.

I immediately spun on my feet to run away from the ambush and certain death—and straight into the legs of Ismerai.

"Whay!" he grunted, grabbing me by the shoulders.

"Get off me! Get off me!" I shouted, fighting at the massive hands now trying to hold me. "Help! He's going to murder me!" I screamed, and a handful of people stopped what they were doing to watch Ismerai carry out his crime.

"Don't be stupid!" Ismerai barked in my ear. "Nobody's trying to murder you!"

"Yeah, not while everyone's looking you're not! Help! Murderer!"

Ismerai shook my body roughly, making my eyes bounce
sorely in my head and bringing me to a stop.

"Listen to me! Listen to me, now!" he ordered. "We were
worried about you, Fawad. All of us were, and that includes
Haji Khan. He sent me to Pir Hederi's shop to look for you."

"Yeah, to find me and kill me!" I interrupted, though with
less strength than before as Ismerai's words began to walk
around my brain, looking for a place to stay.

"Not to kill you, to bring you home. That's all, Fawad. We
just want you home."

I stopped struggling and looked hard into Ismerai's eyes.
They didn't look like the eyes of a killer. They looked like the
eyes of a man who liked to tell jokes and smoke hashish.

"Honestly, son. Nobody is angry with you. We're worried, that's all. It's been a shock for all of us."

I looked at him again, searching his face for any signs of
a trap. "Okay," I said finally, deciding he was probably telling
the truth. Still, a boy can't be too careful, and as he took me
by the hand I turned to the people still hanging around us
and shouted, "If I'm dead tomorrow, he did it!"

"For the love of God," Ismerai hissed, pulling me away.

And I let him drag me home.

As we walked past the guards, one of whom saluted as I
approached, and through the gate of the house, the first thing
I saw was my bike leaning against the wall. Haji Khan must
have brought it with him after I ran away from Wazir.

The second thing I saw was the worried face of my mother.

Ismerai let her hug me and whisper a few words that
melted together in a dozen ways to say "Don't worry, son." He
then asked her to bring us some tea and led me away into the
garden.

There was no sign of Haji Khan, but as his uncle was here
as well as his army of guards, I guessed he must be upstairs

with Georgie, no doubt planting more false promises into her already broken head.

Inviting me to sit first, Ismerai settled into the seat opposite me and lit up one of his cigarettes. His face looked sadder and older than I remembered, his eyes becoming slowly pinched by time and heavy lines.

"He does love her, Fawad."

Ismerai looked at me as he spoke, but I said nothing because I didn't believe him.

"I know you probably don't believe me right now," he continued, "but it's true. I've known Haji Khan for most of my life. We played as children, we fought as men, and we've both known and understood love."

"Then why does he never phone her, Ismerai?" I could hear the sound of tears breaking in my voice as worry, and relief at not being killed, tugged at the bottom of my throat. "Why does he make her so unhappy that her baby died and she can't eat anymore? Why?"

Ismerai sighed, releasing the smoke from between his lips, as my mother arrived with the tea. After saying his thanks, he waited for her to walk away before answering. "You know our culture, son. This is not the West, where men and women live their lives as one person. We live in a society of men, where the women wait indoors and look after the family. The men aren't used to answering to women, and they're certainly not used to checking in with them either. And though Haji is a freethinker and he knows the ways of the West, he is still an Afghan man. And he is too old to change that part of him now, even if he wanted to, even for a woman like Georgie. And even though Georgie is like a member of our family and she knows our ways as good as anyone, she is still a foreigner and her heart and her expectations remain from her own country."

"But she tries so hard . . . ," I said, feeling the need to defend her.

"I know she does, son. We all realize Georgie makes sacrifices for Haji, and her respect for him makes her the person she is and the person we love. But although we know she stays inside the house more than other foreigners and she takes care of herself more than other Western women who drink and party here like it is Europe, she is still a world away from us and always will be. Every time Haji spends evenings with Georgie, every time she comes to his house, he takes a risk. He also commits a terrible sin that rests heavy in his heart for days after. The fact is that people talk, Fawad, and when you're a man whose standing in the community is as important as Haji's, talk is dangerous. It is not something that can be easily ignored. Power is a difficult balance of wealth, honor, and respect. If you lose just one of these elements, you risk losing it all."

"So he's scared of losing his power and his money, then? That's what you're saying. That's how much Haji Khan loves Georgie?"

"No, that's not what I'm saying at all," Ismerai corrected, taking up his tea and blowing hard, which isn't really allowed in Islam because of the germs. "Haji loves Georgie. But what can he really give her? And what can she give him? No, what they should have done a long time ago is give each other up, but they were too scared or too stubborn to let go, and now both of them are trapped in a world where they have no future. They can't walk forward and they can't walk back, so they stand still, holding on to each other with no place to go."

"But why do they have no future if they love each other?"

"What kind of future do you think they could seriously have? Marriage? Here in Afghanistan?" Ismerai laughed harshly and relit the cigarette that had died in his fingers.

"Why not?" I asked.

"It's impossible, you know that, Fawad. They are too different, and both of them are far too strong to change for the

other. Haji once described Georgie as a bird, a bright, beautiful bird whose very song brings a smile to your face and happiness to your heart. Would you have him cage that bird
within our customs and traditions? Do you imagine, even if
she converted to Islam, that Georgie could live as the wife of
a high Pashtun man, locked behind the walls of her home,
unable to go out, unable to see her male friends, unable to
work? It would kill her. You know that."

"They could move . . . ," I offered, silently admitting that
Ismerai was right and that if she did marry Haji Khan in Afghanistan he would probably be forced to shoot her within
a week for bringing dishonor on the family.

"Where should they move to?" Ismerai asked. "Europe?"

I shrugged and nodded.

"And can you see Haji being able to live that life, away from
the country he has fought for, that he has lost family for and
whose soil is as much a part of him as his skin and bones? If
he left to live with a foreign woman, how could he ever return and still keep the respect he and his family have earned
over all these terrible years? He would have to live in virtual
exile, and that would destroy him.

"The fact is, Fawad, Haji and Georgie are two people who
fell in love at the wrong time and in the wrong place. The question they must now ask themselves is what do they do next?"

As Ismerai lit his second cigarette, Haji Khan appeared in
the garden. His brown face was white, and tears hung in the
corners of his eyes, waiting to be freed. My blood froze when
I saw him, and I bowed my head as he walked over to us to
take Ismerai's cigarette from his hands.

"I didn't know," I heard him whisper to Ismerai, who had
got up from his chair. "She never told me, and now I can't reach
her."

"She needs time," Ismerai replied, causing me to look up,
remembering my mother's own words.

"No," Haji Khan corrected, his voice sore and rough. "She needs someone better than me . . . we both know that. But how can I even let that happen? She's my life."

As Haji Khan turned away he paused to look at me, and that's when the tears fell, spilling out quietly from his dark brown eyes like two small rivers, kissing the edges of his nose as they ran to his lips.

18

"WHAT IN THE name of Allah is that noise?" I asked, finding James hiding in the yard after I'd finished the morning shift at school. Afternoon lessons were for girls.

"That, my dear Fawad, is the Sex Pistols," he informed me, which I took to be the name of the noise screaming English words from Georgie's room. "Count yourself lucky," James added. "It was Bonnie Tyler this morning."

"Bonnie who?"

"Big hair, big shoulder pads, big headache—"

"Hey! I like Big Bonnie Tyler!"

Georgie appeared at the door. She was dressed in blue jeans and a tight long-sleeved T-shirt, and she was eating a piece of naan bread, which, if I wasn't mistaken, was painted white with Happy Cow cheese.

"God, I'm starving," she added.

As she walked past us carrying a box in one hand and her lunch in the other, I noticed her finger and her neck were empty of the jewelry Haji Khan had bought her just a few short months ago. I also noticed a pack of cigarettes sticking out from the back pocket of her jeans.

"What's in the box?" James asked as she placed it near the outside trash can.

"Stuff," she replied. "I'm spring-cleaning."

Once she'd disappeared back into the house and into the noise, James and I looked at each other and raced to the box. James got there first, but his legs were twice the size of mine and he'd also pushed me to the ground before we set off.

"Ahhh," he said as he reached it, pulling open the cardboard flaps for me to see.

"Ahhh," I agreed.

Inside was a pile of neatly folded shirts of the finest silk, several perfume bottles, too many rainbow-colored scarves to count, and a bone-carved jewelry box.

On top of them all sat Haji Khan's photo.

As Georgie welcomed in the spring by cleaning away her memories, my mother greeted the season by shaving off my hair. It happened every year, but it didn't make the experience any easier.

May laughed when she saw me. "Who loves ya, baby?"

"Kojak," explained James, which didn't actually explain anything.

"It's for health," I insisted, touching my head to rub away the humiliation my so-called friends were adding to.

"It's for lice, you mean," corrected May.

"Whatever," I said, doing the *W* sign with my thumbs and fingers as James had once taught me in the kitchen after Georgie had teased him about Rachel.

May laughed again.

"Here," she said, throwing me a blue suede coat, "see if you can find a happy home for this!"

"It's beautiful," I replied as it landed in my arms, feeling the softness of it between my fingers and looking at the yellow pattern embroidered around the edges. "Why don't you want it?"

"I so do!" May insisted. "But Ismerai brought it round for

Georgie, and she doesn't want it. Sadly, I don't think she'd appreciate me wearing it either. Women can be unpredictable creatures when they're angry, Fawad."

"You're a woman," I noted.

"Barely," muttered James, who received a punch in the ear from May.

"Why didn't Georgie just give it back then?"

"Ismerai wouldn't take it," May explained.

"But who should I give it to?"

"Anyone, as long as they don't live around here," she said, and walked back into the house just as the gate opened behind us and Shir Ahmad's head appeared.

"Fawad," he hissed, waving at me to come over. "I think someone is looking for you."

"Who?"

"Come see for yourself. I think he's in disguise."

I followed Shir outside, and he pointed to a dark figure across the road, standing a little up the street from us. It was a boy drowning in a giant-sized *patu*, wearing dark sunglasses and apparently reading the *Kabul Times*. He looked suspicious, like a spy, and not a very good one at that because the whole street was watching him.

As the newspaper lowered, I recognized my friend.

"Spandi!" I shouted, which made him drop the paper altogether as he reached for the *patu* to cover his face and turned quickly away to look at the wall.

I ran over to him, laughing. I'd totally forgotten he was still in hiding.

"I've been a nervous wreck," Spandi moaned as we walked toward Shahr-e Naw for no reason other than we had nothing better to do. We'd gone to Pir Hederi's beforehand, but

Jamilla had taken no orders before she left for school, so the old man told us to "go enjoy the sunshine before the government taxes that as well."

"Yeah, sorry about that," I told Spandi. "It left my mind."

"Honestly, I was convinced you'd be dead by now, but I had to check. I'm glad you're alive and all that."

"Thanks," I said. "You're a good friend, Spandi."

"The best you'll ever have."

He laughed. And though I joined in and called him a homo, in my bones I knew he was right.

After we walked past the Ministry of Women's Affairs, trying to sneak a look at the ladies as we went because it annoyed the guards, we moved on toward Chief Burger to pick up a Beef 5—a fried sandwich of shredded meat, potato, and egg that left your lips slippery. After the winter our whole bodies were dry as old twigs, and the grease felt good, like medicine.

With our bellies full, we wandered over to the park where the poor and the hungry gathered to share their misery and jump on anyone fool enough to join them. There, by the side of the wall, opposite the A-One supermarket, we found Pir the Madman, picking through a rotten heap of rubbish with the rest of the city's unwanted dogs. He wore no shoes on his cracked black feet, and his wild curly hair had matted together, making it look like he was wearing a badly made helmet.

"Fleas!" he shouted as he saw us coming. "The fleas return to bite the dog!"

"The only fleas are on you," said Spandi, laughing.

"Fleas on me, fleas on you, all fleas pleased to be fleas," the mental sang, roughly scratching at his head as he did so. "Isn't that so, little flea?"

"I guess," I replied, realizing he was talking to me and

wondering how it was possible to fall so low that you had to spend your day ankle-high in shit.

Nobody really knew Pir the Madman's story. He was just the mental who managed to survive everything Kabul could throw at him. But I guessed it was a bad one, and it made me sad to think that at some time in his life he must have been a boy like me with everything to look forward to.

"Here, Pir," I said, moving over to him and holding out the coat May had given me, and that Ismerai had given Georgie, "a coat for the king of fleas."

Pir roughly snatched it from my hands and tucked it under his arm, quickly shifting away from us, back toward the park, as if he was scared I might change my mind. As he reached the wall, he cocked his head to look at me in a way I didn't understand. Then he jumped over the wall and ran in zigzags across the mud brown grass.

"A coat for the king of fleas!" he shouted. "All hail, the king! The king of fleas!"

"Nutcase," Spandi remarked as we turned to walk back to Wazir Akbar Khan.

"Yes," I agreed.

"Still, that was a good thing you did there, Fawad."

"Not really," I said. "It was just a coat that nobody wanted."

19

"COME ON, FAWAD!" Spandi said, running toward me as I cycled to Pir Hederi's to start work for the afternoon. "Kabul's on fire, and we're missing it!"

"What do you mean, 'on fire'?" I asked, bringing my wheels to a stop to look at the sky for smoke and flames and other fire-type signs.

"The Americans have killed a load of people, and now everyone is rioting," he explained, reaching my side and collapsing against the seat of my bike. "The radio says hundreds of people are marching in the streets and burning everything in sight. Someone told me they even set fire to a Chinaman in Shahr-e Naw."

"No!"

"Yes, really!" Spandi insisted, his cheeks red with excitement where they used to be gray.

"Why?" I asked.

"Why not?" he replied. "It's a riot! There are no rules!"

"Okay then, let's go before we miss it!"

Spandi jumped onto the seat of my bike and grabbed hold of the back of my jacket for balance, and we raced off looking for the riot.

Now, you would think it would be quite easy to find hundreds of rioters setting fire to Chinamen in the city, but by the time we got to Shahr-e Naw the place was empty of anyone looking even a little bit angry. Only the charred remains of police checkpoints, broken shop windows, and stolen goods dropped on the street showed that anything serious had happened there. However, after following the trail and asking a few other boys where everyone had got to, we finally found a small crowd of people in Taimani shouting "Death to Karzai!" and "Death to America!"; they also held posters of the dead Northern Alliance leader Ahmad Shah Massoud high above their heads. We guessed this was about as good as it was going to get, so we joined them.

By the time we fell in behind the snake of people, there weren't that many left and most of them looked like students, but we decided to help them anyway, shouting "Death to America!" because that seemed to be all you had to do to become a member of a riot. A man in black just in front of us turned around with a smile when he heard our voices, which encouraged us to scream even louder. "Death to America! Death to America!" we yelled at the top of our lungs, laughing together in the excitement of it all.

As we marched through the streets like a crazy gang of American-hating brothers, a couple of the older boys tried to pull down any guard huts they found outside houses with foreign signs in front of them. And although Spandi and I weren't strong enough or brave enough to help them, we made up for our weakness in noise, scrunching our faces into masks of hate like we saw the others doing.

"Death to America!"

"Yeah! Die, America! You're rubbish!" Spandi shouted.

"And you smell of cabbage!" I screamed.

"And dog shit!" added Spandi.

"And you fight like girls!"

"And cry like women!"

"And you all eat babies!"

"And shag worm-bum donkeys!"

"And—"

I felt a tug at my neck.

"Just what the fuck do you think you're doing?" an angry voice exploded in my ear.

I turned around to see James behind me. Once again I'd forgotten he sometimes had to work for a living. Along the road behind us were a handful of other white faces holding pens, notebooks, and cameras.

"We're protesting because the Americans murdered five hundred Afghans," I shouted above the other rioters, whose voices seemed to find more power in the journalists' presence.

"You don't know what you're talking about," James shouted back, which was true actually. "This isn't a game, Fawad. Get home now; otherwise I'll take you there myself—and I'll tell your mother exactly what you have been up to."

"But James—"

"Don't 'but James' me," he demanded, which didn't make any kind of sense at all, though it put a stop to the argument.

Spandi and I agreed that we had done our bit to honor the memory of the murdered Afghans, and although it would have been fun to stay with the rioters, they probably didn't have mothers at home who would torture them, and their friends, with hard looks and silence.

And just in case James did turn us in, Spandi and I decided to go our separate ways at the corner of my street.

"Your mother can be pretty fierce," said Spandi.

"Tell me about it."

I walked home slowly, now dreading the return of James, who was usually the easiest member of the house to get along with. However, when he did eventually turn up, about two hours later, he simply nodded at me to join him in the garden.

"Look, Fawad, what you did today was pretty silly," he told me. "People got hurt in that riot, and a lot of families lost people they love. It was a very dangerous situation that could easily have got further out of hand. I'm sorry I shouted at you and all that, but I was worried for you. If you had been injured, I would never have forgiven myself. Anyway, you're safe now, and that's the main thing. So, are we cool?"

"Yes, we're cool," I told him, my heart growing big at the thought that he cared so much. "We're very cool."

After James went inside to write his story, I joined my mother in the kitchen. She was listening to a report about the trouble on the radio as she prepared a stew of sheep's bum and carrots. Georgie and May hadn't come home at all. My mother said they had phoned Shir Ahmad and Abdul, who were both guarding our gates with brave talk that didn't match their faces, to say they had been ordered to stay behind the high walls of their office compounds until everyone was sure the rioters had got tired and gone back to their own homes. Finally, at nine at night, Georgie and May appeared, looking serious, a little drunk, and talking about "the end."

The next day, while sitting on a crate of Iranian yogurt cartons, I found out what had really happened as I read Pir Hederi the report from the *Kabul Times*. Apparently a U.S. military truck had lost control in Khair Khana, where we all used to live, because of "mechanical failure." It hit a load of cars, killing someone. The report said some soldiers, American or Afghan, started shooting as people picked up stones and threw them. That killed another five people. Then, as the protesters marched into the city, even more people died, and offices belonging to foreign aid agencies were set on fire as well as a whorehouse. There was no mention of a Chinaman, though. The newspaper also said the rioters were not all real protesters but "opportunists and criminals" trying to cause trouble. What's more, the government had promised to arrest them—information that made my heart race because it meant that Spandi and I were now wanted by the cops.

Because of the riots the government ordered everyone to stay in their houses after ten at night. This was called a "curfew," said James, and it was the first time Kabul had seen one for four years. Personally, I was quite glad no one was allowed out because it kept all my foreign friends at home, which I thought might be useful if the police came to raid the place looking for me.

"It's getting bloody tense out there," James told Georgie one evening as they sat in the warm night air eating the chickpeas and potatoes my mother had prepared for us all. "You can almost taste the hate growing, on both sides."

"It will pass," said Georgie, who didn't sound too convinced of her words.

"Will it?" James asked her. "The Afghans aren't exactly renowned for their tolerance of occupying forces."

"We're not occupying!" Georgie almost shouted. "Nobody thinks that."

"Not yet they don't," James said seriously. "But it only takes a couple of fuck-ups for that dynamic to change."

I said nothing, mainly because I didn't want the adults to move their conversation inside the house, where I wouldn't be able to hear if James was going to betray me to Georgie, but I knew he was right. In the newspaper reports over the past two weeks I'd read of fighting between the international soldiers and the Taliban. The week before the American truck had done murder through mechanical failure, about thirty Afghans had been killed by bombs dropped from airplanes, a family in Kunar had died the same way, and roadside bombs and suicide attacks were causing death and misery everywhere.

Maybe May and Georgie were right when they first came home after the riots. Maybe this was "the end."

20

"YOU KNOW, HAJI Khan really is very handsome," remarked Jamilla in the singsong voice she sometimes used to annoy me, "like something out of a storybook."

"He's okay," I admitted.

"If you go for that good-looking rich-as-a-king kind of thing," agreed Spandi.

"Oh yes," added Pir Hederi, "he's a heartbreaker all right."

"How can you even know that?"

My hands flew up in amazement at the old man's gift of apparently knowing everything about anything even when he could see nothing.

"I can smell it." Pir laughed. "He smells like a man women would die for . . . and men too for that matter."

"Ugh," I said.

"Gross," agreed Spandi.

"I'd marry him," admitted Jamilla.

"Would you now?"

Spandi jumped down from the counter and moved over to her.

"Well, he's a bit old and all that, but if no one else asked me I would."

"Don't worry, Jamilla, I don't think you'll be short of offers," Spandi told her as he helped her down from the chair she'd been standing on to wipe the rows of cans on the shelves.

"You're a star that shines in the darkest sky, girl. You'll have men falling at your feet in a couple of years."

"Really? You think so?"

"I know so."

"Oh, here we go," grumbled Pir as Jamilla giggled and corrected the scarf to cover the bruise her father had freshly planted on her face. "Stop it, both of you. I'll have none of that romancing in my shop."

"I think I'm going to be sick," I said.

"Don't be such a child!" Jamilla told me, laughing.

"No, really, I think I'm going to be sick," I insisted.

And I was, right on top of Dog's tail.

I'd been feeling hot and sweaty all day and a devil had been sitting in my head playing the tabla drums for the best part of two hours when Haji Khan suddenly walked into Pir's shop saying he wanted to buy a pack of cigarettes. All of us immediately stopped what we were doing—not that we were doing that much in the first place—and we followed him with our eyes. Anyone who happened to be watching us must have thought we were guarding the shop from Kabul's best-dressed shoplifter.

I knew he was lying, of course—about the cigarettes; he had men who brought in boxes of them from Europe. I'd never seen him smoke the Chinese horse shit that everyone else did here.

"So, is everything okay?" Haji Khan asked as we watched him, and as Pir practically spun himself into a woman around him, inviting him for tea, offering him biscuits, and even telling him "it's nothing" when he tried to pay for his Seven Stars, which was the first time I'd ever heard those words fall out of his cracked lips.

I nodded in answer to Haji Khan's question, knowing he was after more but refusing to give it.

"No problems," he tried again, "at the house?"

I shook my head.

"Good. Yes, that's very good. So, everyone's okay then?"

I nodded.

"So, nobody was affected by the riots?"

I shrugged and shook my head again.

"And James? His work is going well? And May?"

"She's fine!" I suddenly blurted out, feeling embarrassed about the whole discussion that was taking place, which was being watched and listened to with great interest by my friends because I hadn't yet told them that Georgie had cleaned out Haji Khan from her life. I could see they were a little confused about what was going on. Big men don't often come into small shops for no reason.

"Good, good," Haji Khan repeated, looking huge and lost in the cramped space of Pir's shop. "I just wanted to, well, you know . . ."

"Yes," I said, "I know."

And Haji Khan nodded and left, leaving the Seven Stars pack on the counter behind him.

"It's probably just something he's eaten." Dr Hugo stroked the top of my head to feel the heat of it before placing two fingers on the side of my neck to look for God knows what. "Plenty of water and some rest," he added, leaning back on our cushions and picking up his tea.

I put my head to one side and looked at him. I'd only heard him doctoring twice, once with Georgie and now with me, and it seemed to me that as far as he was concerned all anyone ever needed was a bit of rest. I seriously wanted to hear what he'd say if someone's leg got blown off.

"Yes, you're probably right," agreed Georgie.

I rolled my eyes.

"What was that look for?"

"What look?" I asked, feeling my cheeks grow even hotter because she wasn't meant to see it.

"That look!" Georgie rolled her eyes around her head.

"Oh, that look," I admitted, rolling my eyes again.

"Yes, that look," she said, copying me.

"Nothing."

"Boys!" She laughed, pulling me into her arms, which were getting softer now she was eating again.

"Women!" I mimicked.

"Are you two always like this?" interrupted Dr. Hugo as he dipped one of our biscuits into his cup. It broke off before it reached his mouth, and fell onto his trousers.

"Nice," said Georgie, rolling her eyes.

Dr. Hugo had been coming to our house quite a lot lately, even during the curfew, because the government had given him a special password to stop him from getting shot at police checkpoints.

I still wasn't sure how good a doctor he was, but I was sure he would be good for Georgie if she let him. He was a bit messy, that was for sure, but he had a good heart. He told me he cried the other day when he had to cut off a woman's arm after her husband shot her during an argument. And though Georgie and I hadn't spoken about him, I guess she liked Dr. Hugo at least a little bit because all the makeup was back on her face. She didn't touch him or stroke his knee or talk with her eyes like she did with Haji Khan, but she smiled when he was near and disappeared when he phoned, which was quite a lot compared to what she was used to.

But then there were the other times, when Georgie's phone

rang and she just let it play its tune. We all pretended not to
notice because we guessed it was Haji Khan reaching out for
her voice and it was up to her if she chose to hide it or not.
However, if she was truly over him, I knew in my heart she
would just tell him.

"I think Dr. Hugo wants to make Georgie his girlfriend,"
I told my mother as we sat watching the *Tulsi* soap opera that
came from India. Tulsi was a young bride who had married
into a rich family, and everybody seemed to spend most of
their time trying to ruin one another, or crying.

"I think you're right," my mother replied as the program
finished in another explosion of tears and sad music.

"And do you think she will let him?"

"I don't know, but I think she deserves to be happy."

"Like Tulsi?"

"Yes, like Tulsi."

"But Tulsi's never happy."

"It's only television, Fawad. It's not real."

"I know that! I'm not stupid!"

"Don't act it, then."

I looked at my mother, who was now reaching for some
sewing she'd stored underneath one of the long cushions.
Sometimes it was really quite difficult to have a normal
conversation with her because she didn't listen that well. I
wondered whether this had anything to do with her being
uneducated.

"All I'm saying is I'm not sure Georgie can love Dr. Hugo
as much as she loved Haji Khan, and I don't know whether
she ever will."

"What makes you say that?"

"A feeling . . ."

My mother raised one eyebrow and looked at me, straight
in the eye.

"Okay, okay. I caught Dr. Hugo trying to kiss her the other night, but she hid her lips from him and he ended up kissing her ear."

"Fawad! I really wish you wouldn't keep spying on people. It's not nice."

"I wasn't spying; I just happened to be there!"

Of course, that was a lie, because it's hard to be in a place by accident when it's close to midnight and you should be in your bed, but my mother let it pass.

"Well, it's early days," she replied. "Georgie may still love Haji Khan, but things change—people change. They just need a little time."

"Time's all good and well," I said, getting to my feet because I was a little mad with all this talk of rest and time and sleeping and everything else adults throw at you when they don't have any proper answers. "The trouble is, Mother, Georgie hasn't got a lot of time left, and she'll have to pick someone to make her happy soon because she's not getting any younger. And neither are you, come to think of it."

"I beg your pardon?" My mother looked up, surprised.

"I'm just saying, that's all."

"Saying what exactly?"

"Look, there's a man outside these gates"—I pointed my finger at the window to make it clear exactly which gates I meant—"and he's learning computering and trying to better himself, and I don't think it's because he wants to be the most big-brained guard in Wazir Akbar Khan, do you?"

"Now look here, young man—"

"No! You look here! Do you people ever stop to think about me? To think about how I feel? Do you ever wonder why my eyes are always half closed in the morning? It's because I'm up all night worrying about who's going to take care of all the damn women in this house!"

"Don't use that language with me!"

"Language! Language! Who cares? It's only words. Actions count more than words. If I'm not worrying about you and who will make you happy when I grow up and get married, then I'm worrying about Georgie, whose head is with one man and whose heart is living with another, and if it's not Georgie, it's May, who hasn't got a chance in hell of marrying anyone unless she unlesbianizes. I mean! Do any of you have even the faintest idea of the kind of stress I am under?"

And with that I stormed out of the room, leaving my mother still as stone, her mouth hanging open, for once empty of anything to say.

21

A FTER MY OUTBURST, Allah punished me with a night of almighty misery that brought every evil in the world to my house so it could move into my stomach and explode from my bum. "Rest," that's what Dr. Hugo had said, which as far as I was concerned absolutely, beyond one hundred percent, proved he didn't know shit about shit—especially the shit that had been pouring from my hole like an open tap every fifteen minutes.

Luckily, my mother did. Having woken up to the sound of my groans and farts bouncing from the walls of the toilet for the hundred millionth time that night, she gave me a spoon of pomegranate dust washed down with a glass of warm milk and took me back to bed, finally rocking me to sleep with the soft sound of her singing.

"I love you, son," was the last thing I remembered her saying.

We don't have much in Afghanistan—apart from drugs, guns, and great scenery—but over the years we've learned how to get by without all the pretty colored pills and buzzing machinery the sick surround themselves with in the West.

If we feel dizzy, we have a glass of lemon juice, water, and sugar. If we have a sore throat, we stick our fists in our mouths three times in the morning to open up the channel to our stomach. And if we have the shits, we eat dried pomegranate skin. Of course, our self-doctoring is not always perfect. I recently read in a cartoon made by an NGO that putting fire ash on top of a wound might actually kill you rather than cure you, and I knew that after taking my mother's medicine I wouldn't go near a toilet for at least three days. But by and large it works.

Like with the drug addicts and the mentals. When it gets too much for their families, they simply chain them up to a holy shrine for forty days so that God can sort out the problem. And, okay, it's not brilliant for the junkies and the crazies because they only get to eat bread and drink green tea for more than a month and most days they get stoned by bored kids, but that also works. If it doesn't, they die, and that must have been God's plan for them all along. Otherwise they wouldn't have been mental or addicted to drugs in the first place; they would have done well at school and become a lawyer, or something. Or, in Pir the Madman's case, they would have grown up to be the king of fleas.

However, absolutely the best thing about being ill is that you don't have to go to school the next day. It's not that I didn't like the lessons; they were easy enough, and I was still getting good marks for my handwriting. But if I had to make a choice between a warm bed and a wooden chair I share with a boy whose armpits smell of beans, the bed would win every time.

And if the front gate hadn't kept banging open and shut, forcing me out of my dreams, I'm sure I would have slept right through until the middle of the following week and missed even more school. But I didn't because the front gate kept banging open and shut. So eventually I got up to see just what the hell was going on.

Walking out into the sunshine that was annoyingly bright and trying to stab my eyes with its light, I followed the hum of grown-up talking. Rubbing at my face and scratching at the soft layer of fur now growing on my head, I wandered into the garden to find Georgie, James, and May sitting on a carpet on the grass, sorting out plates and bread on a plastic mat, getting ready for lunch. With them were Dr. Hugo, Rachel, and a woman I'd never met before. Her hair was short and dark, and her face looked a little hairy.

"Don't you people have jobs to go to?" I asked.

"Afghanistan can do without us for one early lunch," replied May, waving me over to sit at her side.

"I suppose so." I smiled. "Especially in James's case."

"Feeling better then, are we?" James replied, laughing along with the rest of them.

It felt good to be surrounded again by these white-faced people who seemed to like being surrounded by me.

"How we doing, little fella?"

Dr. Hugo leaned over to me, and as he did so I noticed Georgie touch his knee, which surprised not only me but also the doctor, judging by the quick movement of his head to look at her.

"Fine, thank you."

"Fawad, this is Geraldine," interrupted May, placing her hand on Geraldine's knee.

"Hello," I said.

"Hello," Geraldine said back.

I looked over at James. I noticed he was touching Rachel's knee.

Something was definitely going on.

Behind me I heard the gate open and shut again, and Shir Ahmad came in, just in time to help my mother carry glass plates of *mantu* and salad over to us.

"Salaam," he greeted everyone.

"Salaam," everyone said back, and James edged himself closer to Rachel so he could join us on the carpet.

I watched my mother carefully as she came over to join us, lightly lowering herself to sit by Georgie's side, her covered knees far enough away from Shir's hands to stop me from having to make a scene.

Yep, something was definitely going on.

"It's the spring," explained Pir Hederi, "also known as the mating season."

"Oh please . . . ," I protested.

"Just telling it like it is, son."

I looked at Pir, slightly disturbed by the picture he had just painted in my head, and even more disturbed by the orange glow of his beard, which he had freshly hennaed. Why men did this to themselves was a mystery to me, and right now I had enough mysteries on my mind without him adding to them.

After lunch had broken up and everyone had let go of everyone else's legs to return to their jobs, my mother had agreed that some fresh air would do me good, so I'd gone to the shop to pass some time with Jamilla before she went to afternoon school, and to ask the old man about the ways of adults.

I knew it was a mistake almost as soon as I felt the words fly from my mouth.

"Yes," he said, "sounds like the adults are getting frisky."

"Frisky?"

"Yes. It's the effect of another glorious Afghan spring: the sun is bright, the skin grows warm, and the blood heats up after winter. And when the blood heats up it rushes straight to the heart, causing everyone to make a damn fool of himself."

"Isn't that called love?" asked Jamilla, who was trying to clean what was left of Dog's teeth with the wooden brush Pir Hederi used for his own. He'd have gone mental if he could have seen her.

"Some call it love, some call it madness, little one."

"Who calls what madness?"

Spandi walked into the shop swinging his chain of plastic cards behind him. He had been spending a lot of time with us lately, which had made Pir Hederi remark the other day that the place was looking more like an orphanage than a place of business.

"Love," answered the old man. "The stuff of poets, teenage girls, Indian dancers, and overpaid Westerners."

"Haven't you ever been in love?" Jamilla asked him.

"Never had time," he replied. "I was too busy—"

"Fighting in the jihad!" we all finished with him.

"It's true!" he barked. "Besides, it's hard to fall in love when all the women are covered from head to toe and you end up marrying your own cousin."

Despite Pir's crazy old-man ways, and despite the fact that he'd chosen to look like a can of Fanta, there was always something a little real to his words.

Take the other Friday. My mother had dragged me along to her sister's house as they were now talking again. When we got there we were shocked to discover my aunt had another baby growing inside her belly. As she hadn't grown any more beautiful since the last one, I guess my uncle must have been feeling the power of spring in his blood when he made it.

"It's too disgusting for words," Jahid had spat when I congratulated him on getting another brother soon. "I don't even want to think about it."

I didn't blame him. I felt genuinely sorry for him too because sex was usually the only thing Jahid wanted to think about.

"It must be awful never to know love," Jamilla remarked as Spandi and I walked her to school.

"I guess," I said.

"I guess," agreed Spandi.

"Do you think we'll marry for love?" she asked, which was a bit of a shocker.

"Who? Me and you?"

"Not me and you." She laughed. "All of us."

"Oh, I don't know," I said.

"I hope so," admitted Spandi, and we all fell quiet, because in each of our hearts that's all any of us wanted, if we were honest about it.

The trouble is, in Afghanistan marriage is all about deals. Your father, or in my case mother, arranges the match, sometimes even before you're born, and you just have to do it—usually to a member of your own family, so I wasn't sure who I would be married off to, what with all my cousins being boys. But Spandi had girl cousins, so he might end up with one of them, and Jamilla, well, that was a different story. As she got older, the danger grew of her father selling her to someone for drugs. I didn't like to think about that too much because she was my friend and she was a good girl, so I really hoped she could marry for love because I knew that's what filled her dreams at night and it's also what kept the darkness in her life from covering her completely.

"Okay, I'll have to love you and leave you," Spandi said with a wink as we turned the corner at Massoud Circle. "I'm going to hang around here for a while and try and sell some cards to the Americans."

"Okay," Jamilla said. "Maybe catch you after school."

"More than likely," replied Spandi.

"See you later."

I waved and carried on with Jamilla because I had nothing to sell and nothing else to do.

"If you could marry anyone, who would you marry?"

"Jamilla!" I groaned. "I'm not one of your girlfriends!"

"Come on, you must have thought about it," she continued in her best whiny girl voice.

"No way, it's too disgusting!" I lied.

But even as I spoke, pictures of Georgie came running into my mind, followed by Mulallah and then Jamilla, which was worrying.

"I'd marry Shahrukh Khan."

"The actor?"

"Yes, the actor. He is so good-looking. I watched *Asoka* on television last night. It was very romantic! Shahrukh Khan plays a prince who falls in love with a beautiful princess called Kaurwaki. But then he thinks she is dead, and he becomes a vicious conqueror because his heart died with her. In the end he marries another woman, who is lovely, but not as lovely as Kaurwaki."

"A vicious conqueror? Yeah, right. He's probably gay."

"He is not!" shrieked Jamilla.

"He's an actor," I teased. "He's nothing more than a very well-paid dancing boy."

"Take that back!" Jamilla screamed again. "Take it back or—"

"Or you'll what?"

As Jamilla pushed me into a cart loaded with oranges, a bang as loud as anything I'd ever heard exploded in the air around us, slamming us both to the ground. Beneath our hands and knees the earth trembled with pain as our ears thumped with the shock of it and our hearts burst in knowing fear.

Almost immediately, the smell of burning skin filled the air, even as the world stayed silent. I looked backward, back toward Massoud Circle, where the twisted mess of a Land Cruiser and a Toyota Corolla was being eaten by flames; back to the place where we had stood only seconds before; back to where we'd left Spandi.

Spandi!

My eyes raced over the red-hot flames licking the sky like lizard tongues, past the black and bloody faces of people I didn't know, around the mess of skin and bone mashed on the ground, over soldiers shocked and still, until I found him, standing far away from me but close enough to touch because my eyes were now concentrating on him, reaching for him, pulling him in.

He was standing near the wreckage of the Corolla. A small boy caught in a gigantic nightmare. Around him the air was dark with smoke, and I watched pieces of metal and black-red body parts float to the ground like feathers as our eyes met and our lives came to a stop. There was no sound I could hear, just the beating of our two hearts connected by our eyes.

Spandi was alive, and I felt my love for him race through my veins, thumping its message inside my body, from my heart to my ears, in heavy thuds. He was my brother, he was as close to family as it got, and I stared that message into his head with all my strength and power as the screaming started.

Beside me I felt Jamilla jump to her feet, and under the noise of the bomb and its killing I heard her whisper his name.

"Spandi . . ."

Together we ran toward him—just as the bullets began to crack through the air. There was no time to be frightened because there was no time to think—and that's all fear really is: the worst thoughts you can ever imagine coming real inside your head—so we continued to run, side by side, making the world blur as we passed it, forcing ourselves into the hell before us that was trying to swallow our friend.

Then, far away, I heard the shouts start, Afghan and foreign. It was the terrible sound of scared, angry men roaring their hate and fear into the air as people ran from them or dropped to the ground, hit by invisible bullets. Yet still we ran, and all the time I kept my eyes on Spandi, begging him to stay alive, to keep with me, not to be afraid, because we were coming for him, and I felt him take my words and hold on to them. We were getting so close to him it was almost true.

But then those eyes, those eyes I had known almost my whole life, those eyes that were as much a part of me as they were of him, were snatched away as his head suddenly snapped back. I saw a hole open in his chest, spitting blood onto his shirt as he fell to the ground like a broken toy.

"No!" screamed Jamilla, racing to save him as my legs slowed in pain and shock and the deepest blackness. "No! Please, no! He's only a boy!"

22

AFTER SPANDI'S FATHER found him at the hospital, he brought him back to Khair Khana, to sleep forever next to his mother.

That was a good thing, I knew that, and I was happy for him, because he used to tell me how much he missed his mother when he saw me with mine.

So, yes, I was glad he wouldn't be alone.

Really, I was.

But then, in the other part of my head, I wasn't glad, because Spandi was my best friend and now he was gone and somehow, while he was sleeping, I had to carry on with my life, awake and alone.

I couldn't even think how that would be possible.

From this day on there would be an empty hole in our lives, a hole to add to all the other holes this world had punched into our stomachs, and the more I thought about it, and the more I thought of the place where my friend should be but would never be again, the more I thought I could feel my body collapsing in on itself.

I was being eaten by holes.

I wanted to be strong—strong for him and for his father and for Jamilla, who was almost crazy with grief—but I couldn't find the energy anymore. It was all too much. It was all so wrong. And I could hardly breathe through my tears.

Spandi was gone.

Yesterday he was here, talking about love and swinging his cards behind him; now he was being carried to the mosque on the shoulders of his father and three other men.

On top of all that, the damn sun was shining, laughing there, up in the sky, when it should have been crying with the rest of us.

It wasn't right. But nothing was right, and I couldn't think how it could ever be right again.

A suicide bomber did it, that's what James had said, another suicide bomber driving his hate into a convoy of foreign and Afghan soldiers.

According to James, the explosion had trapped an American man inside his burning armored Land Cruiser, and he died in the fire.

So he killed one of them. Well done, him.

Of course, to kill that one soldier, the suicide bomber had also murdered seven Afghans. Then the soldiers, seeing that they were under attack, had shot even more innocent people in their panic to escape.

"The picture is very confused as to who did what," James had explained. "An investigation has been launched by the Ministry of Interior and ISAF, and at this stage it seems that all they know is that some troops opened fire thinking it was an ambush. Who started firing first is unclear. Afghan or international, nobody knows."

I'd nodded as James spoke, thanking him for the information, but I didn't really care. To me they were just details. The only thing that was clear as far as I was concerned was the surprise I saw in Spandi's eyes as a bullet hit him in the chest. Now he was lying in the yard of our old mosque, and all I could do was watch the shapes of men through my tears and the pale curtains that surrounded him.

In whispered prayers, Spandi's family were performing the Qusl-e Maiet, washing his tiny body so that he would be clean to enter Paradise. Their shadows then wrapped him gently in the white cotton of the *kafan* from head to toe. Once they'd finished, the curtains parted and Spandi was brought out, his face and everything he once was now hidden from us. His father, who seemed to have aged about a hundred years and was walking like an old crippled man, placed Spandi on the stretcher lying on the ground so that the mullah could say the Namaz-e Maiet over him, the prayer that would send him on his way to the next life. After that, Spandi was raised high on the shoulders of those who loved him and carried to the graveyard.

Many people had come to say good-bye, and the sad crowd of faces parted and then closed in behind Spandi and his family. All of us were there: me, Jamilla, Jahid, my mother, Shir Ahmad, Georgie, May, my aunt, her family, and James leading Pir Hederi.

And ahead of all of us, walking with the men of Spandi's village, were Haji Khan and Ismerai. How they heard about Spandi's death I didn't know, but bad news tends to travel fast in Afghanistan.

It was at the mosque, before we walked to the graveyard with its tattered flags of fallen mujahideen and rows of stony hills hiding other dead people, that Haji Khan and Georgie saw each other for the first time since their baby died. I watched their eyes meet, but they didn't move forward to touch with their hands, and the space between them added to my sadness because I saw how hard it was for both of them. For a second an idea passed through my mind in the color of red, and I felt the need to shout at them, to grab their hands and force them together, asking them to forget everything that had happened because it was today that was important and tomorrow it could all be too late to fix anything. But I didn't. I couldn't. My throat was full of tears, and there was a hole chewing at my insides. And above all of these reasons I realized I just couldn't be bothered. They were old enough to look after themselves.

When we arrived at the graveyard, the women and the foreigners stayed back a little as the men fell in behind the mullah. The holy man then called Spandi's father forward and asked him to place his son in the grave that had already been dug for him.

My heart nearly broke in two as I watched. As Spandi's father stumbled forward I began to understand for the first time how heavy death was—like a million walls falling on top of you. Although more than half of my family had gone the same way, it had never seemed real; it was more like a TV show that had just stopped playing, or a picture gone blank. But this was different. This was an end, a horrible stop to everything, and I could hardly bear it.

With tears wetting his face, Spandi's father took the white bundle that used to be my friend into his arms and gently carried him downward, into the earth, placing him on the left side of his body in the small hole where he would lie forever. As he let go, he bent low and repeated into his ear the words of the Koran being spoken by the mullah above them both. Then, reaching up, he took the flat stones waiting there and placed them over Spandi's body, locking him into his grave. I could see it was taking every bit of strength he had to do it because each time he lowered a stone his hand hung over his son's body, trembling, and he had to force it down.

Eventually, a man who I think was Spandi's uncle on his father's side moved forward and helped him back up into the light, where the rest of us stood waiting for him. The man then held him tight, his fingers pinching at the arms of his *salwar kameez*, trying to keep him standing because his legs had become weak with tears. Then, one by one, the people passed by Spandi's father to approach the grave and place three or four shovels of dirt on the stones.

As the long line of men stepped forward, a flash of blue caught the corner of my eye, and I moved my head to get a better look. I was shocked to see Pir the Madman staring straight back at me. His eyes were filled with tears, and as they met with my own my sight blurred and his face quickly lost its shape.

It had never even entered my head that a madman might miss a boy, and I was suddenly ashamed of all the things we had done to him over our lifetimes because it was now clear that his heart was as good as any man's here.

I wiped my eyes in time to see Pir move forward to take the shovel from another man so he could place three little hills of dirt over Spandi. As he did so, I caught the confusion in Haji Khan's face as he turned to look at Georgie. Her own eyes had also clouded in surprise at the man in front of them whose feet were cracked and black, whose hair was a ball of filth, and whose body was covered in a fabulous blue suede coat that had obviously been made for a lady.

23

AFTER SPANDI DIED, I think I went a little crazy because my mind refused to stay still. Even when I tried with all my power to concentrate and hold it down, it carried on moving. One minute I was sadder than sad, the next I was as angry as a bee-stung bull, and the next my body was so numb I wondered whether it was God's way of making the hurt go away, like a rat chewing at the fingers of a leper.

I'd always been terrified of the stories Jahid had told me about leprosy—about how the lepers' noses would disappear overnight because of all the animals feasting on their faces—but now it didn't seem too bad, disappearing little by little in your sleep. When I mentioned this to Pir Hederi the day after we buried Spandi, I could see he didn't get it.

"I think you'd best stay at home for a few days," was all he said.

As Jamilla's tears had also kept her away from the shop, I agreed.

Weirdly, all the grown-ups in the house where I lived seemed to think it would be better if I kept busy, so they were forever pestering me to do this and that until eventually, when they pulled out a game called Twister and began to tie themselves in knots on the floor, I had to tell them, "No. Just, no." And I walked away to get some peace.

Back in my room I tried to escape in a book Shir Ahmad had given me about all the famous people in the world, with names like Einstein, Nightingale, Pasteur, Picasso, Tolstoy,

Joan of Arc, Socrates, and Columbus. According to the pages I'd read, they'd all done pretty amazing things with math and medicine, fighting and traveling, and even just thinking. Unfortunately, the book also revealed that they were all dead, which did little to keep my mind off Spandi.

"It will take time, sugar," explained May when I found her in the kitchen.

I nodded.

"Time, Fawad, that's all you need," confirmed James, looking up from his laptop when I saw him in the garden.

I nodded again.

"Everything seems better in time," agreed Georgie when she passed me on the steps on her way to work.

"How much time?" I asked.

"Oh, I guess it depends on the individual, but seeing as Spandi was such a special friend I imagine it may take a bit of time."

So that was clear: I only needed time, and I probably needed a bit of it.

I realized then that it was only my mother who fully understood what I was going through because she said absolutely nothing. She just pulled me into her arms when I came to sit in her room, and she left me alone when I didn't.

The afternoon we buried Spandi we'd all returned to our home to drink tea in the garden, apart from Georgie, who disappeared out of the gate to sit with Haji Khan in his Land Cruiser. He had turned up shortly after us and had sent Abdul to bring her outside.

Normally I would have been dying to know what they were talking about, but my interest had gone and I wasn't sure I would be able to find it again. In fact, I couldn't help thinking that despite their height, adults were just plain unbelievably stupid: men were blowing up other men; soldiers were shooting at children; men were ignoring women they loved; the women who loved them were pretending they didn't; and when I read the newspapers to Pir Hederi, everyone they talked about seemed to be far more interested in rules and arguments and taking sides than the actual business of living.

The Indian actor Salman Khan, who's not quite as famous as Jamilla's future husband Shahrukh Khan, once said in a magazine I found dumped near Shahr-e Naw Park that people should "go straight and turn right" in life. I thought about this for a while, and I ended up thinking he was wrong. But because Salman Khan was a famous actor and I was just a boy whom some people knew from Chicken Street, I tried it out. Walking straight up the main Shahr-e Naw road, I turned right into Lane 3. Going straight and turning right again, I found myself in Kooch-e Qusab, the street of butchers. Going straight and turning right for a third time, I came to Lane 2. Finally, after going straight and turning right yet again, I arrived at the main Shahr-e Naw road, right back where I started. That's when I knew that no matter what Salman Khan had to say, and no matter how many men he had killed and how many women he had made fall in love with him, sometimes in life you just have to turn left.

The third day after we buried Spandi, Haji Khan returned to our house. However, this time he sent Abdul inside not for Georgie but for me.

"I thought we might go together to Spandi's house," he said, standing in the street, watched by one of his guards.

"Okay, I'll tell my mother," I replied.

In Afghanistan, when people die there are strict times for prayers. The first are said on the day of burial, of course, then three days after we say them again, then again after a week has passed, then forty days from the time they went into the ground, and then finally a year later. This was the first time I had ever been properly involved in the business of saying good-bye to the dead, and I wondered how many more I would have to say good-bye to before my own life was over.

I wasn't looking forward to returning to Khair Khana, but in the end I was glad I did because it was almost beautiful. At his brother's house, Spandi's father was surrounded by people who had come to repeat the words of Allah, and speak their own words of help and hope to him. As they fed their love into his bones through handshakes and whispers, I saw the difference it made to Spandi's father, who looked bigger than the last time I'd seen him, not nearly so destroyed. And it helped me too because I could see that away from the politicians and their arguments, away from the suicide bombers and their murders, and away from the soldiers and their guns, people were good. Afghan people were good. And even though I was having trouble controlling my brain, I knew I had to try to hold on to at least that truth.

In the small front room of Spandi's uncle's house, dozens of people I didn't know were taking time out from their own lives and their own problems to remember a little boy who had been my best friend. I saw the sadness in their eyes, and I saw it was real. I heard the soft hum of their words, and I heard they were true.

And so I took these pictures and sounds, and I stored them in my head so that I would always remember that there was more to Afghanistan and Afghans than war and killing.

"When I was about your age one of my best friends died."

Haji Khan was driving and smoking. Beside him was a man with a gun that looked as terrifying as he did. I was sittings in the back, feeling small.

I looked up at his words and caught him watching me in

the rearview mirror. His eyes were dark as night, and his forehead was broken by lines above heavy black eyebrows. He looked both fearsome and kind, which should be impossible, and I remembered Georgie's story about the time he had traveled to see her in a Shinwar village so many years ago.

"How?" I asked. "How did your friend die?"

"We were playing by the river in Surkhrud, a village just outside Jalalabad where the water runs red from the mountains. He fell in and drowned."

"It must have been a deep river."

"No, not really. I think he hit his head on some rocks when he slipped because, when I realized he wasn't fooling around and I tried to pull him out, there was a deep cut on his head."

"You thought he was playing?"

"Yes, I'm afraid I did. Hey! Mother of a cow!"

Haji Khan suddenly swerved the car to avoid a one-legged man riding a bicycle almost into our path. After sounding his horn and frowning at the cripple, who would soon lose the other leg if he wasn't more careful, Haji Khan looked at me apologetically.

"Sorry about that," he muttered. "Best not tell Georgie I said that."

"Said what?" I asked.

And he looked at me in the mirror again, smiling with his eyes.

"So, how did you feel when your friend died?" I asked.

"Not good."

"I don't feel very good either," I admitted.

"You won't right now," Haji Khan replied with a shrug, "and maybe you never will. I still think of my friend even today."

"Ho . . . that's a long time."

"Yes," Haji Khan agreed. "Sometimes I think the dead have it easy. The difficult part is staying alive and, more than that, wanting to stay alive."

When we arrived back at the house, Haji Khan reached into the space between the two front seats of his Land Cruiser where a little drawer was hidden. He pulled out a book and passed it back to me. It was covered with the softest leather, like a baby's skin, and inside were about a hundred handwritten poems in Pashto. When I flicked through the pages I saw the verses were all about love, each and every one of them.

I looked at Haji Khan, not sure what to say.

"It's not for you." He laughed, obviously picking up on the worry that had crept into my head. "It's for Georgie. But maybe you can read these poems to her now and again because she's been very lazy and hasn't learned Pashto."

"Okay," I agreed, relieved. "Did you write them?"

"Me?" He laughed again. "No. A man from my village wrote them. He's blessed with the gift. I am only blessed with the money to get him to write his words down on paper."

"But Georgie doesn't understand one word of Pashto," I reminded him.

"No, she doesn't. But she knows the sound of love, and she knows the word for love."

Mina. Love. My sister.

"Also," Haji Khan added, breaking into my thoughts, "will you tell her that I've prepared the house for her, ready for when she comes? Ismerai will be there."

"Where will you be?" I asked.

"I'll be . . . giving her time."

Back in the house, I couldn't deliver Haji Khan's message because Georgie was nowhere to be found. As it was still early, I guessed she was probably still in her office sorting out goats to comb. It came as no surprise to me that James was at home, however. As I fetched myself a glass of water, he jumped on me.

"Psst! Fawad! Come here!"

I sighed, heavily and dramatically so he would understand the full force of my tiredness.

"I'm not playing any of your stupid games," I told him. "And besides, I'm sure they're against Islam."

"What on earth do you mean?" James asked, looking slightly hurt. "Twister, my dear fellow, is not against Islam. It is a competition involving skill and agility—that's sort of like being good at moving—and great courage."

I looked at James and raised my eyebrows in the way May did when she knew he was talking rubbish.

"Okay, okay," he admitted, "it also allows you to touch ladies' bottoms."

"See! I told you it was against Islam!"

"Details, Fawad, only details. Now come with me, I want to show you something."

As ordered, I followed James into the living room and over to the table where May liked to do her work. On top of it sat a small box and some green and silver paper.

"Right," he said, "take a look at this and tell me what you think."

He passed me the box. I opened it and found a beautiful ring inside, a silver circle with a cover of gold on top that had been carefully marked with tiny scratched flowers.

I looked at James, not sure what to say.

"Don't give me that look!" He laughed. "It's for Rachel. I just wanted to see if you think she would like it before I wrapped it up."

"I'm sure she will. Are you getting married?" I asked, surprise making my voice climb high.

"What? No! No, of course not," James replied with even more surprise. "It's for her birthday."

"Oh."

"Fuck! You don't think that she'll think that I'm proposing, do you?"

I shrugged.

"Oh, fuck!" whispered James, pulling at his hair, which could really have done with a wash. "Fuck! Fuck! Fucking fuck!"

A little after the sound of evening prayers had floated across the sky and my mother had skipped across the road to see Homeira "about something," Georgie came home with Dr. Hugo following behind her. This gave me something of a problem. I really liked the doctor—he was gentle and kind, and he closed the holes in children whose legs had been blown off by land mines—but I was a bit mixed-up as to who I liked best, him or Haji Khan. Dr. Hugo saved Afghans, but Haji Khan was Afghan. Either way, I didn't think I should give Georgie the book filled with poems right there in front of him, and as I knew I couldn't hide my heart from my eyes, or even keep my mouth shut, I stayed in my room.

Within ten minutes Georgie came to find me.

"Why are you hiding in here?" she asked after I shouted permission for her to come in when she knocked at my door.

"I'm getting some rest," I lied.

"Really? Had a busy day, did we?"

And of course I couldn't stop the truth from slipping out.

"Yes, it was quite busy actually. Haji Khan came for me, and we went in his car to Khair Khana with a man with a gun to pray for Spandi. Then he brought me home and told me about his best friend who died after hitting his head in the red river when he was a boy, and then he gave me a book and he said I should read it to you sometimes because you're lazy."

"Oh, he did, did he?"

"Yes."

"I see."

I reached for the book hiding under my pillow and gave it to her. Georgie gently took it in her hands, stroking the skin of it with her long white fingers before opening it carefully.

"It's beautiful," she whispered, and I nodded.

"He also told me that the house was ready for you and that Ismerai would be there."

Georgie nodded. "That's kind," she said.

"I didn't know you were going to Jalalabad."

"I've some work to do there. I'll be leaving tomorrow because I need to speak to Baba Gul about his goats again." Georgie looked a little sad. "Hey! Shall we ask your mother if you can come with me?"

I thought about it for a second and, because I didn't really feel like traveling and I felt I should concentrate on Spandi a little more, I was going to say no, but then I remembered Salman Khan and I turned left instead of right.

"Okay," I said.

"Great!" Georgie smiled and moved back toward the door, holding the book Haji Khan had made for her in one of her hands and hanging the other in the air for me to grab. "Now come with me," she ordered. "I think something interesting is about to happen."

In the front room of the big house a mat had been set on the floor and food had been brought in from Taverne du Liban and placed on paper plates in front of May, her hairy friend Geraldine, Dr. Hugo, James, and Rachel, who must have sneaked in when I wasn't looking, which kind of proved that I wasn't feeling myself yet.

James looked like death.

"Hello, Rachel, happy birthday!" I said.

"Hello, Fawad, thank you very much. How are you doing?"

"Oh, okay, not too bad," I replied.

"Good," she said in her special singsong voice. "Sometimes we all just need a little time."

Because it was Rachel's birthday I swallowed the "tut" rising in my throat and smiled. I then went to sit next to her as she had moved over to make room for me. It was quite lucky, really, because James was opposite us and it gave me a fantastic view of his face. His skin was whiter than paper.

As ever, the food from the Lebanese restaurant disappeared down our throats faster than a boy born before his father. However, James hardly touched a thing, and as we washed down our meal with fizzing Pepsi—laughing because it made Geraldine do the loudest burp I'd ever heard come out of a woman's mouth—the journalist got quieter and quieter until his face nearly turned green and I thought he was going to vomit.

"Present time!" shouted Georgie, with a wink at James.

"Yes, yes," agreed James, who didn't sound like he wanted to agree at all.

When Rachel clapped her hands and squealed like a girl, he pulled back, as though he'd just been bitten.

I was finding it quite funny.

Georgie was the first to hand over her present, a beautiful green scarf that really looked pretty on Rachel. Next, Dr. Hugo gave her a little plastic case that held bandages, some needles, some ointment, and other things that might be useful in an emergency but were hardly the stuff of dreams. After Dr. Hugo, May presented Rachel with a framed photo of some *buzkashi* players from Mazar-e Sharif, saying it was from her "and Geri."

"And, erm, here's a little something from me," said James finally. "Many happy returns."

He didn't sound too convincing, and his arm looked weak as jelly as he held out the little box covered with sparkling green and silver. Not that Rachel seemed to notice.

"Oooh," she said, tearing open the package and carefully opening the box.

As the silver and gold shone in her eyes, everyone stopped talking and held their breath. Rachel slowly picked up the ring and turned it in her fingers.

"It's beautiful, James," she said quietly. "And I'm so honored, really I am. It's such a wonderful thing to do. But . . . really . . . I'm sorry . . . there's absolutely no way I can marry you."

James groaned. "I was afraid this might happen," he said. "It's just a ring, Rachel, I didn't mean—"

He stopped midsentence because everyone was laughing at him, Rachel the hardest of all.

"I know, James!" she said. "I'm joking! Georgie told me about your little panic attack!"

James groaned again and slapped his forehead, which brought some of the color running back to his face.

"But the ring really is beautiful," Rachel told him. "Thank you. I'll treasure it always."

"My pleasure—I think."

James grinned as he leaned across the floor mat to give her a kiss.

"Hey," he said as he moved back to his place, "what do you mean you wouldn't marry me?"

Rachel giggled. "Look at you! You're a mess, darling, a big scruffy—and most of the time drunken—mess. How could I ever take you home to meet my parents?"

"Now hang on—"

"And besides, your surname is Allcock!"

"That's a very noble old English name, I think you'll find."

"That may be so, James, but I can't go through the rest of my life being known as Mrs. Allcock!"

And everyone burst out laughing, apart from James, who looked disappointed, and me, because I thought Rachel would make a lovely Mrs. Allcock. Judging by the small shadows now crossing James's face, I think he did too.

24

A s we wound our way around the gray mountains down to the blue of Surobi and into the flatness of green that took us to Jalalabad, it struck me that this was a journey that usually followed some kind of disaster in my life—first it was James's knife in the Frenchman's ass, and now it was Spandi's death—and I couldn't help wondering what catastrophe might pour soil on my head if I ever came this way again. Would my mother have died? Would Jamilla have been sold for a night of hashish? Would I have woken up one day to find a rat running around Kabul with my nose in its stomach?

The more I thought about it, the more it spoiled the journey, to be honest. I was also sweating in the backseat like a fat man wrapped in a *patu* because the air-conditioning was broken. Even though Jalalabad was only a few hours away from Kabul, the sun was about one hundred times stronger, and the heat of it filled my mouth in the closed space of the Land Cruiser that had come to pick us up before lunch.

Georgie did little to make the journey any more fun as she sat in the front seat talking to her office most of the time, because the mobile phone reception kept disappearing halfway through her conversations.

"Are you hungry?" she asked me eventually, snapping her phone shut as we came to a stop in front of the Durunta tunnel. Two giant trucks were trapped inside facing each other, unable to pass and unable to go backward because of all the other cars, taxis, and Land Cruisers that had arrived to block them in.

"I'm starving actually," I replied.

That morning I'd eaten only a little bread and honey because eggs were now off the menu thanks to a report my mother had heard on the news. Apparently we were all about to die from bird flu, so anything that had anything to do with chickens was now officially banned from the house.

"Good, let's get out then," Georgie said.

We left the car with the driver because we knew it wouldn't be going anywhere fast and jumped into the chaos of the street. Around us, the air was thick with bad-tempered shouting and angry car horns as a group of policemen tried to sort out the mess. As usual, everyone was pretty much ignoring them, even getting out of their vehicles to bark their own orders, while other cars tried to overtake and squeeze past one another, hoping somehow to force their way into the tunnel.

I imagined that if I was a bird looking down from the sky, the road might look like it was covered by a giant blanket of metal.

Weaving our way past rattling engines, we reached one of the fish restaurants lining the road. Outside, a man stood in front of a metal bowl that was spitting oil. He waved us inside, away from the smell of burning fat and heavy car fumes.

We walked past him, through a small room where a group of men sat on the floor tearing apart bits of fish with their bread or picking bones as thin as needles from their mouths. We nodded at them, they nodded back, and we walked out through a door at the back of the restaurant.

In front of us, Durunta's blue-green lake shone its colors before a jagged line of brown mountains. It was incredibly beautiful. And it would have been incredibly peaceful too if the air hadn't been filled with the sound of men insulting one another's mothers.

A small, thin man with a small, thin mustache and no beard waved us into another small room balanced on the edge of the lake. Inside there was a massive window, and the man got to work with a cloth, shooing away a cloud of flies that buzzed around in circles before landing back in their original positions.

We sat down on bright red cushions dotted with greasy fingerprints, and Georgie ordered two cans of Pepsi, a plate of naan bread, and some fish.

I looked out of the window that didn't have any glass in it and saw a tiny boat covered in pretty colored ribbons playing out on the water. Below us I also saw a small boy, about my age, scrambling up the hill from the lake. The top half of his body was naked, and his trouser bottoms, patchy with wet, had been rolled up.

"Well, at least the food is fresh," Georgie commented, because the boy was holding a plastic bowl filled with flapping bony lake fish.

"Yes, that's one thing," I agreed, falling back onto the dirty cushions. "So, why do you need to see Baba Gul again?"

"I need to finalize some details," Georgie replied. "The organization I work for just received a load of money, and we've got a great opportunity to really move this cashmere project forward."

"In what way?"

"Well, we've been trying to get businesspeople to invest, and an Italian company has shown an interest in buying into a factory here. That would bring a lot of jobs, Fawad. It would also create a demand for cashmere, giving hundreds of thousands of farmers an extra source of income. I want Baba Gul and his family to be a part of that. Besides, I thought it would give you a chance to say hi to your girlfriend."

"She's not my girlfriend!" I protested, hitting Georgie with a fly swatter that had been left on the floor.

"But you know who I'm talking about, don't you?"

"Oh, shut up, Georgie!"

"Oh, shut up, Fawad!"

Smiling, we both began to pick at the bony fish that had arrived on paper plates. And as I ate I thought of Mulallah running through the fields with her red scarf streaming from her neck like the tail of a firework, and I wondered whether Georgie was right and whether Mulallah would become my girlfriend.

After lunch we didn't stop at Haji Khan's house; we kept on driving right through Jalalabad, beeping nonstop at the people, cars, and *tuk-tuks* racing like ants around the yellow streets, on past the picture of Haji Abdul Qadir and into the tunnel of trees until we came to the turn that took us to Shinwar.

As we got nearer, my stomach began to tickle as Mulallah's face came into my head, and I prayed that Baba Gul's hut would still be where we had left it months before.

As we bounced up the stony track—the main road, as far as I could see—I thought I recognized the field where we had played together in the winter sun, but I couldn't see any sign of the old man's goats or my friend. Under my skin, my heart began to move faster as we missed the turn I was sure took us toward Baba Gul's hut. I looked at Georgie, who also seemed confused.

"Zalmai," she said to the driver, "where are we going?"

"Baba Gul has a new place," was all he said.

Ahead of us the mountains that joined with Pakistan grew larger before our eyes, and we passed strange rocky fields that looked like ancient steps until we turned left at some stone walls bordering fields of flowers. About ten minutes later, up a dusty track that kicked clouds of sand into our mouths through the open window that Georgie shut too late to save us, we came to a stop outside a small house. In front of it stood rows of young trees, fenced off from the mouths of the hungry goats that grazed nearby. They were Baba Gul's goats, and they looked much thinner than the last time I'd seen them because their coats had now been taken from them to be made into coats for people.

We followed Zalmai out of the car.

"Agha Baba Gul Rahman!" he shouted.

Mulallah's mother came out of the curtained doorway and into the sunshine. She looked fatter than I remembered, and the weight seemed to have ironed out some of the creases in her face. She came over to greet Georgie, smiling widely with her hands stretched out. When she reached her she stood on her toes to take hold of her face, then she kissed her six times, three on each cheek.

Georgie kissed her back, but I could see the confusion covering her eyes as Mulallah's mother spoke to her in quick, happy Pashto.

"She says may Allah bless you with a thousand wishes—you are her sister," I explained as Georgie was pulled toward the house.

"Tell her that's very kind and I hope God repays her kindness in a million more happy ways," Georgie replied, so I did.

At the door we kicked off our shoes and followed Baba Gul's wife inside, where we found Mulallah and two of her brothers sweeping the dust from the long cushions, ready for us to sit down.

"Salaam aleykum," Mulallah said, grabbing Georgie's waist in a huge hug before giving her hand to me. Her brothers shyly held out their own hands and giggled their welcome.

Baba Gul was nowhere to be seen.

"You live here now?" I asked, surprised and happy at the

family's good fortune. Either they had combed a lot of goats that spring, or Baba Gul had found the luck of the devil in his card games.

"Yes, it is beautiful, isn't it?" Mulallah replied. "And to think I was ready to die a few months ago."

Over cups of wet tea and plates of dry cake, Mulallah and I shared the job of explaining to Georgie the words of Baba Gul's wife. It was almost unbelievable what had happened to their family in such a short period of time, and I was glad their story had a happy ending because I don't think I could have coped with another tragedy.

After the winter, Baba Gul had apparently got into serious trouble with his gambling, and one day he returned home unable to look his own wife in the eyes. Without a word to anyone, he took Mulallah's hand and practically dragged her to the next village, leaving his wife beating her chest in the wooden hut and crying rivers of tears.

As they walked down rocky lanes, Baba Gul said nothing to Mulallah. She grew increasingly afraid the more he refused to answer her questions until her own eyes filled with tears for a reason she didn't know.

When they got to the village, she found out why her father could not speak: he was dumb with shame because he had traded his debt to another man using his daughter. Mulallah nearly fainted with horror when she realized what was happening. Her father had sold her to a man she would soon have to call "husband."

As she backed into the wall of the house she was now expected to live in, the man shook hands with her father. His fingers were thin and dark, and they bent inward with age. With a terrified scream at the thought of those fingers touching her, Mulallah pulled open the door of the house and ran for her life, even though she knew this was the biggest insult she could ever have shown her father, not to mention the man who was about to become her husband. As she ran she knew she was as good as dead because by saving herself she had brought dishonor on her family.

Disappearing into the fields surrounding the village, she sank to her knees and crawled through the growing plants, not daring to raise her head for hours on end as her hands and knees became ripped on the sharp rocks beneath her. For two whole nights she slept under bushes and inside holes that time had made in the hills and mountains, surviving on the berries and raw potatoes she stole while everyone else was asleep in their beds.

By the third day Mulallah realized she could not live like this forever, but she couldn't go back to her family or the man she had been sold to. So she looked deep inside herself and chose to take her life. Even though it was a terrible sin, one of the worst in fact, she prayed that God would forgive her because she was still a child.

As she waited for night to fall, sitting in a cave hidden by bushes, she made her plan. She would sneak into the village when the sun had gone and steal a can of gas from one of the houses. She would then set herself free in fire.

Of course, Mulallah was terrified by what she was about to do. She knew it would hurt, and she was afraid that God wouldn't forgive her at all, and she would continue to burn in the next life. On top of that she was heartbroken at the thought that she would never again see her mother, and as she quietly cried to herself she imagined her mother's voice calling her. "At first I thought I was dreaming," explained Mulallah, "even though I wasn't sleeping. And I thought maybe this was the way of death when you had made the decision to embrace it. But it sounded so real. I really felt my mother calling for me."

Unable to stand the craziness her mother's shouts were producing in her head, Mulallah moved from the cave where she had been hiding and looked down into the valley. A small woman dressed in green with the blue of her burka pulled back from her face was wandering through the grass. She was shouting Mulallah's name, and Mulallah realized she hadn't been dreaming at all. Her mother had come for her.

Unable to stop herself, even though she was certain she would be taken back to the old man who was to be her husband because her mother could never defy her own husband, Mulallah ran out and threw herself into her arms. Wrapped in her mother's love, she cried and cried until her exhausted eyes could no longer make any more tears.

"It's okay, it's okay," her mother cried with her, placing soft kisses all over her daughter's face. "We are safe now, Mulallah. You are safe."

As Mulallah quieted, her mother took her hand and walked her back to their home. On the way she told her how she had almost been broken by grief by what her husband had done, and by the news that Mulallah had run away. But then the pain turned to crazy anger, and in a fit of blind rage she walked all the way to Haji Khan's village almost half a day away to plead with him to do something. He was the strongest man in the province, and if he intervened, then maybe Mulallah could be saved.

Amazingly, Haji Khan was there when she arrived, and when he came to the door of the house Mulallah's mother fell exhausted at his feet, begging him for help. When Haji Khan heard what had happened, he gently told her not to worry and that she should go and find her daughter and bring her home. He then traveled to the man who had bought Mulallah, and he paid for her freedom.

But his kindness didn't stop there. Baba Gul's wife said Haji Khan had spoken such hot words to the goat herder when he turned up at the hut that he had actually put the fear of God into him, for real, and from that day on Baba Gul never went near the cards again. "He spends almost every waking breath in the mosque these days begging Allah for forgiveness while he still has time to save himself from Hell," Mulallah told us with a smile.

And after saving Baba Gul's daughter, as well as the old man's eternal soul, Haji Khan moved the family to their new house. Baba Gul's wife said he charged them a rent for the house that "was almost as free as the air," and he gave them enough rice, oil, and beans to fill the whole family's bellies to bursting for the next month. Even better than that, some men had turned up at the house a few days after they had moved in to plant the trees we had seen in their garden; apparently, one day their branches would be filled with oranges, plums, and pomegranates, which would give Mulallah's family another way of earning money.

"It's all Haji Khan's doing, and it's all because of you," Mulallah's mother finished, reaching up with her hands to bring Georgie's face toward her. She then kissed her sweetly on the forehead.

On the way back to Jalalabad I was filled with talk about Haji Khan's kindness, and in the mirror I saw Zalmai smile as I excitedly told him the story he must surely have known already.

Amazingly, though, Georgie stayed silent. I could see only the back of her head, but it seemed her eyes were reaching out across the fields ahead of us as if she were looking for something she had lost, and her lips were tied shut no matter how hard I tried to include her in my chatter.

Just as Haji Khan said it would be, when we finally arrived at his house in Jalalabad we found Ismerai waiting for us. By now the sun had dipped below the mountains, and the house was a ball of light in the dark. It was also very quiet with only the three of us there, and the midget man we had seen before, flitting around serving us food and sweet tea.

After the excitement of the day and the hours of driving we had gone through, my eyes quickly became heavy with sleep. Of course, this may also have had something to do with the thick smoke of Ismerai's special cigarettes. I leaned back on one of the cushions in the golden room to rest my eyes for a minute.

"Do you want to go to bed?" Georgie asked, breaking away from her conversation with Ismerai.

"In a minute," I said, too comfy to move.

"Okay, in a minute then," she replied, and pulled me forward to place my head on her knees.

I closed my eyes in warm happiness, feeling the softness of coming sleep while listening to the gentle hum of adult conversation. Georgie and Ismerai were talking about politics and the growing troubles in the south and the east.

"We live in difficult times," Ismerai told her. "Personally, I'm at a loss as to what Karzai's plan is. I can see the need for a strong central government, but this is Afghanistan—it's not as simple as moving people around on a chessboard. You move the traditional authority out of an area, the men who share a culture and a history with their own people, and you create a vacuum. There are no longer any restraints; there is no longer any loyalty; there is only money."

"Is Khalid's position in jeopardy?" Georgie asked.

I heard Ismerai click his tongue to say no. "They can't move Haji," he said. "How could they? He doesn't hold a government position; he's his own man. But that's not to say he's not faced with a million problems of government."

"Such as?"

"Well, you know he's thrown his weight behind the governor's poppy eradication plan, don't you?"

"No," Georgie admitted, "I didn't know that."

"Well he has. There will be no poppies planted on his land this year, and he's pushing the strategy at the Shuras, trying to convince other landowners and elders to join, but it's not easy. Haji's trying to find the right path to travel down, for the good of everyone and for the good of Afghanistan, but it's a path blocked by a many-headed enemy, Georgie. You've got the farmers who face the prospect of their yearly income being slashed by at least two-thirds, you've got the smugglers themselves, and you've got the insurgents looking at one of their main sources of money drying up."

"What will they do?"

"What, besides try to kill him?"

"You're not serious?"

Georgie moved sharply, but I pretended not to notice in case she packed me off to bed. But I felt the concern in the act, and I felt it in my own heart too.

"Well, no, maybe I'm being dramatic," Ismerai soothed. "But these are not easy times for him, Georgie. You need to be aware of that."

Despite the sadness in Ismerai's voice, Georgie stayed silent. I guessed she must have been taking his words and turning them over in her head before she answered him. But when she did open her mouth, almost a full two minutes later, I nearly choked in my pretend sleep.

"Khalid has asked me to marry him," she said.

25

Y OU KNOW, I really didn't mean to say anything, absolutely nothing at all, and for hours I didn't even say a
word—which was a kind of torture if you stopped
to think about all the questions that must have been shouting in my head demanding to be answered. But as the saying goes, "A tree doesn't move unless there is wind," and by
the middle of the next morning I realized I might have to do
a bit of blowing.

"Is there something you want to tell me?"

Georgie was sitting in the front seat of the car. As I
was pretty intelligent for my age, and a master in the art of
spying, I spoke in English so that Zalmai couldn't understand.

"Like what?" she replied, turning in her seat to look at me.

"Like . . . stuff . . . ," I replied, stealing a line I'd heard James
use a million times before when he was trying not to say
anything.

"Oh . . . stuff . . . ," returned Georgie.

"Yes . . . stuff . . . ," I kicked back.

Georgie yawned, leaned back in her seat, and pulled down
the sunglasses from her head to cover her eyes.

"No, not really, Fawad. But if you hear of anything interesting, do wake me up, won't you?"

Which basically translated as "Don't stop a donkey that
isn't yours."

I shook my head. She really was irritating sometimes.

Back in Kabul, my desperation to talk broke out like fleas under my skin—itching, tiny-legged words that crawled up my nose, marched around my head, and rested in my mouth ready to jump out at the slightest opportunity. But there was no one to talk to!

Spandi would have been my first choice because he was my best friend and I knew he could keep a secret. As for Jamilla, well, there was just no way. She had already confessed to being a bit in love with Haji Khan, and on top of that she was a girl, which made trusting her pretty much impossible, especially when it came to subjects like marriage. And though Pir Hederi might have been an old man, he was worse than Jamilla when it came to this sort of thing. If I told him everything I knew, I wouldn't be surprised if by the end of the day, as he tossed out the rotten fruit for the goats to feed on in the morning, he had Georgie and Haji Khan already joined and expecting their sixth baby.

So that evening I decided to have another go at Georgie.

And I would have done it too if Dr. Hugo hadn't beaten me to her.

After a delicious meal of *Kabuli pilau*, cooked by the expert fingers of my mother, I was heading to the garden, where I knew Georgie sat reading a book in the fading sun, when the doorbell rang and the gate opened to let in the doctor.

Even before I knew Haji Khan was making a proper fight for Georgie, I was having trouble being in Dr. Hugo's company because he was so nice, and it was obvious that he liked Georgie a lot because his eyes hardly ever left her face when they were together. But "nice" and "like" weren't that much competition for an Afghan man in love, and I guessed the only thing stopping Haji Khan and Georgie getting back together was Georgie. And even though Haji Khan's ways had killed Georgie's baby, we had just found out that he recently saved a whole family, which, if you looked at it like a game of *buzkashi*, gave him a few more goals than the other team.

So, unable to face Dr. Hugo without my eyes giving away the fact that I thought he had lost the war, I shrank into the shadow of the wall just as his messy head of hair appeared in the yard. Hugging its edges, I crept around the house to the "secret passageway" at the back that led to the garden. There I took up my position, as I'd done so many times before, sitting down on my heels to peep through the rosebushes that once again were bringing their brilliant colors to the world.

As Dr. Hugo walked over to Georgie, she put down her book and smiled, lifting her head to offer him her cheek rather than her lips. Dr. Hugo hesitated, but took it.

"Thanks for coming," I heard Georgie say.

"Thanks for coming? That sounds very formal," replied Dr. Hugo, trying to laugh.

"Yes, sorry, I . . . it's just that . . ." She sighed. "I think we need to talk."

"Okay, now this sounds not only formal but serious."

"Yes, it is. At least I think it is; maybe you will think differently. I don't know. I'm not sure how you might feel about it, to be honest with you."

"Well, why don't you try me?" Dr. Hugo replied, and I could hear a tightness stretching his voice.

The doctor took a seat and moved it so it was directly opposite Georgie, rather than at her side. It made them look as though they were at a job interview. As I sat there spying on Dr. Hugo's embarrassment, I felt a bit sorry for him, although I was pleased he was moving things along because Georgie was starting to lose her thoughts in her apologies and I was dying to hear the good stuff.

"Okay, now, Hugo, please let me finish before you say anything."

"Okay."

"Good." Georgie sighed again and sat forward in her chair, pulling the *patu* around her even though the weather was warm and she couldn't have been in the slightest bit cold.

I noticed it was the gray *patu* Haji Khan had given her.

"Well," she began, "when Fawad's friend Spandi died we went to the funeral in Khair Khana, as you know, and I saw Khalid there. It was the first time since the miscarriage, and, as you might expect, coupled with the occasion, it was quite an emotional moment. We didn't speak at the funeral, it wouldn't have been right, but he turned up at the house a little later and I spoke to him outside in his car. He was distraught, Hugo. If you could have seen him, it would have broken your heart. It was as if—"

"Fawad!"

My mother's voice rang out like the crack of a bullet in the graying sky, and I slammed myself flat against the ground.

"Fawad!" she shouted again. "Fawad!"

Cursing my bad luck, I crawled farther into the shadow until I was clear and could get to my feet and walk around to the yard without being seen coming from the garden.

"Oh, there you are," she said when I emerged. "Come, I need to speak to you."

I wasn't very happy about it, but I followed my mother into her room. It was clean and tidy, and the television stood silent for a change. I also thought she looked unusually nervous, as if she had done something wrong, which was normally my job in our life together.

"What's happened?" I asked.

"What do you mean 'what's happened?'" she asked back, seating herself on a cushion and holding out her arms for me to join her.

"You look . . . weird," I said.

"Ho, that's a nice thing to say to your mother, isn't it?"

"It's the truth," I protested.

"Well, I suppose that's okay then."

She laughed, and I noticed how pretty her eyes were looking that night, like beautiful green lights.

"Okay, Fawad." My mother leaned forward and took both my hands in her own. "I need to speak to you about something, and if you don't like what you hear, then you just tell me and I promise I won't mention it again. Not ever."

"Okay," I said, feeling a coldness creep into my insides—the same coldness that must have crept into Georgie when she was about to tell Dr. Hugo that Haji Khan wanted to make her his wife, causing her to hold on tighter to her *patu*.

"Wait a minute," I added, an idea suddenly turning the shiver in my heart into something much nicer and warmer, "are you going to get married?"

"What? How . . ."

My mother pulled away, clearly shocked, and I felt immediately terrible for saying something she found so ugly to hear.

"I'm sorry," I said, "I was just thinking out loud."

"No, don't be sorry, Fawad. I'm . . . I'm just surprised you asked, that's all, because it's sort of what I want to talk to you about."

She paused.

I paused.

In the silence, our eyes held, and I felt how strong our love for each other was.

"Shir Ahmad has asked me to marry him," she finally said, "and I want to know what you think about the idea and about him becoming your father. If you say no, that's it, son. We'll never discuss it again, and I won't think any less of you. But you have to know he is a good man, Fawad, and I think he can offer us a real future. It's a chance for us to live some kind of normal life, as a family, as an Afghan family, not a crazy mix of Afghan and foreign. I want to be settled. More important, I want you to be settled. But you are my son, and this marriage can only ever go ahead with your permission."

When my mother stopped talking, I felt the trembling in her fingers and I let go of them to get to my feet. Slowly, I walked over to the window, where I stood looking out for a time, shaking my head and rubbing at my eyes as if a great pain had suddenly invaded my body. I then sighed, loud and hard, and turned back to look at my mother.

Her face had turned downward, and she was staring at the floor.

"It's okay, Fawad," she whispered, "don't worry. I'll tell Shir Ahmad—"

"Yes, Mother! Tell him yes!" I shouted, jumping over to her and grabbing her around the neck to plant a thousand sweet kisses on her face. "It's about time!" I added, laughing hard because my mother had grabbed me by the waist and was tickling my stomach in punishment.

26

I'D NEVER HAD many secrets in my life, mainly because people don't trust children with things that are important, so most of the time I just made them up. But now that I actually had a head full of the damn things, they didn't seem half as much fun as they should have been. After thinking about it in bed, right up to the point when my eyes gave up and closed for the night, I decided the main problem with having a secret is that you're not allowed to tell anyone about it. And when you can't tell anyone about it, well, what's the point in even having it?

And I didn't just have one; I had loads of them. So far, Haji Khan had asked Georgie to be his wife, but I couldn't say anything because I was pretending to be asleep when I heard about it. Dr. Hugo had almost certainly been told something "formal and serious," but I couldn't ask him about it because I was spying when he got told. I couldn't tell anyone about my mother's news because after she told me she made me promise to keep quiet until she'd been to Khair Khana to visit her sister. I couldn't even have a man-to-man talk with Shir Ahmad about his future prospects or where he imagined we might live because my mother was torturing him with silence. I hoped for her sake that he didn't ask another woman in the meantime. Sometimes Afghan men just want to get married, and it's not really important who says yes to them.

In Afghanistan there are quite a few ways for men and women to get married: it can be arranged between, and inside,

families; it can be a business deal or, as Mulallah nearly discovered, the payment of a debt; and there's even a system
called *badal* where families make a trade—one family gives
their daughter to another so she can marry their son, and in
return that family gives their daughter to them so their son
can marry. This way nobody has to pay for anything. But although it's cheap, it's not the best system in the world because
it can get very complicated, and in the end everybody has
blood with everybody else and this makes their babies die.

I think this is maybe what happened to Pir Hederi and
his wife. He once told me they had never had a child that had
lived over the age of two years, and this came down to the
"bad blood" between them. Pir said that when their blood
mixed, it turned to fire in the bodies of their babies, damag-
ing their brains, until eventually it killed them.

I felt a bit sorry for Pir when he told me about his dead children because I reckoned that given the chance he would have
been a good father. You only had to look at the way he treated
me and Jamilla, and the way he used to take care of Spandi.

"You live, you lose, you die," Pir grumbled one day as the
radio spoke of another bomb that had come to eat away at
some families in Kandahar. "Who in their right mind would
bring a child into this world of ours?" It wouldn't have been
nice to remind Pir Hederi that he and his wife had in fact
tried and failed to do just that, so I said nothing.

Of course, Pir Hederi wasn't the only man without a son;
there was also Shir Ahmad. But at least he had his computer
school to keep his thoughts busy. And maybe one day he would
make a baby with my mother. Who knew? In fact, who knew
anything for certain?

The only sure thing in this life as far as I could see was
that no one would ever be able to hold two watermelons in
one hand.

The following day after school, which had been as boring as a room full of women, I was surprised to find Haji Khan waiting in his Land Cruiser for me at the gate. I then realized it was a full week since we had buried Spandi and it was time for prayer.

Even though it was another sad occasion, my face couldn't help smiling, because Haji Khan had not only remembered my friend, and me, but also recently saved Mulallah from an old man with curled fingers; he'd helped her mother put the fat back on her bones; he wanted to marry Georgie instead of shame her as a girlfriend; and whether he was a drug lord or not, he had this year decided not to be one.

"Ready?" was all he said as he brought down the window to speak to me.

"What about my bike?" I asked.

Haji Khan mumbled something behind him, and the big man with the big gun who had traveled with us to Khair Khana the last time appeared. He picked up my bike and placed it carefully in the back of the Land Cruiser. Haji Khan then nodded at me to get in.

Inside, I leaned forward to give him my hand.

"How is everyone?" he asked.

"Good," I answered. "Georgie was very happy because of the help you gave Mulallah's family."

"Was she?"

"Yes."

"I'm glad. The family deserved a little luck."

I was going to make a joke about luck and Baba Gul's cards, but then I remembered myself.

"Haji Sahib?" I asked. "Why don't you have as many bodyguards with you these days?"

This was now the third time I'd seen Haji Khan with only one of his men instead of his usual army.

"Because it is better this way," he replied. And when he looked in the mirror and saw the next question arriving in my eyes, he added, "At some point, if you're trying to convince people that the country is changing for the better, you've got to start believing it yourself—and even if you don't, you've at least got to give the impression that you do."

When we returned from Spandi's prayers, Haji Khan dropped me off at Pir Hederi's shop because I was already late for work. As soon as I set foot in the door I could see the old man was up to one of his schemes, and by the grin on his face it was going to involve me.

"We're going into the food business!" he told me as I came to sit on a crate of Pepsi beside him. "That's the future, Fawad—Pir Hederi's Take-out Service."

"Don't people already take out food from the shop?" I asked.

"Well, yes, in a way they do . . . but I'm talking snack food, that sort of thing. It was your friend James who gave me the idea."

I groaned in reply. James was almost as crazy as Pir Hederi with his get-rich-quick schemes. Lately, after talking to someone, the journalist had become convinced that one of the mountains in the Hindu Kush had a secret door leading to a cave filled with treasure, so he spent all of his time looking through old papers from the Mines Department and learning how to rock climb with the help of the Internet. My guess was that if there was treasure hiding in Afghanistan's mountains, it would probably be on sale in a Pakistani market by now, along with all the rest of our old stuff.

"So, what's the idea?"

"Well, your friend James came in here looking for this thing called 'sandwich.' Apparently, that's bread filled with something."

"I do know what a sandwich is."

"Good! Then we're halfway there! Apparently all the foreigners are crazy for these things. So I've been trying some out."

Pir pulled out a tray from underneath the counter. It was piled high with folded-over pieces of naan bread.

"What happened to the ones at the end?" I asked, picking up one of Pir's homemade "sandwiches."

"Let me see." Pir reached out, and I placed the ragged piece of naan in his hand. "Oh right," he said. "Dog must have got to that. Anyway, have a taste and tell me what you think."

"I'm not eating that one," I said, pushing Pir's hand away.

"Don't be so gay," he replied, taking a bite—and quickly spitting it out again. "Allah wept. No wonder the old boy didn't finish it off. Write it down, Fawad: onion and mango don't mix."

"Onion and mango?"

"Why not? James said the more exotic a sandwich is, the better."

"He was messing with your head!" I said, although in truth I'd seen him eating banana in bread before, which I didn't think would be the choice of most normal people.

"Okay," Pir continued, never one for giving up, "try the ones on the tray. Jamilla made most of them before she went to school."

Because I was hungry, and because this was my job—such as it was—I did as he ordered. Fifteen minutes later we had two lists. Cheese and tomato, peanut butter, cucumber and mutton, strawberry jam, yogurt and kebab, egg and chicken—

they all worked. Lettuce and cream, mashed-up apple, honey and onion, honey and cheese, mustard and egg, and boiled carrots definitely didn't.

Pir clapped his hands, waking Dog, who was asleep on the step of the shop.

"We'll get the wife to cook up more of this stuff tonight, and Jamilla can do the sandwiching tomorrow, and when you return from school you can go out and sell them."

"I thought you said this was a take-out service!"

"Ah yes, I did, didn't I? Okay, you take out half of what we've made at lunchtime, and when you've sold them you can come back for any I've got left."

"Great . . ."

"Isn't it?"

"I didn't mean . . . oh, forget it." I couldn't really see any point in arguing with the old man because it was quite clear he had made up his mind. "You do know I'm in mourning, don't you?"

People are always dying in Afghanistan. That's just the way it goes. And maybe because people are always dying, the ones who are left alive don't spend that much time thinking about the ones who are dead. They just get on with things. And even though I knew Pir Hederi liked Spandi a lot—I'd even seen his white eyes lose tears at the burial—he was now getting on with things. More to the point, he was making me get on with his things.

Despite my strongest prayers the night before, when I returned to the shop the next day after school I found him waiting for me at the door. He had a metal tray in his hand loaded with his "sandwiches." Rather rudely, I thought, he hardly gave me the chance to wheel my bike inside before he was pushing me out of the door.

"We've got no time to lose," he shouted, trying to keep Dog's face away from the food with his free hand, "lunchtime is nearly over. Get yourself over to the Pakistani Embassy. There's always a massive line of people outside, and they'll be starving, I bet."

"*I'm* starving," I told him.

"Oh." Pir paused to think about how this piece of news might affect his plan to take over the take-out world before telling me, "Okay, you can eat on the way." He passed me the tray. "Only one," he warned as I walked out the door, "and make sure it's egg. They're already starting to smell like hell."

I walked across the main road, past Wazir's mosque and the small row of shops selling airline tickets to places in the world I'd never even heard of and would probably never get to see, and turned right, onto the street with the Pakistani Embassy. Pir Hederi was correct: there were tons of people lining up against the wall, all hoping to get visas. Looking at them, I wondered what it was that made so many people want to go to a place they pretty much blamed for everything. But I guessed anywhere was better than nowhere when you had nothing.

Of course, when you had nothing you weren't going to waste the money you didn't have on sandwiches.

"How much?" One man laughed when I told him the price of two hundred afs that Pir Hederi had set. "I could buy a damn sheep for that."

"Yeah, but you couldn't get it slaughtered, sliced, and placed between bread for the same price," I countered, quickly dodging the back of his hand.

"I'll give you ten afs," another man said.

"That's very kind of you," I replied, "but you'll still have to pay for a sandwich."

As I began to draw quite a crowd—mainly those who wanted something for nothing—a policeman came over and told me to move along. I was causing a disturbance, apparently. And, apparently, he could arrest me for that. As I was too young to spend the rest of my life in prison for a tray of sandwiches nobody wanted to buy, I did as I was told and walked off toward the barricaded openings of the American camps nearby.

I sat down by the side of the road to wait for passing soldiers and told myself that after nearly losing my freedom I deserved more than one crappy naan bread filled with egg turning green. I opened up a few of the newspaper-wrapped parcels and settled for cucumber and mutton. Although the bread was getting hard around the edges, I had to admit the sandwich tasted pretty good.

"Hey, little fella!"

I looked up into the glaring sun and kind of saw the blacked-out face of Dr. Hugo.

"Hey, Dr. Hugo! Do you want a sandwich?"

"Okay," he said.

He picked the top sandwich from the pile and opened it up.

"Peanut butter," I said. "Nice choice. That will be two hundred afs, please."

Dr. Hugo smiled and came to sit by my side.

"No, I'm serious," I said.

"Oh." He dipped into his pocket and pulled out five dollars. "Keep the change."

"Thanks, I will."

For a while we sat there saying nothing because our mouths were too busy trying to chew Pir's sandwiches. As I had a head start on the doctor, I finished first.

"So, what are you doing here?" I asked.

Dr. Hugo swallowed hard and coughed a bit. "I was seeing the Americans about some medical supplies—nothing that interesting."

"Oh."

He continued eating. Then he stopped chewing, pushing his mouthful into a cheek in order to speak.

"Look, Fawad, I've been meaning to ask you something . . ."

"Okay."

I hoped to God it wasn't another damn secret coming my way.

"Well . . ." Dr Hugo looked a bit embarrassed, and as he searched for the words and gulped down his sandwich he put a hand through his hair, leaving in it a smudge of peanut butter. "Do you know where Haji Khalid Khan has his house in Kabul?"

I looked at the doctor, trying to work out in his eyes what he was up to as I nodded my head slowly.

"Good. That's excellent news. That really is. Now, can you possibly take me there?"

I picked up another sandwich and bit into it. Tomato, onion, cucumber, and honey—not a combination I remembered being on the list Pir and I put together. It tasted like rat vomit.

"Fawad?"

"Look," I said finally, "I don't think that would be a very good idea."

"I only want to talk to him."

"What about?"

"Georgie."

"Then that *really* isn't a good idea. I don't think he'd like it very much."

"Be that as it may, young man, but I have to. If I don't, she'll leave."

I turned my head at his words, surprised and just a little bit pleased.

"Is Georgie going to live in Jalalabad?"

"No, of course not," Dr. Hugo replied, looking confused. "She'll go back to England."

"England?"

"Yes, England. And I'm sure that, like me, you wouldn't want to see that happen, would you?"

It hadn't even crossed my mind that Georgie might leave Afghanistan—or rather that she might leave me.

"No, I don't," I admitted.

"In that case, take me to Haji Khan."

Although I knew it was a bad idea to take Dr. Hugo to see Haji Khan because he would almost certainly be killed, there were now more urgent worries crowding my head than the life of a foreigner. There was *my* life with a foreigner. I couldn't imagine Georgie not being near me; more than that, I didn't want to imagine it. After recently losing one of my best friends, I couldn't face losing another, so if Dr. Hugo thought he could fix the problem by getting killed, I wasn't going to stop him.

"Here it is," I said, pointing to the green metal door in front of us, where a guard with a gun sat on a green plastic chair.

"Okay, let's do it," Dr. Hugo said.

"Okay, it's your funeral."

The doctor looked at me for a second to see if I was laughing, but I wasn't. Amazingly, though, he still got out of the Land Cruiser, and I followed him, slightly impressed, holding my tray of sandwiches.

Dr. Hugo told his driver to wait for him, and we walked toward the guard.

"We want to see Haji Khan," I told him.

"Who's the foreigner?" he asked.

"A doctor," I replied.

The guard nodded his head and disappeared inside, leaving us waiting outside.

Two minutes later he was back.

"Okay," he said, and he stepped back from the gate to let us through.

Haji Khan was in the garden with about six other men dressed in expensive *salwar kameez* and wearing heavy watches. He got up to greet us and held out his hand to Dr. Hugo first.

"Salaam aleykum," he said.

"Waleykum salaam," replied the doctor. "I'm Hugo."

"Nice to meet you, Hugo," Haji Khan replied.

It was quite obvious he hadn't the faintest idea who the British man was, and I smelled trouble coming.

As Haji Khan invited us over to the carpet to sit with him, he asked after the health of my mother and told me he hoped I was fine, doing well, and keeping happy. "If you were hungry, we could have made you something here—you needn't have brought your own food," he added, looking at my plate of unsold sandwiches. I tried to laugh, but because of the situation it came out as more of a squeak.

All of us then sat there on Haji Khan's carpet with his friends gathered nearby, watching one another and saying nothing. Haji Khan must have been wondering what I was doing there with a doctor he didn't know, but he didn't ask because it wouldn't have been polite. We had been invited into his garden, and we were his guests.

Now, if we could just continue to sit there, all nice and quiet, and drink the tea that was being poured for us, I thought we stood a pretty good chance of walking out of the gate in one piece. But then Dr. Hugo started talking.

"You're probably wondering why I'm here," he stated.

Haji Khan shrugged his shoulders in a way that said well, yes, actually, I was wondering.

"Well," Dr. Hugo continued, coughing a little as he did, "I'm a friend of Georgie's."

Haji Khan said nothing.

"I also know that you are a good friend of hers, and over the years you have become quite, um, close."

Haji Khan again said nothing, and because his silence was turning the air weird I tried to concentrate on my tea.

"Well, the fact is that I know things have changed between you two and, um, you're not as close as you once were. But it's quite clear that she still feels an awful lot for you, and I think it's time you, um, well, you know, backed off a bit."

Haji Khan continued to say nothing, but his eyes were growing dark and his eyebrows were moving inward. This was not a good sign, not a good sign at all, and I prayed the doctor would stop his talking, drink his tea, thank my friend for his hospitality, and go.

But he didn't.

"I'm saying all this to you because Georgie is thinking of leaving for England, and the fact is I would prefer her to stay, for obvious reasons."

"What reasons?"

It was the first time Haji Khan had spoken since the conversation began, and I heard the anger cooking in his voice.

"I think I'm in love with her," Dr. Hugo told him, almost matter-of-factly.

It wouldn't have been the first reason I'd have given.

"Have you slept with her?"

Haji Khan's voice was quiet and careful, and I noticed his friends shifting themselves on the carpet.

"Sorry, but I really don't think that's any of your business."

"I said, have you slept with her?"

"Well, no. No, I haven't slept with her, but that's not really the point here. The fact is we have become close, and I'm sure that if you just gave her some space, if you finally let her go, I know I could make her happy. I mean, come on, what could you give her here, in Afghanistan, in your culture—"

Suddenly, Haji Khan let out a roar so loud I dropped my cup of tea.

The doctor sprang to his feet in shock, and Haji Khan

flew at him, grabbing him by the neck and pinning him to the wall.

"Are you mad?" he raged, spitting each and every word in Dr. Hugo's face. "Coming to me and talking like this? Do you not know who the fuck you are dealing with?"

"Of course I know who you are," Dr. Hugo gasped, struggling for breath and ripping with both hands at the one hand that held him. "I'm not scared of you!"

By now I was also on my feet, and from where I was standing Dr. Hugo didn't look scared—he looked terrified.

"You stupid, stupid, *stupid* motherfucker!" Haji Khan screamed back at him, slamming his fury into his face. "You think you're in love with Georgie? You *think*? Well, let me tell you something: I *am* Georgie! That woman is my heart; she is locked in my bones, in my teeth, even in my hairs. Every inch of her is me, and every inch of her belongs to me. And you? You come here with your schoolboy dreams to convince me to 'back off.' Are you insane? Are you *fucking* insane?"

Haji Khan threw the doctor to the ground, leaving him choking for air at his feet.

"Get him out of here," he snarled in Pashto to one of the guards who had crept closer at the first sign of trouble. "Get him out of here before I rip his throat out."

He then walked away, into his house.

27

O N THE DRIVE back in the car Dr. Hugo was very quiet, which was fair enough—he had just been half strangled after all. His hands were also trembling, and the middle of his eyes looked bigger than normal.

"That man's a bloody animal," he finally muttered, "a maniac. What the hell does she see in him?"

I guessed he meant Georgie.

"Well, he is very handsome, and last week we found out that—"

"It was a rhetorical question, Fawad."

"Oh."

I didn't know what *rhetorical* meant, but I guessed it might have something to do with a question that did not want an answer.

Still, if nothing else, Dr. Hugo's visit to Haji Khan had made up my mind about one thing: the doctor was nice and all that, but a woman needs a man who can fight for her, especially in Afghanistan. And although I knew it was wrong, because my mother told me "Violence is never the answer," I was beginning to think that Haji Khan was pretty "down-with-it-cool," to use James's words. I didn't say anything, though, and for the rest of the journey Dr. Hugo also said nothing. He only rubbed at his hands now and again, and sometimes his neck.

About ten minutes later we stopped in front of my house, and he leaned over. His voice was almost a whisper in my ear.

"I'd appreciate it, Fawad, if you didn't mention any of this to Georgie."

"Okay," I agreed, because I felt sorry for him. But I was far from happy about it. When I got back to my room, I'd have to write everything down on paper just so I could remember all the things I was now not supposed to tell anyone about.

I was hoping to avoid anyone who might make me lose the secrets hiding in my head but, because life is never how you want it to be, I came into the yard to see the whole house, including my mother, sitting in the garden. She immediately jumped to her feet. As she moved, I noticed an Afghan woman next to her who I thought looked like someone I knew, but I couldn't think from where.

My mother's eyes were wet, but her face was happy—incredibly happy in fact. And then I noticed that everyone else looked incredibly happy too, and I guessed that my mother must finally have said yes to Shir Ahmad, which at least meant I could scratch one secret off my list.

"Fawad!" my mother cried, grabbing me by the arm and practically dragging me to the garden. "There's someone I want you to meet."

Obviously I'd not been involved in my mother's first marriage, so I thought I was about to go through some kind of formal introduction to the man who would soon become my father. But it still seemed odd. After all, I'd been speaking to Shir Ahmad for the best part of the year, every day of it. In fact, without me they probably wouldn't have been getting married.

I passed Georgie, James, and May, whose faces looked stupid with joy, and then the woman my mother had been close to when I first came into the yard got up from the ground to greet me. Close up I could see she was beautiful. She was also young, much younger than my mother, and, rather weirdly, she shared her green eyes.

"Fawad," my mother said in a shivering voice, coming to a stop in front of the woman. "This—oh, son!—this is your sister, Mina."

Well, if anyone ever needed further proof of God's great love and compassion, he only had to look at the beautiful face of my lost sister. After so much darkness she came into our lives like sunshine, and it showed that even though God sometimes took away, he also gave back.

Although I was amazed and feeling brilliant at the sight of Mina, for a full hour I was knocked dumb. My heart was so swollen with happiness, no words could find a way past it to come out of my mouth. For months I'd been wondering whether my sister would hear Georgie's message on the radio, and when she never turned up I began to accept that she was probably dead, along with the rest of our family. But now I knew that every day she'd been getting taller and more beautiful in a house in Kunar.

Apparently, Georgie had known about Mina for a full two weeks but hadn't told anyone because she had been trying to arrange a way to get her to Kabul to surprise both my mother and me. Really, I had to congratulate her on that because there was no way on God's earth I could have kept *that* secret to myself.

Now that she was here, nothing else seemed to matter, and over a never-ending chain of cups of tea that James and May were mainly in charge of producing, as my mother had some serious mothering to catch up on, we all listened in amazement as she told us what had happened to her after she'd been stolen by the Taliban. It sounded absolutely frightening and, even though I was still learning about life, I guessed she left out much of the story, because when she fell over her words or they stopped for a bit my mother would take her hand and pass on her strength to her.

Mina said that after being thrown into the truck with the rest of our village's girls, she was taken west. In a gentle voice, she described how men with guns guarded them all through the journey so that they couldn't escape. When one girl did jump off the back, having gone mental with fear, a Talib simply pointed his gun at her and shot her dead. "We were like sheep going to slaughter," she said. "Nobody told us anything. We had no idea where we were going, and most of us assumed we would soon be killed . . . or worse than that."

As Mina spoke, our mother bowed her head. I felt the water come to my eyes too. My sister waited for us to finish our sadness, and then kissed us before continuing.

For three whole days she and the friends she had known from the day she came into this world were trapped in the truck, forced to survive on scraps of bread and leftover food that was chucked into the back for them to eat whenever the Taliban stopped for a meal. Then at last, as they began to grow weak and sick and their clothes stank with their own dirt, they arrived in the province of Herat, where the men who had ripped them from the arms of their families dragged them from the back of the truck—beating the ones that were screaming into silence—and forced them to wash.

Once they were clean, the girls were taken to a room in a building in the middle of nowhere where they were made to stand in a line. Men began to arrive, to look at them and pinch their bodies. One by one the girls around Mina began to disappear, sold to men they didn't know as new wives, or as future brides for their sons, or as slaves.

Mina awaited her turn, but when no man came to grab her by the arm and push her out the door she thought she might have escaped because she was so much smaller than the rest. But it turned out that she had been bought the very night she had been forced onto the back of the truck and driven away from Paghman.

"When almost all of my friends had gone, a man came in. He looked like a Talib with his long beard and turban, but he told me not to be afraid and he held out his hand."

Unable to do anything else, Mina followed him.

The man took her to a nearby Toyota pickup and told her to jump in the back among the sacks of rice and beans and cans of cooking oil he was transporting. He then got into the front seat and started driving back along the road Mina and her friends had just come down. The farther they traveled, the more Mina dared to believe that the man might be taking her home, because he hadn't once touched her or moved to beat her; he'd even given her a kebab after stopping at a tea shop. But then, instead of going straight toward Kabul, they started moving south. When they finally stopped, in front of a big house in a small dusty village, Mina was told she was in Ghazni.

Grabbing a sack of rice from the pickup, the man nodded his head for Mina to follow him into the house. Inside, an older woman was waiting with her children. When she looked at Mina her face immediately clouded, but she didn't say anything. The man then left Mina with his children, some of whom were older than she was, and took his wife away into another room. About thirty minutes later both of them returned, and whatever the man had said to his wife she seemed to accept it. Though she was never friendly to Mina, she never beat her either. However, she did make her work, and for the next four years my sister practically had a twig brush glued to her hand.

"Considering what could have happened, it wasn't too bad, and they were decent enough people. And though I was never happy in that house, after the first week I was never afraid in it either."

Mina said the man who had bought her, for a price she had never been told, was called Abdur Rahim. His wife's name was Hanifa. She was a strong woman and proud of her husband and her children. She ruled the house with the force of a king when her husband was away, which was quite a lot. During the first year she coped with Mina by treating her like "a stray dog"; she was fed and watered and given a corner of the kitchen to sleep in. She was also warned never to go upstairs into the family's main living space—unless it was with a brush in her hand. Abdur Rahim's children were quite nice to my sister. They would often come and talk with her, and even help her with her chores when she grew tired or ill. "They were a good family, so life was okay. It just wasn't much of a life, that's all."

But then everything changed again.

One day, Abdur Rahim called Mina to his side and told her it was time for her to leave. He said he was sorry, and he looked genuinely upset. He then told her that he had made a promise to himself to protect her in some small way so that he could compensate her for the sadness he had visited on her life—it turned out that Abdur Rahim had been in our house the night the five Taliban knocked down our door. "He told me he had seen you, Mother, fighting so hard for all of your children, and then when he turned to walk away he had been trapped by the wide eyes of a small boy and he became consumed by guilt and shame. That must have been you, Fawad. Abdur Rahim told me that it was because of the look in your eyes, the complete fear and horror of the night mirrored in them, that he decided to buy me. He felt the dishonor of what they had all done that night hanging around his neck, and he needed to save me in order to save himself. And because of that his wife agreed to shelter me also."

Apparently, his wife's willingness to help her husband lasted only as long as Mina was a girl. When she began to show signs of becoming a woman, Hanifa demanded she go. Abdur Rahim protested that he thought of Mina as a daughter, but his wife was convinced that over time he would think that way less and less. As her shape changed and she grew into her beauty, there was no blood link to stop him from taking her as a second wife.

Reluctantly, Abdur Rahim agreed to Hanifa's demands. However, he told Mina that he had found her a good man to live with, and even though he would be her husband rather than her guardian, he would not beat her because he was a true Muslim.

Although Mina appreciated the old man's thoughtfulness, and the fact that he had done no harm to her over the years, she said she still could not find it in herself to forget or forgive the wrong he had done in the first place, so after he told her she was going she simply collected her small bundle of clothes and without a word or a gesture, apart from a nod to his wife, Hanifa, she walked out the door and never looked back.

Outside, her new husband was already waiting to pick her up. He was younger than Abdur Rahim by a good ten years, and one of his arms was smaller than the other as a result of a disease he had caught as a child. Without a word he collected Mina's things with his one good arm and put them in his Toyota Corolla. He then drove her eastward until they arrived in Kunar.

Although the journey was long, the only thing Mina learned on the way was that her husband's name was Hazrat Hussein and the Taliban were no longer in power in Afghanistan, and hadn't been for the past two years. "Although I was pleased to hear the Taliban had been defeated, I was also angry that, as far as I could see, nothing had changed. The Talib who had bought me was still in his big house and I was still the prisoner they had first made of me."

When Mina arrived in Kunar, she was taken to a small house, and, as she'd half expected, there was already another woman in it. In fact there were two more. The older woman was Hazrat's mother, and she was as sour as the milk from a poisoned goat. The other woman was Hazrat's wife. Her name was Rana. She was tiny and very ill, and she had been unable to give her husband any children. After taking one look at the pitiful creature she would have to call sister, Mina knew what was expected of her.

She didn't disappoint. A year later she handed Hazrat a son. They named him Daud. "Hazrat was delighted, and really he was, and is, a very good father to our son. And thanks to our son, my life is filled with some measure of joy now." More amazingly, Hazrat's mother melted like butter whenever she held her grandson, which softened her heavy-handed ways around the house. Even Rana gained strength and happiness with the arrival of Daud.

Even though life had forced the two of them together, Rana and Mina quickly became one as they united against their shared husband's mother, and because my sister saw the pain in Rana's eyes that came from her body, she did everything she possibly could to make life easier for her new sister.

It was because of my sister's kindness that when Rana was listening to the radio one day, as Mina was busy cooking in the kitchen, and she heard Georgie's message, she immediately told her about it. "I couldn't believe it could be true. I was certain you had all been killed because I remember seeing the houses burning in the night as we drove away from Paghman, and I remember clearly the hate that had been painted on the faces of those men who took us. Then all of a sudden I get this message that you didn't die after all, that you were still looking for me, even after all these years."

For days after hearing Georgie's message Mina bounced from joy to grief as she thought of us and then the miles between us that could have been a million as far as she was concerned, because she didn't even dare to think that her husband would agree to her coming to Kabul.

But my sister hadn't reckoned on the might of Rana. Day after day Hazrat's first wife begged her husband to be merciful, and she cried real tears as she told him how happy this one act of kindness would make her—"she who had known nothing but the love of a good man and the anguish of an empty womb and failing health," Mina whispered. "She was amazing. I owe her so much."

Sadly, Rana died a month back from the illness that had been eating her insides. Wanting to honor the last wish of his dead wife, because he really was a good man just like Abdur Rahim said, Hazrat Hussein contacted the number Rana had written on a piece of paper and spoke to Georgie.

28

A FTER MINA CAME back from Kunar, and back into our lives, she stayed the night with my mother, sleeping in her room.

I wanted to stay with them because I didn't want to leave my sister after just finding her again. It was all so strange and confusing. Mina was different. I recognized her, but at the same time I didn't. In my dreams, when I had prayed so hard for her to come back, I always imagined her as a little girl. But she wasn't a little girl anymore; she was a woman.

"You are so grown up!" Mina told me, pulling me to her because I was sitting by her side, not sure what to do. "I can hardly believe it! My little brother now a little man, all quiet and serious."

"He's not usually so quiet," my mother said with a smile.

"Well," Mina said, kissing me on the cheek, "it's a lot to take in. We must get to know each other again."

As Mina spoke I let myself fall deeper into her body. Though she was right and our eyes and our heads needed time to learn about each other, my heart already knew all there was to know, and it loved her.

When my eyes struggled to stay open, my mother told me to go to my room so she could speak to Mina alone. I wanted to stay, but I didn't say so because I saw it was important to my mother, and as I waited for sleep to take me I listened to them talking and crying together. I guessed my sister was slowly getting the story of our life—and slowly getting used to the idea that she had lost our older brother, Bilal.

When the sadness of the night was over and the sun woke up to shine its happiness back on their talk, my mother decided that my sister's return was a blessing from God that she should marry Shir Ahmad. I was pretty relieved when she told me because it stopped the guard from marrying someone else and it also allowed me to tick another secret off my list—well, almost. Apparently we still couldn't tell any of our friends because we had to travel to Khair Khana to my aunt's house first.

For two women who not so long ago couldn't stand the sight of each other, they were sure as hell seeing a lot of each other now. But of course there was a reason for it. After all, this is Afghanistan, and rules have to be followed.

There in my aunt's house, in front of the mullah who had said the prayers for Spandi, my mother and Shir Ahmad performed the marriage ceremony, *nekah,* accepting each other three times before Allah. As well as the holy man making sure they did everything right, my aunt and her husband were allowed to watch, as well as two of Shir Ahmad's brothers, and my sister Mina and her husband.

Hazrat Hussein had turned up at our house earlier that morning, expecting to take his wife home but finding a wedding invitation in his hand instead. To my surprise, he was a lot bigger than I had imagined, and his face was soft and kind. And although his arm looked strange, as if God had tied a child's one onto his body rather than a man's, I was relieved to see it was the left one, which meant there were no embarrassing problems when it came to shaking hands.

As all the adults stood around being polite to one another, I heard that Hazrat had spent the night in Kabul, staying with a business partner of his. Apparently my sister's husband did clever things with wood—so clever, in fact, that he could sell them. And in Khair Khana he presented my mother with a beautiful brown chest carved with flowers and singing birds.

Unfortunately, we didn't get to see my sister's baby, Daud, because he was in Kunar with his grandmother, but Mina promised she would bring him on her next visit. As she spoke she quickly looked at her husband as if she had forgotten something, but he nodded his head and it put the smile back on her face.

In the short time I'd known him I already liked Hazrat Hussein, which I suppose was just as well now that we were family.

When my mother and Shir Ahmad performed the *nekah*, the kids were made to wait outside, because those were the rules. Jahid's brothers immediately went off to play in a ditch in front of the house because there was a dead cat in it. Jahid and I disappeared around the corner, well away from the house, so he could teach me how to smoke.

Although cigarettes were pretty disgusting and tasted of dead *bukharis*, I realized that if I was ever to become a man there were a lot of disgusting things I'd have to get used to. Hair downstairs was one of them, according to Jahid. Worse than that, one day I would wake up to find my cock had been sick.

"Your sister's pretty good-looking," Jahid said as he tried to blow smoke rings. "I tell you what, if she hadn't been kidnapped, I wouldn't have minded marrying her myself—being blood and all that."

I looked at Jahid, with his rolling eye, lazy leg, and stumpy brown teeth, and thought that if my sister had accepted his offer, I'd have handed her over to the Taliban myself.

"So, how's the job going?" I asked, wanting to change the subject before my cousin forgot himself and started making sexy talk about the sister I'd only just got back.

"Slow," he admitted, "but I'm starting to do more filing now, the paperwork and all that, and my boss says he'll get me on one of those computer courses soon."

"Shir Ahmad's been going to computer school."

"Well, it is the future." Jahid nodded. "There's not an office in Kabul that doesn't have a computer these days. And you wouldn't believe the amount of porn you can find on them. There are pictures, even films, of every kind of shagging you've never even thought of. There's women shagging men, women shagging women, men shagging men, women shagging midget men, women shagging dogs, and I've even seen women sticking marrows up their—"

"Fawad!"

My mother's voice rang out loud and clear, and Jahid and I quickly killed our cigarettes. "Here," he said, handing me some chewing gum that was supposed to taste of banana but actually tasted of plastic. It was pretty disgusting as well. We used to sell it to the foreigners on Chicken Street for a dollar, proving people will buy anything if you look sad enough.

After my mother's *nekah*, we said good-bye to Mina, who had to return to her baby. As we all held on to one another, it was both happy and sad, but Hazrat Hussein gave my mother a telephone number so we could call her any time we liked, which then made it more happy than sad.

Shir Ahmad returned to his house and my mother to our house. The next day, after the wedding party, my mother would finally move to her new house, and I would follow a week later—for a reason I didn't want to know. While she'd spend the week doing stuff I didn't want to know about, my mother thought I might like to stay at my aunt's house. She couldn't have been more wrong if she'd tried.

"Mother, the last time I was in that house Jahid's father hit me on the head with a water jug, and one of their kids peed in my bed, and let's not forget that my aunt's food nearly killed you. Really, I'm not sure you've properly thought this through. But that's okay, I know you're not thinking straight, what with your mind being on your new husband rather than the happiness of your son and his chances of living to the end of the week."

My mother smiled at me—which showed how much she had changed since she spat at her sister's feet and left Khair Khana—and she played a little with my hair.

"Okay, Fawad, you win. If Georgie gives her permission, and promises to look after you, you can stay in the house for a week. I suppose it will give you time to say your good-byes."

We have a saying in Afghanistan: "One day you see a friend, the next day you see a brother." After nearly a year living with the foreigners, I now had two sisters and one brother, and though their ways were sometimes strange and their behavior not in any way to be copied if you were a good Muslim, I loved them all dearly, each and every one of them. So when my mother and I returned home to tell them in Dari (with my English translation) that she had got herself married and would be moving out the next day and taking me with her a week later, they all looked at us with blank faces.

I think they call it shock.

Georgie was the first to recover her mind and remember her manners, and she gave my mother a hug.

"Congratulations, Mariya," she said. "That's fantastic news."

"Yes, wonderful. Congratulations," added James.

"Absolutely! Congratulations. I hope you have a wonderful life together," said May. Then, just as everyone was getting used to the idea, she added, "I might as well tell you all now. I'll also be leaving soon. I'm pregnant."

If my mother's news had been a surprise, May's announcement hit everyone like a grenade. I translated May's words for my mother. Her eyes grew wide, but she said nothing.

Again, Georgie was the first to recover.

"Congratulations, May! That's . . . amazing."

"It's not just amazing; it's a bloody miracle," added James, stepping forward to give her a hug. "Who's the father?"

"Well . . ." May smiled shyly. "The baby will be mine and Geri's, but there's a small chance it could be born with a French accent."

I shook my head. In many of their ways the foreigners were just like Afghans. They laughed and cried, they tried to be good with one another, and they loved their families. But in other ways they were just plain crazy and trying their absolute hardest to burn for all eternity. Worse than that, they all seemed so damned pleased about it.

29

IN MY COUNTRY we wear the *salwar kameez*—basically a long shirt over baggy trousers. There's a lot of cloth involved, more than you would believe, and it's our traditional dress. These days I usually wear jeans like the older boys who copy the Iranian pop stars on TV, but there are times—say, at your mother's wedding party—when the top of your trousers dig into your stomach because you've eaten so much it's grown to the size of Kandahar, and it's quite possible that at any moment you will be cut in two by the waistband. That's when you realize that Afghans are a lot cleverer than Westerners. Not only do we believe in the One True God; we also make clothes big enough to fit Kandahar *and* Helmand.

"What's the matter with you?" James asked as I fell into the seat next to him.

"I think I'm dying. I shouldn't have eaten so much."

About an hour after we arrived at the Herat Restaurant in Shahr-e Naw, we had started filling our faces. First it was *ash*—a soup of noodles, yogurt, kidney beans, and chickpeas—followed by potato and green onion *bolani*, eggplant in yogurt, *Kabuli pilau*, lamb kebabs, and finally *firni*, a delicious plate of cold custard. Really, it was no wonder that everyone enjoyed a wedding. It was probably the most food they got to eat in a year.

As I groaned under the weight of kebab lying in my stomach, James leaned over and moved his hands toward my trousers.

"What do you think you're doing?" I asked, not too full to be shocked.

"Loosening your belt to help you breathe better."

I looked at James in disbelief. "I don't think so, James," I said as I tugged the top of my trousers out of his hands.

Honestly, foreigners had no sense of shame, not even at a wedding.

Of course, it was my own fault, because I hadn't stopped eating from the moment I sat down at my mother's table until the moment I left her to collapse next to James in the men's room. As was only proper, the men and the women were separated at the party. Only my mother and Shir Ahmad got to sit together, in a little room set aside for them where they could greet the family guests who came in to see them.

Although the party wasn't huge and there was no music or dancing because it was a second wedding for both my mother and Shir Ahmad, she still looked amazingly beautiful in her pretty pink dress with her hair fixed in curls under her matching scarf. Her eyes were huge, painted in pink and black with sparkles around the edges and giant-size eyelashes that a woman had glued to her face back at our house.

As I was her son, I could tell my mother was really happy, even though she didn't smile much because that was only proper too. In Afghanistan, when a girl gets married she has to look unhappy at her wedding. Her sadness shows everyone how much she loves and respects the family she is leaving. Of course, in some cases it's also real because the girl is terrified of the family she is about to join. But real or not, an unhappy bride is a good bride, and if on the wedding day she can squeeze the tears out from her eyes, that makes her even better. Of course, in my mother's case the tradition seemed a little backward given that she had left my grandparents a long time ago, and they were both dead anyway. But the fact that she still followed the rules marked her out as a "good woman." A "good woman" marrying a "good man"—that's what everyone kept saying. And I think they were right, because Shir Ahmad had loved my mother for ages and he had changed his life so he could marry her, bettering himself at computer school and fixing up his home to make it ready for her even before he asked her to be his wife.

Yes, he was a good man, and I was pleased. He looked very handsome at the wedding banquet in his white suit and white shoes, and when he served my mother's food to her, to show his respect, all the other women watched with smiles on their faces and nods of approval.

As well as me, my aunt, and Jamilla, Georgie and May sat in the marriage room, along with May's woman-husband Geri. Out of all the Afghans at the wedding, only my mother and I knew of the baby hiding in May's stomach, and before we left the house my mother begged the foreigners not to talk about it in public. If that news had got out, all of us might have been stoned to death, which wouldn't have been a very good ending to my mother's special day.

Despite having lived in the same compound as my mother for the best part of a year, James wasn't allowed into the marriage room because he wasn't a relative, and because he was a man. When I joined him he was sitting with Ismerai, Pir Hederi, and some friends of Shir Ahmad's, looking lost because there was no one there to translate for him. Even though he had lived in Afghanistan for more than two years, James's Dari hadn't improved much from the few phrases he had learned when he first arrived, such as "Hello," "How are you?" "Where's the toilet?" and "Take me to your leader." Mainly he got by with his hands flying wildly and the pocket dictionary he carried around with him.

I could only imagine how long it must have taken him to

mess with Pir Hederi's head over the business of the sand-wiches.

When I began to feel a little better—without the need to run around the restaurant half naked—Ismerai asked me to go and fetch Shir Ahmad and bring him to the men's room. He had a gift for him, apparently. I did as I was told because Ismerai was an elder. I was also excited to see what the present would be. Georgie had already given my mother a mobile telephone so she could call Mina whenever she wanted to, which I thought was pretty damn brilliant of her. But I could hardly imagine what Ismerai and Haji Khan were bringing to the table.

Shir Ahmad muttered his apologies to the women for having to leave them, but I could tell he was secretly pleased because I think they were starting to do his head in. Slowly, I led him to where Ismerai was waiting. It took quite a bit of time because of all the handshaking he had to do on the way.

Once in the men's room, Ismerai asked Shir Ahmad to sit down and presented him with a white envelope. "From Haji Sahib Khan," he said. "He apologizes for not being here in person to celebrate your wedding with you, but he had to return to Shinwar to attend to some urgent business."

Shir Ahmad accepted Ismerai's words with some kind ones of his own and opened the envelope. Inside were about four or five pieces of official-looking paper.

My new father looked at Ismerai, confused. I looked at Ismerai, disappointed. I was expecting to see money.

"It's a contract," Ismerai explained.

"Oh, a contract," we all said, continuing to stare at Ismerai.

Laughing, the old man took the papers off Shir Ahmad and slowly explained what they all meant. It turned out that Shir Ahmad and Haji Khan were now in business together—the joint owners of Kabul's latest Internet café.

30

AFTER THE WEDDING party, my mother left with her husband to get our new house ready for the start of our new life, and the rest of us returned to Wazir Akbar Khan.

Back at the house, Georgie, James, and May opened a bottle of wine because apparently they were all "in need of a drink," and one by one they tried to convince me to move into James's room for the week.

"It won't be so lonely for you," explained Georgie, coming in from the kitchen carrying my tea.

"Your mother would want you to sleep there," May tried.

"It will be fun!" cried James.

But I was having none of it. I wasn't a child anymore, and my mother had only gone to another house; it wasn't as if she'd nearly died or anything—not like the last time she'd left me alone with the foreigners. And besides, my mother had a TV in her room, and I was moving in there.

After getting a little cross with my friends and all their nagging, I picked up my kettle of tea and left them to their wine so I could settle myself in my mother's room and finally get some peace. And as I arranged the cushions for the best view of the television, I felt pretty grown up about it.

"This is the life," I said to myself, sipping at my drink and stretching out on my mother's bed.

I plumped up the pillow and relaxed for the film that was about to begin.

Eight hours later I was woken by the sound of Georgie calling me to breakfast. The television was silent because the electricity had gone off, and as my head caught up with my surroundings I realized I'd fallen asleep before I'd watched even five minutes of the movie, which annoyed me slightly because it seemed such a waste of my new freedom.

I climbed out of bed, washed myself, changed my clothes, and went into the big house for breakfast. Only Georgie was there, as May had already left for her office and James wouldn't come out of his room for another three hours at least.

"Did you sleep well?" Georgie asked, pushing a plate of bread and honey in my direction.

"Yes, thank you. Did you?"

"Yes, thank you."

I poured myself a cup of sweet tea.

"So, did you enjoy the wedding party?" Georgie asked.

"Yes, it was pretty good. What about you?"

"Yes," she agreed, "it was pretty good."

We then continued eating in silence until Massoud turned up to take Georgie to her office and I jumped on my bike to go to school. Although it was always nice to spend time with Georgie, neither of us was really a "morning person."

As usual, I went to the shop after class to earn my money, such as it was, and to tease Jamilla before she went to school.

"I read yesterday that Shahrukh Khan got married to another man," I told her.

"Where?" Jamilla asked. "In Fawad's Special Newspaper of Lies?"

"No, in an Indian temple, of course."

"Very funny," she said, fixing her scarf before walking out the door.

"I thought so." I laughed. "See you after school, Jamilla."

"Whatever," she replied, in English, making the sign that James had taught me and that I had taught her.

As she walked out the door, I suddenly noticed she was starting to get taller than me, which didn't please me one bit. I'd scratched a mark on my bedroom door when I first moved into the foreigners' house, and I didn't seem to be getting any higher. It was starting to play on my mind, so much so that I'd recently got to wondering whether I'd end up like Haji Khan's midget man. Even Jahid had commented on my height when I saw him at the wedding.

"Hey, runt," he'd greeted me.

I ignored him, obviously, because in God's great plan for us all he hadn't come off too well either. But it was still annoying.

"How old are you now?" Pir Hederi asked when I mentioned it in the shop.

"I don't know." I shrugged. "Maybe ten, maybe eleven."

"Oh, well then, boy, you've got nothing to worry about. Come back to me when you're maybe twenty-five or twenty-six, and you're still no higher than an ailing calf."

"I'm not likely to be here when I'm twenty-five or twenty-six, am I?"

"Where the hell else are you likely to be?"

"Well . . ." I stopped to think about it, and realized I had no idea. "Somewhere else," I said eventually, now even more disturbed by the thought that I might end up as a man-midget working in Pir Hederi's shop for the rest of my life.

"Look, if you're seriously worried, my advice is to get your mother to boil up a chicken in hot water, throw in some chickpeas and a spoon of scorpion juice, and take a glass of the water every morning when you wake up."

"We're not allowed to eat even chicken these days because of the bird flu, never mind scorpions," I told him.

"In that case, you're screwed," was all he said.

"You have absolutely nothing to worry about," Georgie told me when I returned home later that afternoon to drink tea with her in the garden. "Girls mature faster than boys—that's a fact. In a couple of years you'll catch up with Jamilla, and then you'll overtake her. And really, Fawad, you're far too clever to end your days in Pir Hederi's shop, so calm down."

"Do you really think I'm clever?" I asked.

Georgie laughed. "Fawad, you're the most intelligent boy I've ever met! You are . . . what is the phrase in Dari? I don't know. In English we would say that you're 'bright as a button,' meaning you're amazingly clever and lively for your age. Honestly, I've met adults who haven't got the sense you were born with. You are a very special little boy who will one day grow up to be a very special man. And you're also very handsome."

"Wow, I'm pretty good then, aren't I?" I laughed.

"You sure are, Fawad."

As I looked at Georgie, her lovely face sweating in the summer sun, I suddenly felt a cloud of sadness come over me. Things were changing so fast, and they would probably never be the same again: May was moving back to her country to have her French baby; I was moving to Kart-e Seh to begin my new life; James was worried about who was going to cook for him now my mother was gone, and why Rachel didn't want to marry him; and Georgie—well, nobody knew what Georgie was up to.

"Are you going to leave Afghanistan?" I asked, watching her carefully.

"Who told you that?" she asked back, surprise making her voice grow high.

"Dr. Hugo told me before he got beaten up by Haji Khan."

"He what? Khalid did what?"

My heart stopped. I'd gone and done it again.

"It was only because he loves you," I added quickly. "And really it was all Dr. Hugo's fault because he was trying to make him 'back off,' and Haji Khan said that you were in his teeth and he called Dr. Hugo a motherfucker and then he got really angry. But he didn't kill Dr. Hugo or anything, even though he told his guards that he was going to rip his throat out."

Georgie stared at me over her sunglasses.

"I'm in his teeth, am I?" she asked finally.

"Well, that's what he said."

"How romantic," she replied, but she spoke the words in a flat way like it wasn't romantic at all.

"So, are you leaving Afghanistan?"

Georgie shrugged. "Right now, I don't know, and that's the honest truth. Maybe it will become clearer on Friday when I go to Shinwar."

"You're going to see Haji Khan?"

"Yes."

I didn't say anything because I couldn't, but I guessed she was about to give Haji Khan his answer.

"Can I come with you?" I asked.

"Well . . . I don't know. I've got a few things to sort out."

"Please, Georgie. What if you do leave? This might be the last chance I get to see Mulallah."

"To be honest, Fawad, I'm not sure I'll have time to visit Mulallah and her family."

"Okay then, Haji Khan."

My friend looked at me through her glasses.

"I don't know . . ."

"Please, Georgie. I'll be ever so good, and I won't make any trouble, and I'll play by myself when you need to speak to Haji Khan and—"

"Okay, okay, you can come!"

"Great!"

"But only if your mother agrees."

Using Georgie's phone, I immediately called my mother to ask if I could go to Shinwar for the Friday holiday. She agreed, as I knew she would, because when it came to a choice between Shinwar and leaving me in a house with James and a pregnant lesbian, Shinwar would win every time.

"Don't forget your prayers, and be good!" she yelled in my ear.

"I won't, and I will," I promised, making a note in my head to show her how to speak properly into a phone when I next saw her. She was shouting so loud I could have heard her in Tajikistan.

As with our other journeys, it was Zalmai who arrived at the house to drive us to Shinwar, but this time Ismerai came with us and we were taken in a Toyota pickup with a guard in the front and two more outside in the back.

"Expecting trouble, are we?" Georgie asked when she saw our escort.

"No, not really," Ismerai replied. "Haji just wants to take precautions with you both, seeing as you are such special guests."

"Oh, come on." Georgie laughed. "What's happened?"

"Beyond the usual?"

Ismerai took off his *pakol* to scratch at the few bits of hair left on top of his head.

"Okay. Last week the governor escaped a roadside bomb and there have been a few other incidents, but nothing to get worked up about."

"Because of the poppy ban?" Georgie asked.

"Poppies, power, the time of the year . . . who knows?

This is Afghanistan. We don't do peace that easily, as you well know."

As we traveled to Shinwar, Ismerai tried to take our mind off roadside bombs and "other incidents" by pointing out the places where people had been blown up in the past. "This is where the mujahideen ambushed a Russian convoy toward the end of the jihad," he said as we came out of Kabul and into the mountains. "Here there was a mighty battle that lasted a full week . . . here we had some of our best sniper positions . . . here we dug tunnels into the hills to escape from the Communists . . ." He then pointed out the death sites of fallen friends and forgotten heroes and basically sent us all into a bit of a depression.

As we slipped down into Nangarhar and on into Shinwar, the sun burned hot through our windows, making it difficult to talk without completely exhausting ourselves, so we fell into our own thoughts and daydreams until we arrived at Haji Khan's home.

I'd never been to his Shinwar compound before, and though it was smaller than his place in Jalalabad, it was much nicer—more like a home than a palace. Of course it was a home filled with guards carrying guns, but they were more in the shadows than at the other place.

As the Toyota came to a stop in the driveway, Georgie was the first out. Bending to the ground to stretch out her back, she then lifted her arms to the sky, holding them there for a moment, high above her head, as if she was feeling the air between her fingers.

"God, I love this place," she said to no one, sighing. Then, turning to me, she added, "You know, Fawad, this is where I first fell in love with Afghanistan."

"And with Haji Khan," I added for her.

"Yes," she accepted, "with Haji Khan too."

I smiled, because this was important. If Georgie was to

make the right decision about her future, she needed to be reminded of everything she loved, not of all the other things that had come to make her sad.

Ismerai came over to join us.

"Go sit on the carpet, and I'll join you in a minute," he said. "I've just got a couple of phone calls to make."

Georgie and I nodded, and we walked over to a red carpet that was lying under a huge tree. The air was much cooler under the leaves, and above our heads birds sang to us. Life just didn't get any better than this.

"It would be sad never to see this place again," I said to Georgie as she kicked off her sandals and sat back to stretch out her legs.

"Yes, it would," she admitted. "You know, it's a shame that so many people don't get to experience days like this."

"Yes, it is," I agreed. Then, after thinking about it a bit more, I asked, "Why?"

Georgie smiled. "Well, there's so much more to your country than war, as you can see, but unfortunately we rarely get to hear about it. I don't think people get the full picture— about what Afghanistan is like, and what Afghans are like."

"Yes, it is pretty good here," I said, "as long as you're not hungry."

"Or no one's trying to kill you."

"Or you don't get sold by your family."

"Or you don't lack electricity or clean water."

"Or . . . or . . ." I was struggling now. "Or you don't get your head blown off by a gas cooker."

Georgie put her chin to her chest and looked at me over her sunglasses.

"It happened once, to a woman in our street," I explained.

"Oh," Georgie said, lifting her head back up to the sun that winked at us through the leaves, "well then, you're right. It's a pretty good country if you don't get your head blown off."

"Or your legs," I added. "There are still a lot of land mines."

"Or your legs," Georgie agreed.

"Actually, what is so good about Afghanistan?" I asked, and we both started laughing.

"Okay," Georgie said, stopping first. "For one, I've never lived anywhere where the sky is so blue it can leave you speechless."

"It can get very blue," I agreed.

"And though life is hard here, much harder than we can imagine living in our nice house in Wazir Akbar Khan, there is also kindness hiding behind the walls of these houses, and love."

"What do you mean?"

"Okay, let me think how to explain. It's like the books about your country. Most of them would have you believe that Afghanistan is a land of noble savages, heroic men who kill at the first provocation, and in some ways maybe they are right. There is a quick anger within you all and a brutality that is sometimes shocking to us, but mainly the Afghans I've been lucky enough to encounter have been simple people with good hearts who are just trying to survive."

"I wouldn't call Haji Khan simple."

"Well, no, you're right, again," Georgie admitted, "but although he's not poor, he still has a good heart. Khalid means well, I know that, it's just that sometimes . . . Well, hey, come on, let's not even go there."

Georgie reached for her cigarettes, and as she suggested, I decided "not to go there" just in case "there" was the place where all the bad memories sat waiting.

As Georgie blew the smoke from her mouth, Ismerai returned. His phone was closed, and he had a smile on his face.

"Come," he said, struggling a little for breath. "We've got something to show you."

Zalmai drove us to a place about fifteen minutes away from Haji Khan's house. Bouncing off the main track, we came to a stop outside a half-finished building where workmen were still busy building walls and moving dirt around in wheelbarrows.

As we stepped out into the air, Haji Khan appeared from the house talking to a man holding a large notebook. When he saw us, he shook hands with the man and walked over, with a smile on his face. He certainly looked a lot happier than the last time I'd seen him, and as usual he was dressed in the finest *salwar kameez* of pale blue with a gray waistcoat matching the color of his *pakol*.

I decided that if I ever got bored of wearing jeans, I would definitely find out who his tailor was.

"So, what do you think?" Haji Khan asked when he reached us. He spoke in English, and I guessed it was to stop the workmen from listening to his conversation.

"It's a beautiful area," Georgie said. "Are you building another house then?"

"Yes, I am building a new house," he said, "but this house is for you. If you choose to accept it or not, this is also a matter for you."

I was pretty amazed by his words, and I felt my mouth drop open with the weight of a million questions wanting to spill out but not being allowed to.

Georgie said nothing.

"Look," Haji Khan continued, "come inside and let me show you."

Before Georgie could refuse him he walked away. So we followed.

Stepping over bags of sand, we entered the house and walked into a square-shaped hall that was cement gray all around, with bits of wire hanging out of the walls. It wasn't what you might call "pretty."

"This will be the seating area," Haji Khan said, looking at Georgie and waving his hand around the room. "It will be for your guests when they come. When it is finished, the walls will be a very beautiful green—this is my thinking—like the meadows of Shinwar, so that when it is cold you will always have spring."

Without waiting for Georgie to react, Haji Khan moved to the left where two holes were waiting for doors.

"This room is the kitchen," he explained, "and the other room is where your guests sleep. I am making also a very beautiful toilet place, side by side—what is it you say?"

"En suite," replied Georgie.

"Yes"—Haji Khan nodded—"yes, in sweet. I think this is a good idea. Very Europe. Come."

Haji Khan crossed the hall to where a staircase was being made between the ground floor and the top floor. It wasn't finished yet, and a ladder leaned against the balcony above so the workmen could get up and down.

"This will be the staircase," Haji Khan said, which made me laugh because we weren't stupid. "Your rooms will be upstairs. One is your bedroom, one is a large seating area, and the other room is for maybe the children."

Haji Khan looked at Georgie from under his heavy eyebrows. I could see he was taking a chance with his words, seeing as he had practically killed their last child.

"Here you can relax and see a wonderful view of the mountains to help keep your mind happy," he added, and Georgie smiled, which made Haji Khan smile, and because both of them were smiling I smiled.

So far it was going very well, and I thought that if the new house filled with the promise of their children couldn't keep Georgie in Afghanistan, nothing would.

"So, what is your thinking?" Haji Khan finally asked.

Georgie looked around.

"I think it will be wonderful, Khalid, but—"

"Please, Georgie," he interrupted, frowning as his eyes fell sad, "not with the 'buts.' Please, first, let me show you one more thing."

Haji Khan moved away and out the door, speaking again as he stepped outside.

"You see this garden to the river and to the road over there? This will all be yours. We will build the walls so you have privacy, and we will put beautiful roses in the ground along here"—he pointed to the left side of the garden—"and here"—he pointed to the right—"and here"—he pointed in front of him. "This way all of the day you will be surrounded by color and beauty."

Georgie slowly looked around, probably imagining the colors that might shine in her world and what her life might be like surrounded by flowers in the garden and spring in her hallway.

As she considered things, Haji Khan moved away from us, his head bent low and his hands reaching out to each other behind his back. He was really trying, anyone could see that. I could almost feel the hope he was holding inside his hands. I knew that if Georgie really loved him there was no way she could refuse him, but when I searched her face she was looking away into the distance and I saw the worry in her eyes as she lifted a hand to block out the sun.

"Shit!" she suddenly shouted.

I looked to where she had been looking and saw something dark move along the roof of a nearby house. I looked back at Georgie, but she was gone, running toward Haji Khan and shouting at him to get down. As he turned to face her, she threw herself straight into his body. He stumbled backward before catching her in his arms, just as the bullets cracked in the distance and began to scream over our heads.

I threw myself to the floor as Haji Khan's bodyguards opened fire, killing our ears with the noise of their guns.

Scared beyond scared, I raised my head to look for Georgie and saw her lying in the arms of Haji Khan. Blood covered her clothes, and her face was pulled into his chest. He was shouting at the guards firing around him. "Get the car!" he yelled, but his words were barely heard over the noise of battle.

"Georgie!" I screamed, and I got to my feet to run toward her.

When I reached them, Haji Khan pulled me flat to the ground. "Keep down, Fawad!" he shouted. His eyes were wide with pain, and I saw blood rushing from his shoulder.

"Georgie," I whispered, and I pulled myself closer to her face so I could hold it in my hands.

Her life was pouring from her body like a river. Splashes of it colored her skin, which had grown white. Underneath my fingers she trembled as if a terrible wind from winter had suddenly blown over her.

I didn't want to believe it. I squeezed my eyes hard shut and prayed to my God with all my strength. But I knew she was dying. We were going to lose her.

"Please, Georgie, please," I begged, "we haven't time. You have to say the words. You must believe!"

All around me the bullets kept flying, whistling and cracking over our heads and kicking up dirt around the garden that was waiting for Haji Khan's roses. Above me I could hear him ordering his men and still calling for the car, but all I could see was Georgie's face, and her dark eyes now hearing my voice and reaching for me.

We had one chance, just one chance, and it was slipping away so fast.

"Georgie, please believe," I whispered, and I felt the tears tumble from my eyes, blurring her face. "You must believe, or you are lost! Georgie!"

"Fawad," she breathed into my face, but her sound was too soft and I had to put my ear close to her mouth. "Fawad, don't worry . . . I believe . . . I promise you, I believe."

"It's not enough," I screamed back at her, because I couldn't be gentle. There was no time to be gentle. We had only seconds. "You've got to say the words, Georgie! Please, you must say the words!"

And as my tears fell onto her lips, I saw her grab at the power deep inside her and she looked at me hard.

"La ilaha," I told her, pushing the wet hair from her face and pressing my ear to her mouth.

"La ilaha," she copied.

"Il-Allah," I said.

"Il-Allah."

"Muhammad-ur-Rasulullah."

"Muh . . . Muhammad-ur-Rasulullah."

There is no God except Allah; Muhammad is the Messenger of Allah.

And as Haji Khan's car arrived, kicking up the dust in front of us, she closed her eyes and Georgie was gone.

Epilogue:
One Year Later

THIS SUMMER THE Taliban leader Mullah Dadullah was killed in Helmand. He was a nasty piece of work who paid money to the disabled and mentals to carry out suicide bombings in our country. In the past he'd also killed thousands of Hazaras, just because he didn't like them. So when he finally got what was coming to him, everyone was pretty surprised, so much so that the governor had to put his body on TV so they knew it was true.

More amazing to me, though, was that he had only one leg.

"You would think that if he had only one leg they would have caught him a lot quicker," I mentioned to James after he'd sent his story over the computer to England.

"Fawad, for the past five and a half years no one's been able to find Mullah Omar, who's a six-foot-four-inch bloke with one eye riding around on a motorbike, so why the surprise? And if the rumors are to be believed, Osama bin Laden's running around Waziristan clutching a kidney dialysis machine. I'm telling you, Stephen Hawking could outrun this lot."

"Who's Stephen Hawking?"

"He's a clever man in a wheelchair who speaks through a computer."

"Really? Like Professor Charles Xavier in *X-Men*?"

James released the weights he'd been struggling to lift to his chest—one of his latest plans to win Rachel's hand in marriage—and looked at me with his hands on his hips.

"You, my boy, have been watching too much television," he said, breathing heavily.

And he was probably right.

After Pir Hederi's sandwich business failed to make him any money, he had turned half of his shop into a DVD store. Amazingly, it was a fantastic success. Now, instead of spending my afternoons walking around Wazir Akbar Khan advertising "cak," I was checking films for him so that he wouldn't get a visit from the Vice and Virtue Department.

It was the best job I'd ever had.

Jamilla was also pleased with the development because she now got to spend most of her mornings mooning over Shahrukh Khan, much to Pir Hederi's disgust.

"Doesn't that man ever stop singing?" he shouted one day because even Dog was refusing to come into the shop.

Jamilla turned down the sound but kept on watching regardless. She wasn't that interested in his singing in the first place.

Despite having moved halfway across town, most days I still came to work at Pir Hederi's shop because I had my bike and Shir Ahmad would come and pick me up when he'd finished at the Internet café. As I thought it would, his business with Haji Khan was going well—so well, in fact, that he now drove his own car, we had a generator in the house, and last week he even bought my mother a fridge.

Really, we were getting quite rich by Afghan standards, but I still liked to come to Pir Hederi's because it gave me an excuse to catch up with James and Rachel, who were now living together in my old house and pretending to be married, "for appearances' sake and because she can cook," explained James.

He was such a fat liar. Despite his words, I knew he wanted to make Rachel his wife because she told me that every time he was drunk—which didn't seem as often as when I lived with him—he would get down on his knees and propose.

"Why don't you just say yes one day?" I asked.

"You know, Fawad," she replied, turning to me with a wink, "one day I just might."

As I was seeing James at least once a week, I also got to find out what had happened to May after she left Afghanistan to have her baby.

"It's a boy!" James had shouted when I stopped by to drop off the *Four Weddings and a Funeral* DVD he'd asked for—no doubt another part of his scheme to trick Rachel into marriage.

"What's a boy?"

"The May-Geri-Philippe love child!" Laughing, he lifted me over his head and then dropped me again because this was before he had started working on his muscles. "They want to call him Spandi. What do you think?"

I took a moment to think about it, as he asked me to, weighing up all the good points and the bad points of giving my best friend's name to a boy who would most probably be lesbianized before he reached the age of five.

"I don't think so," I said finally. "It's a nice idea and everything, but Spandi was a good Muslim and it might be dishonorable. Maybe they should call the baby Shahrukh."

"Shahrukh, eh?" James nodded his head. "Okay, I'll e-mail and say it's a no to Spandi but you'd be happy with Shahrukh."

"Yes, I'd be very happy with that."

Of course, Jamilla would be furious when she found out, which made it even funnier.

Even though Jamilla was now a full head taller than me and her mind had become filled with things like lipstick, we were still the best of friends. More important, her life had started getting a lot less painful as we got older because her father no longer left so many marks on her face. I half suspected this was because he was frightened of ruining his chances of selling her, but Jamilla said the drugs were starting to affect his mind rather than his fists and half the time he couldn't remember his own name, let alone that he had to beat up his own children.

Even though nothing was said, I got the impression that Pir Hederi was hoping to give Jamilla his shop when he died because Mrs. Pir Hederi had started giving her lessons in bookkeeping. I was kind of annoyed about it at first, seeing as I was just as good at math as Jamilla and I had got her the job in the first place. But I calmed down when I saw how happy it was making her, and I guessed I'd probably inherit Shir Ahmad's Internet café eventually anyway—if I didn't become a journalist like James. To me this seemed the best of all jobs, other than checking DVDs. I'd been watching James's career with interest for quite a long time now, and I had come to the thinking that if you were a journalist you could spend most of your working life in bed.

Another person who was spending most of the time sleeping these days was my mother. Secretly I knew this was because she was becoming exhausted with the brother or sister I had growing in her stomach, but I couldn't tell anyone about it because it would have been disrespectful to my mother. Babies just appear in Afghanistan; how they got there is something good Muslims don't talk about. So, right now, the only other person, apart from Shir Ahmad, who knew about my mother's news was my aunt, who was also carrying a new baby in her arms. Amazingly, she had brought a little girl into the world, which of course filled my heart with nightmares. One day they might ask me to marry her. She was quite cute, though, for a baby and for a girl, and at least her eyes were pointing in the right direction.

As were Jahid's nowadays. Behind my back he had gone to speak to Dr. Hugo about his rolling eye, and as the doctor couldn't really tell him to get a good night's rest he had passed him on to another doctor who actually knew what to do about rolling eyes. After a few appointments Jahid finally got his cure: a pair of the most enormous glasses I'd ever seen that made his eyes look as big as saucers. Jahid was happy, though, because for once he could look at things and not see three of them.

"I'm getting my teeth fixed next," he told me.

"How can you get your teeth fixed?" I asked, not sure that even Allah could sort out that mess.

"I read about it on the Internet. In America everyone wears false teeth, so that's where I'm going."

"How are you going to afford that?"

"The marriage money I've been saving," he whispered. "Now that I've got my eyes sorted out, all I need to do is fix my smile and the ladies will be falling over themselves to get a taste of the Jahid love snake."

As he spoke he thrust his hips in my direction, which didn't look quite as sexy as he probably meant it to on account of his lazy leg.

At least he'd stopped fantasizing about my sister.

Since my mother's marriage we had seen Mina five more times—four of them in Kabul and the other in her own home in Kunar. Now that was a hell of a drive, but every painful bump of it was worth it because my sister grew more beautiful each time I saw her. It was kind of sad that we had missed so much of our life together, but despite what had happened to her, Mina seemed calm enough, if a little lost in her eyes, as if she had been caught remembering something. Thankfully her husband continued to be a good man, and he brought her with him to the capital whenever he came to hand over his wood to his business partner. But what really brought the light to her face was baby Daud, who was a loud, fat, happy child who wouldn't have looked out of place running around Homeira's house.

Of course it was still difficult for my mother and my sister to have spent so many years apart and still to be cursed with so many miles between them, but when they couldn't be together they clung to each other on their mobile phones. I think the chatter and the cost of it was doing Shir Ahmad's head in because if he wasn't at his shop he was out in the street buying Roshan cards. To be honest, my mother could have done with Spandi still being around—at least he might have been able to cut her a deal on the cards, or showed her the tricks some of the other boys knew to get their calls for free. And I'm sure Haji Khan wouldn't have minded. He didn't seem to be that fussed about anything these days, not since his head had become full of his new wife.

To our surprise, Haji Khan had married Aisha Khan as spring came to break through the dead of winter. Although some people in his district grumbled that she wasn't good enough for him, on account of the fact that she didn't wear gloves when she went out in her burka—as a woman of her standing should—and because she sometimes worked for a company in Kabul—and, even worse than that, men would come to her home who weren't male relatives—Haji Khan didn't take much notice of them because he loved her. What's more, most other people loved her because she had made Haji Khan so happy, in a way none of us thought would have been possible after his brother was jailed for his attempted murder.

Although nobody would have thought any less of him for putting a bullet through Haji Jawid's head after he was caught running his drugs out of Shinwar and plotting the murders of those trying to stop him, Haji Khan insisted his brother be tried and sentenced, as an example to the people. He then married his bride and everyone rejoiced—even though she couldn't give him children because her insides were damaged—because it was a true love story and they had become famous in the province.

You see, not only had Aisha Khan risked her life for that of her husband-to-be, she had also converted to Islam, earning her the name of the Prophet Muhammad's wife (Peace Be Upon Him).

Of course to me she was still plain old Georgie.

Make a Difference

Years of war have left many Afghan children mentally and physically scarred. Many parents have been killed or disabled, whole families have been displaced, and the poor still struggle to make ends meet. As a result, many parents have had to sacrifice their children's education in order to put them to work.

The nongovernmental organization ASCHIANA, based in Kabul, was founded in 1995 to educate street and war-affected youngsters. And for as little as twenty dollars a month, you can make a very real difference in the life of an Afghan child.

For more information, e-mail aschiana@yahoo.com.au or visit its Web site at www.aschiana.com

Glossary

af slang for afghani, the currency of Afghanistan

bakhsheesh a gratuity, tip, or bribe

bolani flat-bread stuffed with spinach or potato

bukhari a steel or aluminium stove

buzkashi a team sport where the players on horseback attempt to place a goat carcass into a goal

chador a headscarf worn by women

ISAF the NATO-led International Security Assistance Force

ISI Pakistan's Inter-Services Intelligence

kafan sheets of clean, white cloth that wrap a body before burial

kafir an unbeliever

kuchi a nomad

madrassa a school for teaching Islamic theology and religious law

mantu steamed dumplings filled with minced meat and topped with white yogurt

pakol a round-topped hat worn by Afghan men, typically made of wool

patu a woolen shawl

Ramazan the Muslim holy month of fasting more commonly known as Ramadan but pronounced "Ramazan" in Afghanistan

Acknowledgments

I have so many people to thank whose lives and stories inspired me in a million different ways to reveal a side of Afghanistan that is all too often ignored. In spite of the hardships—and there are many—this is a land filled with laughter and light, compassion and spirit. It is a land that has inspired many before me and will inspire many who will come after. And it is a land that I have fallen deeply in love with.

AFGHAN

First and foremost, I want to thank the family and friends of Haji Abdul Qadir, who showered me with warmth, affection, and good humor from the moment I first set foot on Afghan soil in 2001. Special thanks also go out to my "brothers" Fida and Israr, Haji Daud, Zalmai, Bilal, Tiger, Mustafa Khan, Ahmad, Daoud, Nadar, Pir Hederi, Fareydoon, Pir Bakhsh, Ibrar, Haji Almas, Massoud and family, Monir, Qasi Naeem, Safi, Gulbaz, Bashir, Zaman, Assad, Sayeed, Anwar, Sharab, Sayed Ikram, Koochi, Najib, Mohammad Sharif, and the Mohseni family.

My love and gratitude also go to three very special children who brought a rare magic into my life: Fawad, Ali Reza, and Shabnam. Although the story I've written bears no resemblance to their own, these children with their infectious smiles and huge hearts were a tremendous source of inspiration, surprise, and delight. *Born Under a Million Shadows* is my small tribute to them.

NON-AFGHAN

I have been blessed with some truly wonderful, committed, brave, and beautiful friends whose support, advice, and encouragement helped me turn a dream into a reality. Special thanks go to Frauke, Matthew, Alastair, Jerome, Jeremy, Rahilla, Chris, Tom, Rachel, Tim S., Jo, Nick, Richard, Meghann, Kristian, Marco, Mark, James, Paddy, Tim A., and Dominic.

Elsewhere, I am grateful for the fantastic support given to me by my agent, Charlie Campbell, and his costars at Ed Victor Ltd.; my editor, Helen Atsma, and the team at Henry Holt and Company; and the unwavering love and friendship of Janey and Lucy. Also, all my love and thanks go to my mother, Jean, my father, Mike, and my sister, Louise, who followed this book chapter by chapter.

And finally, I must thank Lorenz—who switched on the light and made me start writing. I love you.

etc.

extras...

essays...

etcetera

more author
About Andrea Busfield

more book
About *Born Under a Million Shadows*

...and more

Jerome Starkey

Meet Andrea Busfield

Andrea Busfield is a British journalist who first traveled to Afghanistan to cover the fall of the Taliban in 2001. She is now a full-time writer living in Bad Ischl, Austria. *Born Under a Million Shadows* is her first novel. ∎

Until recently, I lived in Kabul. To the outside world, Afghanistan's capital was a city creeping into lawlessness. The Taliban had burst back onto the scene with a series of headline-grabbing suicide attacks. According to reports, Kabul's expatriate community was living in fear, barricaded behind bomb-proof barriers, inside fortified compounds. But the reality was very different. Kabul was fun.

After shaking off the shackles of the fundamentalist regime following 9/11, the capital pulsed with life and possibility. Young men no longer hid handsome faces under fist-length beards. Afghan women were able to walk the city freely, to get an education, and to work for the first time in years. Shopping malls mushroomed, restaurants grew in sophistication, bars opened for business, and Western NGO workers and security personnel descended on the city in their thousands. Afghanistan promised opportunity, tax-free wages, and excitement—and Kabul offered postwar thrills with few of the risks of Baghdad.

In 2005, I applied for and won the post of print editor on the fortnightly newspaper *Sada-e Azadi* (The Voice of Freedom). The publication was a hearts-and-minds exercise financed by the NATO-led International Security Assistance Force (ISAF). The premise was simple: sixteen pages documenting the reconstruction effort in order to bolster support for the government and its military backers. In reality, most Afghans dismissed it for the

Andrea Busfield's Kabul Chronicles

Reprinted by permission of British *Vogue*.

propaganda it so evidently was and used it to line vegetable boxes and drafty windows. The job was a means to an end—I had been itching to move to Afghanistan ever since I was sent by a British newspaper to cover the War on Terror. From the moment I set foot on Afghan soil, I was hooked; the country was breathtakingly beautiful and its people proud, fierce, and gallant. By the time I moved to Kabul, the place felt like home.

I was well aware of the challenges I might face as a

> I was well aware of the challenges I might face as a Western woman in an Islamic country precariously balanced between recovery and relapse.

Western woman in an Islamic country precariously balanced between recovery and relapse. I always took care to respect the customs and I also learned the language. Most ordinary Afghans were not even remotely hostile to Westerners. When men stared at me in the street, it was out of curiosity, not malevolence. I was never made to feel unwelcome or vulnerable, which is why I declined the free accommodation offered behind the barbed-wire walls of the ISAF headquarters. I planned to spend at least two years in Afghanistan and sharing a metal container with another expatriate was not the way I planned to do it. So I hired a driver, employed a cook, and moved to a house on Lane 2, off Street 15, in Wazir Akbar Khan, a relatively plush suburb that was home to embassies, NGO compounds, and good restaurants.

By the time I moved in, spring had arrived and I was as happy as I'd ever been. I had a much-longed-for puppy, Blister; a two-story home opposite a Thai restaurant; a man to cook and "guard" the place; a decent job; and a mobile phone that buzzed with gossip and invitations. Kabul gave me a life I could never have dreamed of. Which is not to say that it didn't have its difficulties.

In Kabul, electricity was a rare visitor that appeared for five hours a night every forty-eight hours—or every seventy-two hours when the rivers ran dry and the hydroelectricity dams shuddered to a halt. As a consequence, the capital hummed with the constant buzz of generators, which invariably broke down or ran out of fuel when you needed them most.

Being 5,900 feet above sea level, the winters were exceptionally harsh, hitting −20°C outside and −15°C inside. Pipes would freeze, water had to be drawn from a well, toilets were flushed manually using a bucket, and heating was a source of frustration and danger. One night, my diesel fire exploded, startling my dog and me, as well as the guards from the compound next door. They came running to help, suspecting some fiendish Taliban plot, only to find me in my pajamas, my face smeared with black soot, watching my crippled *bukhari* (stove) burn out.

Once the snow thawed and the sun came out, everyone followed it. In the center of town, Chicken Street would wriggle with Westerners bartering over Persian carpets, scarves, *pakoul* hats, and antique guns dating back to the Afghan-Anglo wars.

On nonwork days, I would meet up with my best friends—Frauke, thirty-nine, a Dutch woman working for an NGO promoting textile and cashmere projects, and Rachel, thirty-five, a BBC producer. We would do lunch at Le Bistro before trawling the shops for new scarves, tunics, cosmetics, and toiletries, all the while followed by a small posse of children offering their services as bodyguards or bag carriers. But it was when the sun set and the call to prayer died on the breeze that the city turned magical. Shops decked with fairy lights and brightly colored bulbs gave evenings a festive

5

air; smoking charcoal from kebab stalls wafted along pathways; and, from Wazir Akbar Khan to Shahr-e Naw to Qala-e Fatullah, Land Cruisers clogged the streets, ferrying people to dinner invitations, restaurants, and bars.

At night, we would discard our headscarves, rearrange our cleavages, apply our lipstick, and head for favorite spots such as the restaurant-bars L'Atmosphère, Gandamack, and La Cantina. (Afghanistan is, of course, an Islamic country but the alcohol ban only applies to Muslims. The only rule imposed on Western revelers was one of leaving firearms at the door.) Although spring signaled the start of renewed Taliban assaults—following the traditional hiatus in hostilities over winter—the main topics of conversation among the women I knew involved hairdressers, waxing, and men. Life was normal. Even in Kabul.

> The only rule imposed on Western revelers was one of leaving firearms at the door.

A typical day began at seven o'clock, when I would be woken with coffee by my cook, Mohammad Sharif. He lived in a hut at the back of my house. He had asked me for a gun, thinking this would be an easy request given my military contacts, but the most dangerous weapon I allowed on the premises was the gas burner. In Wazir Akbar Khan, the streets crawled with heavily armed guards and I didn't feel it necessary to add to the neighborhood's arsenal.

At 7:45 a.m., I would jump into a Toyota Corolla expertly driven by my driver, Sharabdin, through nightmare traffic jams and sudden road closures, as politicians and dignitaries sprang from one fortified residence to another. If we happened to come across an ISAF patrol, we kept our distance. They were a target for suicide bombers and if they came under attack we might get caught in the crossfire.

By eight o'clock, I would be at ISAF headquarters, attending the "huddle"—a daily meeting to issue orders and recount hostile incidents. Following the huddle, work began on the newspaper, but, as the whole publication could be written in two days, time was usually spent debating lunch venues, going for coffee, and scheming up ways to leave the office early.

Occasionally, the UN and the larger NGOs imposed curfews on their staff following Afghan protests triggered by perceived injustices, or after attacks on Westerners. In May 2006, the Afghan government stamped a weeklong curfew on the city after riots broke out following a fatal collision in the north of Kabul involving a U.S. military truck. At the time, rather than being fearful, much of the expatriate community was only irritated by the 10 p.m. lockdown. Most restrictions were short-lived, however, and, within days, L'Atmosphère's swimming pool would again be decorated by women in bikinis.

This wasn't bravado; Kabul veterans honestly believed they had little to fear from insurgents. Although tragedies such as a shooting of a female South African Christian aid worker in the west of the city were not unheard of, they were nevertheless rare events, and quite random. Everyone in Kabul accepted that there was a risk, but most crimes committed against the expatriate community were opportunist, not planned, and therefore the general feeling was one of "wrong place, wrong time." No matter what happened—or to whom—our work continued and the parties never stopped.

I adored Afghanistan. I enjoyed the frantic pace of the city, the enormity of the circling mountains, and the camaraderie I found there.

I adored Afghanistan. I enjoyed the frantic pace of the city, the enormity of the circling mountains, and the camaraderie I found there. And in the autumn of 2006, something happened for which I was totally unprepared: I fell in love.

Lorenz was a captain in the Austrian army, and he was deployed to the hearts-and-minds section of the ISAF machine. Although I recognized that he was good-looking, he was a soldier and therefore of little interest to me. He was also six foot three with blond hair and blue eyes: not my type. Then one Thursday night, I pitched up at L'Atmosphère and found him drinking beer in civilian clothes. I decided to make him my boyfriend.

For the first time in Afghanistan, I lived my life not as a single woman—dodging curious questions from my Afghan friends about when I planned to marry and have children—but as part of a couple. Despite the threat of an instant disciplinary action—and probable dismissal—Lorenz snuck out of the ISAF camp every night. At 5 a.m., the alarm would sound in my bedroom and he'd pull on his jeans, sit on the bed, snap his gun into its holster, and pull on his T-shirt. Although Mohammad Sharif was initially aghast at having a man staying overnight, he soon grew fond of Lorenz—no doubt because he possessed his own gun.

While Lorenz was in Kabul, it was like seeing the city with new eyes. We hired a Land Cruiser and drove the tourist trail, visiting the bombed-out shell of Darul Aman Palace, the spectacularly renovated Babur's Garden, and the Shah M bookstore (of *The Bookseller of Kabul* fame). We spent every evening together and our nights keeping each other warm through the long freeze of winter. By the time Lorenz had to leave, I knew my time in Kabul was coming to an end. I loved the city, but I also loved him. And so in January 2008, I resigned from my job and began the sad work of saying good-bye—to my friends, expatriate and Afghan, and to Kabul. However, in that same month, gunmen attacked the supposedly bombproof Serena Hotel. Six people died and six others were injured. The incident threw a grenade into the lap of the expatriate community. Embassies and NGOs imposed immediate lockdowns, only allowing staff out on "mission-critical" business, and the city turned into a ghost town.

Leaving now felt like a betrayal. I spent my last few days walking my dog, as I had always done, along Wazir Akbar Khan's streets—causing one of my exasperated friends (the country manager of a risk control company) to send me a map of the embassies and NGO compounds in my area that were deemed to be bomb targets, entitled "Andrea's IED [Improvised Explosive Device] Dog-Walking Route."

As I divided my furniture between Mohammad Sharif and Sharabdin, I was filled with sorrow. I was leaving a country that felt like home at a time when she needed all the support she could get. Afghanistan had been generous to me. I went there single and curious, and I left two and a half years later richer and wiser, with a dog and a boyfriend. One day, I will return—and perhaps with the husband and children my Afghan friends so dearly wish to see me with. *Inshallah.* ∎

> I was leaving a country that felt like home at a time when she needed all the support she could get.

Born Under a Million Shadows came out of the two and a half years you spent living in Kabul. Was there a specific child who was the inspiration for Fawad? If so, could you tell us more about him?

If you are a first-time visitor to Kabul it is almost certain that you will be befriended by a child—they are everywhere. This is, of course, a sad indication of where the city is at, since all of these children will be asking you for *bakhsheesh* (charity). Anywhere there is an abundance of U.S. dollars—from the military bases and foreign embassies to the tourist hub of Chicken Street—you will find groups of youngsters "working" to feed their families. As a rule, the kids are pleasant, charming, and hugely entertaining. They also speak ridiculously good English.

The first time I set foot on Chicken Street, I was befriended by an eight-year-old boy called Fawad who presented himself as my "bodyguard" and who insisted on carrying my bags as I moved from store to store. Right from the start, I found Fawad, quite simply, amazing. A beautiful-looking boy with an easy smile, he worked the foreigners with his friends under the watchful eye of his older brothers and widowed mother. The family was obviously poor, yet Fawad was always a ray of sunshine. His love of life was astonishing—and incredibly humbling.

Therefore, when I first thought about writing a novel, and more precisely a novel narrated by a young boy, I wanted my hero to be as charming and as intelligent as the real-life

Fawad from Chicken Street. This is why I took his name—it is my small tribute to a very special little boy.

Today, Fawad and I are still in regular contact—he calls and lets my phone ring twice before hanging up when he wants to say hello; I then call him back—and, though I've tried to explain why I've used his name in my book, I'm not sure that he realizes what a wonderful impact he had on my life. Hopefully, when he is older he will come to understand that.

I wanted my hero to be as charming and as intelligent as the real-life Fawad from Chicken Street.

The community of expatriates living in Kabul is vividly depicted in your novel, and Georgie and her two roommates are quite involved in their local community. Georgie's romance with Haji Khan is particularly moving. Did you witness many romances between foreigners and Afghans when you lived in Kabul?

Although marriages between Afghan men and Western women have been documented, it is by no means the norm. Even though I have heard of relationships taking place, it is rare to witness such affairs because they are conducted in private and well away from the public eye, out of necessity. Afghanistan remains a very conservative society and there are rules to follow, both traditional and religious. There is no dating culture in Kabul!

In my experience, Afghan men are charming, chivalrous, and hard as nails—both inside and out. I know this because I count some of them among my best friends! If a Western woman seriously wanted to enter into marriage with an Afghan man it would be extremely testing—and she would almost certainly have to conform to the strict rules of Afghan society and ideally convert to Islam. However, when you truly love someone anything is possible and, I guess, that's the beauty of it.

On the more general topic of expat relations with Afghans, most of the foreigners I know in Kabul enjoy genuine friendships with the locals they work with or meet by chance. The strict rules that pose such an obstacle to a romantic relationship do not apply to the same degree in a social context. It would be hard to find a more hospitable place on earth than Afghanistan.

One thing your novel explores is how vibrant the city of Kabul is, despite the poverty of many of its residents. When you lived there, was it difficult to face the lack of resources of many of the Afghans? Was it difficult to write about?

I didn't flaunt my comparative wealth while I was in Afghanistan—while some had armored Land Cruisers I traveled in a battered Toyota Corolla. However, it's hard not to feel like a heel when you are being driven to work in the depths of winter and you spy a child walking in the snow in bare feet. The poverty is appalling, but you do what you can to help where you can.

> The average life expectancy is forty-four. This is the reality. The other reality is that Afghans are bewilderingly stoical.

I certainly didn't find it a difficult subject to write about; poverty is a fact of life for the majority. You can't ignore it. Besides, I wanted people to understand how challenging life is for ordinary Afghans. Afghanistan has the world's second-highest infant mortality rate. The average life expectancy is forty-four. This is the reality. The other reality is that Afghans are bewilderingly stoical.

Your work as a journalist has taken you all over the world—what prompted you to turn to writing fiction? Was it a challenging switch for you to make?

I've written for various media outlets, but I also spent nine years working for tabloid newspapers, so some might argue that the transition to fiction wasn't that great a leap to make! Of course, I'd beg to differ.

Like most reporters, I'd always harbored romantic dreams of becoming an author, but it was only in Afghanistan that I seriously decided to have a crack at it. To cut a very long story short, my boyfriend, a captain in the Austrian army, had finished his tour in Kabul—where we met—and I was desperately trying to work out a way to join him in his homeland. (There's not much call for non-German-speaking ex-tabloid hacks in Vienna.) So, one morning I decided I would write a book. I knew it would have to be about Afghanistan because it was a country I had grown to love and one that I felt was little understood. Although there are numerous fantastic history books, travelogues, and novels about the place, I wanted to capture the beauty I found there—the fun, the laughter, the love. Therefore, I opted for a romantic plot and decided it should be narrated by a hero who was still young enough to see the good in life—and bounce back from tragedy. Within forty minutes I'd sketched thirty chapters and that evening I started writing. Four months later the first draft was finished. And two months after that I said good-bye to Kabul.

In all honesty, I found writing *Born Under a Million*

Although there are numerous fantastic history books, travelogues, and novels about the place, I wanted to capture the beauty I found there—the fun, the laughter, the love.

Shadows a hugely enjoyable experience. I loved seeing my characters come to life and I wanted people—readers—to care about each and every one of them. It was challenging to consistently write as an eleven-year-old boy because there are times when you simply want to show off. However, after a break I'd come back and scrap any pompous pretense of literary greatness and return to character.

What do you hope your readers take away from your novel?

Ultimately, that Afghans are deserving of our continued support—and as the last page turns that they discover a little piece of Afghanistan in their hearts. ∎

1. *Born Under a Million Shadows* is narrated by Fawad, a young boy, rather than by an adult. What is the purpose in having the novel narrated from a child's point of view? Are events in the novel clarified or obstructed by the use of this perspective? Can you think of any examples?

2. How is the Taliban depicted in this novel? Did the novel change your perceptions of the Taliban? Of the Afghan people?

3. Fawad, Jamilla, and Spandi are very close friends. Does their friendship help to protect them from some of the dangers of Kabul? How does poverty affect their bond?

4. What are some of the major differences between Afghan and Western societies shown in the novel? Are there certain aspects of Afghan society (its famous hospitality or deference to elders, for example) that you'd like to see more of in Western society? What about vice versa?

5. Ismerai tells Fawad, "Education is the key to Afghanistan's successful future." The importance of education is one of the novel's main themes—how is this shown? What does Georgie do that makes this clear? What about Pir Hederi, Haji Khan, or Shir Ahmad?

6. The "foreigners" in the novel form a close friendship—a family, really—despite being from different backgrounds and having differing opinions. Do you think their bond is stronger than it might have been otherwise because of their expatriate status? Have you ever made friends with someone you might not have usually

because you found yourself in the same position as that person?

7. Fawad notes that "Afghanistan is famous for two things: fighting and growing poppies." Jahid declares, "This 'stop growing poppy' shit is the West's problem, not ours." Do you think that's true? Would Afghanistan be better off without poppy farming, or is it merely the West's "war on drugs" that has made poppy farming so contentious? How is drug use portrayed in the novel?

8. What role does Fawad's stabbing of Philippe play in the novel? Is it just comic relief or is it more than that?

9. Haji Khan and Georgie's love affair is one of the central points of the novel. Do you think they're meant to be together? Did your opinion of their love change as the novel progressed? Can two people from totally different worlds really put their differences aside and live happily ever after? Do you think you would be able to make the sacrifices Georgie makes for Haji Khan or the sacrifices he makes for her?

10. What role does religion play in the novel? Georgie calls herself a "Godless *kafir*" at one point, but by the novel's end she has professed her belief and converted to Islam. Do you think that she truly believes?

11. How does Spandi's death affect Fawad? Fawad says, "Although more than half of my family had gone the same way, it had never seemed real." Can you remember the first time death seemed real to you?

12. How does the ending reinforce some of the novel's major themes? Is it an ending worthy of Laila and Majnun, the couple in Jamilla's mother's story? Do you think it's a hopeful ending—not just for the characters of the novel but also for Afghanistan?

◆ *An Unexpected Light: Travels in Afghanistan* by Jason Elliot

This is a remarkable and beautifully written account of Elliot's travels in Afghanistan, first in the midst of the Soviet occupation and then during the emergence of the Taliban. It is one of the few books I have read twice and it's like falling into a vat of chocolate—luxurious, lyrical, and deeply satisfying. There are also some laugh-out-loud moments such as Elliot's wonderful examination of Afghanistan's relationship with her neighbors.

◆ *Emergency Sex (and Other Desperate Measures)* by Kenneth Cain, Heidi Postlewait, and Andrew Thomson

I started reading this shortly after moving to Kabul and almost regretted not having gone to university—a largely insurmountable barrier to joining the United Nations. The book is the work of three civilians who worked for the UN and the Red Cross and who first met in Cambodia. It is a wonderful, fast-paced, and often humorous account of their growing friendship against a backdrop of some of the world's worst war zones. At times funny, shocking, and tragic, it is a very personal story that left me inspired.

◆ *Kestrel for a Knave* by Barry Hines

This is the first book that broke my heart. It's the tale of a disillusioned teenager growing up in a small Yorkshire mining town who finds a kestrel hawk he names Kes. It's a slim novel that grabs you instantly and leaves you battered. I read it in one sitting and twenty years later just thinking about it raises the hairs on my neck.

◆ *Birds Without Wings* by Louis de Bernières

If I am writing, about to start writing, or even thinking about writing, I absolutely do not, under any circumstances, pick up a Louis de Bernières novel. Quite simply, I think the man's a genius and I suspect a part of me actually wants to be him, albeit with more hair and less manly. *Birds Without Wings* is perhaps my favorite of his novels. Set in the period when the Ottoman Empire was collapsing, the story centers on a small community in southwest Anatolia where Christians and Muslims have peacefully coexisted for centuries—until the outside world intrudes. A long and sometimes complicated tale, this is a novel that requires your absolute attention because there's a cast of characters to get your head around. But, as ever with a Bernières work of art, those who persevere are always rewarded. Tragic and magical.

◆ *The Curious Incident of the Dog in the Night-time* by Mark Haddon

I fell in love with this book on a beach in Tunisia. A quick read packing a massive punch, it's the tale of a teenager with autism who is determined to uncover a crime (the title should give a clue as to what crime has been committed). Engaging and human, it is one of the few books I've read that deserves to be described as hysterically funny. It is a joy from start to finish and in my mind an absolute masterpiece because there's a fine line between laughing at someone and laughing with them, and in *The Curious Incident of the Dog in the Night-time* you are firmly in tune with the hero. ■